T0374323

The words, "the threesome", are translated in the following five different languages: Spanish, Korean, Japanese, German, and Chinese.

The story is so diverse that the cover's various translations of the title words indicate the diversity.

The
THREESOME

Dion Gooden-El
with
S. W. Greene

authorHOUSE®

AuthorHouse™ LLC
1663 Liberty Drive
Bloomington, IN 47403
www.authorhouse.com
Phone: 1-800-839-8640

Published by AuthorHouse 04/17/2014

ISBN: 978-1-4685-7234-6 (sc)
ISBN: 978-1-4685-7233-9 (e)

Library of Congress Control Number: 2012905622

This book is a work of fiction. Names, characters, places and incidents are the
product of the Author's imagination or are used fictitiously. Any resemblance
to actual events, locales, or persons, living or dead, is entirely coincidental.
Sale of this book without a front cover is unauthorized. If this book is
coverless, it was reported to the Publisher as "unsold" and/or "destroyed". As
a result, neither the Authors nor the Publisher has received payment for it.

Any people depicted in stock imagery provided by Thinkstock are models,
and such images are being used for illustrative purposes only.
Certain stock imagery © Thinkstock.

This book is printed on acid-free paper.

DEDICATION

First, to Sheila W. Greene: Because you love me without any regrets. You're the real reason this book—and its predecessor—were written. Without doubt, I love you beyond description.

Second, to Clifton M. Greene: Because you're always willing to take the long trips. You're the only uncle I honestly know.

Third, to the late Verona Yvette Bullock (26 October 1968 – 28 September 1996): I will always love you, my second love, and will forever treasure our Liberty Park days in Norfolk, Virginia, throughout the early-1980's. Enjoy your Divine Journey on the Soul-Plane as well as the Spirit-Plane, Verona.

Fourth and finally, to Marguerite L. Calabrese: You are, and will always be, my first love. The mid-to-late 1970's were truly a beautiful era. Lott Carey Elementary, Norview Junior High—who could ever forget those days?! I know I won't, my dear Marguerite.

~ Dion ~

ACKNOWLEDGEMENTS

As with any book, there is always someone to whom the author is indebted. I am deeply indebted to two specific individuals and a group of individuals; therefore, I take this opportunity to acknowledge and thank them all:

- Sheila W. Greene of Maryland, my Personal Affairs Manager and favorite aunt, who picked up from where "The Good Doctor", Audrey Marie Gooden, left off.

- Lynette Warren of Virginia, my Book Agent with Warren & Associates who typed the final 555 handwritten pages of this novel, proving she was well worth the fee.

- Book Readers and Fans all across North America who appreciated my creativity and imagination enough to read my last book and who, I would hope, are still appreciative enough to read this one as well.

With respect to these individuals, mere words could never fully describe how grateful I am. I can only hope that by acknowledging them in this book, they all understand their importance.

INTRODUCTION

This is a story about three men. Each led a different life and came from a different background but they all had several things in common: Each of them would lose a close family member—their mother—and each would experience similar tragic injuries. Each of them would even father an illegitimate child. Most chilling, though, is that each of them would …die.

To most, there is nothing strange about dying. Such is true. With this threesome, however, it would be dramatically different. Death would come in the deepest meaning of the word. And, ironically, they would all die at the exact same time…together.

James L. White, affectionately called Jimmie Lee, was a law-abiding young drifter from Georgia who would spend a decade traveling the country, working odd jobs as he went, attempting to cover all fifty states. Being single and childless proved advantageous as he trekked across the nation. But when severely injured while toiling as a day-laborer in Memphis, Tennessee, his entire life changed. Attempting to find himself, he moved to Little Rock, Arkansas. Here, instead of finding himself, Jimmie Lee would find love and a career opportunity. He would be split on whether to embrace his former or latter find, or both, or neither.

Dr. Deloren "Dee" Powell, a writer who lived just south of the District of Columbia, reportedly held two doctorate degrees: one in psychology, the other in education. In 2000, he would set out on a special writing assignment in Miami while working on his third book. The polished and uppity African-American bachelor was finally leaning towards his first national bestseller. Little did he know that he would find love-at-first-sight. Unfortunately, the pains of a very dark past would find their way to Dee as well.

Andrew "Andy" Smith was a totally different story. Reared in a broken home by a loving mother who suffered from acute mental illness and epilepsy, this bright lad found his way into a life of unforeseen criminal mischief, beginning at age 15. Then, after having more than ten years of his life snatched away for crimes against the peace and dignity of the Commonwealth of Virginia, it would seem he was finally finding his way to a full life of freedom and success. Or was he? In the twinkling of an eye, things changed. A night of anticipated social entertainment turned into homicide. And all Andy could do was run.

Three men, three losses, three debilitating injuries, and three unplanned pregnancies. What brought these men together? Was it coincidence or something else? What led them into the same tunnel of life—on a quiet street in Opa Locka, Florida—to jointly experience the same ultimate fate? Only the Threesome—Jimmie Lee, Dee and Andy—know the answers. So, let's find out from them.

Dion Gooden-El
December 31, 2002

CHAPTER I
Winter 1980
Suwannee, Georgia

"Jimmie Lee," the bed-ridden woman called out, "that you comin' in the door?"

"Yes, ma'am," the young lad answered, slamming the door as he wiped his feet.

"Boy, what I tell you 'bout slammin' that door like that?!" she scolded.

"Yes, ma'am; sorry," he said sincerely.

"Put a kettle on the woodstove, fix two cups of tea, then come on back here," she instructed.

"Yes, ma'am," he answered to the unseen voice.

Eleven-year-old Jimmie Lee Johnson was becoming accustomed to caring for his ailing mother who had been confined to her bed for more than a year. Her small business, Johnson Cleaning Service, had been around for quite some time, and most of Gwinnett County knew little Jimmie Lee had been doing all six of his birth mother's accounts. Lilla Mae Johnson, however, had begun to wonder in recent months how such a young boy could finish cleaning a half-dozen houses after a 7-hour school day and still be home by six each evening. She often pondered whether Jimmie Lee was doing a thorough job. Indeed, her reputation was at stake. Opening a business in the late-1950s anywhere in Georgia was tough for an African-American woman. But, after 22 years in business, it seemed as though everyone was still pleased with her work. She did not want that attitude to change.

"Boy!" she called out, "that tea ain't ready yet?!"

"No, ma'am, not yet," he yelled from the kitchen. "It's comin' though."

"Well, while we wait, come on back here and rest yourself. I'm fixin' to—as city folk would say—'inquire of you' 'bout some things."

Jimmie Lee's 43-year-old mother sounded serious. He wondered what was to come. As he entered his mother's bedroom, he discovered she was not alone. A chic, brown-skinned woman with salt-and-pepper hair stood idly near Lilla Mae's bed. Her all-white J. C. Penney skirt set, black pumps and matching black hand bag graced her with an aura of pure professionalism. Clutched in her left hand was a thin manila folder. On the label, Jimmie Lee saw his full name, "James Lee Johnson" and his birth date, "11-29-69."

"Jimmie Lee," his mother began, "this is Mrs. Ivanna Rosser Moore. She's Deputy Sam Moore's pretty new wife. Say 'hello'."

Jimmie Lee walked closer to shake hands with the attractive woman who looked to be between 27 and 29, catching the scent of the world's most popular women's perfume, Chanel No. 5. He instantly recognized it because his mother used to wear it all the time. With an honest smile, he greeted her in his mannerable Southern drawl, saying, "Hi, ma'am."

"Well, hello, James," saluted Mrs. Moore, her smile as beautiful as a garden of roses. "And how are you this evening?"

"I'm fine, ma'am."

"Boy," interjected Lilla Mae, "you remember Deputy Moore, don't you?"

"Yes, ma'am," he answered with a huge grin, "me and him cut pulp wood together last summer. He gave me five whole dollars a day and we only had to work from sun-up to sun-down!"

"That's him," his mother stated, then corrected her only child's bad English, advising, "but it's 'he and I' cut pulp wood, not 'me and him'. Bad enough your momma's English is not good."

"Yes, ma'am," he acknowledged.

Lilla Mae raised half-way from her wooden-framed, full-size bed, supporting herself with pressed fists to the ivory-colored, cotton bed sheets purchased during one of K-Mart's Dollar Day Sales. She looked squarely into Jimmie Lee's personable eyes and said, "Mrs. Moore is from the county school board. She tells me that you never entered the sixth grade back in September. You've been absent from school for the past 70 days. Being that it's December now, I believe you got some 'splaining to do, wouldn't you say, boy?"

Jimmie Lee's mouth dropped open, his head tilting slightly towards the floor, a look of confusion set about his face. The raising of his mother's tenor-level voice quickly snapped him back to reality, however.

"I said, 'I believe you got some 'splaining to do'."

Half-turning towards the bedroom door, he said, "I

think I hear the kettle whistling," and began to make a fast exit.

"Freeze!" his mother expertly commanded, the rising anger in her voice becoming unquestionably apparent. For a brief instant, the cancer that ate daily at her body seemed no longer to exist, for the strength of her voice sounded like the good ole days when she was active, bubbly and, of course, healthy.

Very slowly Jimmie Lee turned to again face his mother. As he did so, a single tear—more so one of fright as opposed to sadness—trickled down the young country boy's right cheek. Realizing that honesty was the only thing Lilla Mae would accept, Jimmie Lee opened his mouth to render his explanation.

CHAPTER 2
June 1982
Portsmouth, Virginia

The massive applause—coupled with the standing ovation—that consumed the gymnasium of I. C. Norcom High School was electrifying. The speech of the valedictorian Deloren Powell had moved the 211 graduating seniors in such a way that it would be remembered by most, if not all, of the students in the years to come.

"That was absolutely spectacular, Deloren!" commented Principal Matthew Abington as he embraced the 18-year-old Advanced Placement student. Both strolled off the stage together, where Deloren's parents and eight siblings met them. Hugs or kisses were exchanged between the college-bound honor roll student and his immediate family and then off they went to join the festivities in Norcom's cafeteria.

Deloren "Dee" Powell was going to attend The College of William and Mary in Williamsburg in the fall, where he aspired to learn to one day become a teaching psychologist. There was a part of him, however, that wanted to be a writer. Then, of course, there was his father, the devout minister of a large holiness church in downtown Portsmouth who believed the science of psychology was the work of the Devil. "Figuring out man's problems in life is God's work," he would always say. "Anything else is of the Devil." But, Dee, forever the optimist, believed his 46-year-old father, the Reverend Tyler Powell, would someday come into the understanding that psychology was necessary to create the balance between mental competency and mental illness or defect.

In the cafeteria, Dee joined a reserved table with twelve chairs. Seated were his parents, to include his mother, seamstress Brittany Powell, and a circle of siblings: brothers - Brandon, Zachary and Jacob and sisters - Emily, Megan, Samantha, Brianna and, of course, twin Delorna. Emily, the oldest at almost 23, was seated next to her husband of the past eleven months. Dee sat in the vacant chair to the East.

While everyone feasted on fried shrimp and duck soup, Dee reflected on his family life. His parents were married on Christmas Eve, 1957; about six months after his father had graduated from seminary school. He was twenty-one and Brittany—then a Vinson—was just eighteen. The couple's first child, Tyler Jr., died at birth nine months and a week after the nuptials. Emily was born in September of 1959, Brandon in December of 1960, Megan in the Spring of '62, then Dee and his twin sister were born on March 28, 1964. They were followed by Zachary, Samantha, Jacob and Brianna between 1965 and 1968. His parents had been busy in the baby-making area, producing ten children in a decade. Now, after nearly a quarter-century of marriage, it seems their offspring were all headed in the right direction. No trouble with the police or school, except for Jacob who had an occasional brush with his high school vice principal from time to time. Dee was pleased with his strict upbringing for it kept him from picking up bad habits and incorrigible ways. Indeed, the honor and veneration he had for his parents, especially his mother, suggested as much. Now he only hoped his future as a psychologist would not damage the critically important bond between him and his father. Hope was all Dee had. To him, it was his beacon light.

CHAPTER 3
April 1983
Norfolk, Virginia

"Has the jury reached a verdict?" The judge asked the forewoman.

"We have, Your Honor," she answered. "We, the jury, in the above-mentioned cause, as to the sole count of the indictment, murder in the first degree, doth find the defendant, Andrew Smith, a juvenile, as follows: 'Not Guilty.' So say us all."

The standing-room-only courtroom on the second floor of Norfolk's circuit court building burst into applause and celebration as 16-year-old Andrew was acquitted of a homicide committed fourteen months earlier. Many watchers were unsure if Andrew would be set free. Although there were no clear eye-witnesses, Andrew confessed to the homicide—as well as three other unsolved murders—after twelve hours of police interrogation. The reason for confessing was bizarre: Andy, as he was called by his mother, had nothing to do with the killings but wanted the media attention so he wrote letters to police, confessed to four murders, then signed the letters, "The Pale Horse, Revelation 6:7-8." To take it a step further, Andy even called police from his high school, not leaving his name but instead leaving a note at the phone booth. He was eventually arrested, charged and indicted on one of the murders, the 96-year-old owner of a local cab company. The presiding judge ultimately allowed the lengthy confession into evidence, the only concrete evidence against Andy. Now the jury had spoken and the youth would be heading back home to his mother.

During the ride home, Kayla Smith told her son, "I'm glad this is over, Andy."

"Yeah, me too," Andy agreed.

Andy and his mother lived alone in Norfolk's uptown. The two moved into the Section Eight rent-controlled apartment complex three years earlier after spending many years in the harsh ghetto of the city's Huntersville section downtown where poverty, addiction and crime were so prevalent that hopelessness was all but expected and suicide was welcomed. But Andy's mother was different. She escaped drugs but not mental illness. In fact, she battled depression from the age of 16 and was diagnosed some years back as being paranoid schizophrenic. Top that off with epileptic seizures once or twice a month and what you have is a catastrophe waiting to happen. And Andy's antics, such as confessing to unsolved murders all over the city, did not help matters.

"I sure wish your father was still around," commented Kayla as she turned the car's radio to WPCE-AM 1400, a local gospel station.

"Why, so he can deny me as being his son?" He remarked.

"Andy, that's not nice. Your father was an immature fellow who needed some direction in life."

9

"Actually, Mom, he had some direction," Andy sarcastically responded. "He was directed by his conscience to walk out on you when I was only three."

Kay was all too familiar with her son's bitterness towards his absent father, Larry Knight, who denied Andy was his and deserted them both in 1969. She desperately tried to empathize with Andy's pain; however, her strong faith in God and adherence to His principles prevented her from speaking ill of Larry. Andy often asked, "Why did his mother appear to deny the no-good nature of his father?" Kay's response was typically simple, and then followed by a Bible quote: "It's not that I'm denying Larry's nature, Andy, but the Bible says, 'Where there is no wood, the fire goes out; and where there is no talebearer, strife ceases'."

Back in their two-bedroom apartment on Sewells Point Road, Kay and Andy spent the rest of the evening catching up on old times. After all, Andy had been held in the city's juvenile detention home since February 1982, more than a year. This quality time with his mother—and only friend—was quite refreshing. But just before midnight, when the two were preparing for bed, Kay came down the hall to her son's bedroom to leave him with an odd message:

"Andy, I'm not going to be around all the time. You're going to be eighteen in another year and some change and I may not be there to celebrate it with you. You're a very smart boy. Don't let that go to waste. Life is full of choices and decisions and determination is the longest word in the dictionary. The Bible offers guidance and Psalms 139 will pull you through when it comes to those decisions. Like I said, I'm not going to be around all the time." Without more, she turned from his doorway and retreated to her own bedroom.

Andy searched within himself, looking for an answer to what his mother meant by her words. It was more to it than what she had said. He knew his mom well and could distinguish between a lesson of life and a subliminal message, the latter of which was what he had just been hit with. "Did she receive some bad news?" He wondered. "Did she fail her annual physical last autumn?" Andy went to bed worrying; tossing and turning throughout the night was all he could do. His mother loved him beyond measure and for the first time in his life, Andy Smith tried to imagine what life would be like without her. The thought scared him.

CHAPTER 4
July 1985
Suwanee, Georgia

"For none of us lives to herself, and no one dies to herself. For if we live, we live to the Lord; and if we die, we died to the Lord. Therefore, whether we live or die, we are the Lord's …." The humble words of the Southern Baptist minister flowed like a river. The light drizzle of rain that fell gave his words a calming effect. The three dozen or so onlookers bore solemn countenances, especially 15-year-old Jimmie Lee Johnson whose damp eyes held a look of sadness so deep that it would appear nothing or no one could ever make him smile again. Continuing, the minister stated, "Lord, we commit the body of Lilla Mae Johnson to you for your safe-keeping. Ashes to ashes, dust to dust."

Emma White, owner of Suwanee's only full-service diner, Lou-Lou's Diner, gently pulled Jimmie Lee to her and whispered, "Listen, Jimmie Lee, I talked to the county social services folks yesterday and told them you were welcome to come live with me instead of going into a foster home. Your mother's first customer was my late-husband. That was 27 years ago. He never had a complaint. I think you'd love living with me on the plantation. What do you think?"

No words came from the teen's mouth. He merely hunched his shoulders to indicate that he didn't know. Looking up at Emma White, Jimmie Lee tried to speak anyway. Instead, he cried.

***

The cold January wind blew fiercely as young Jimmie Lee trekked his way through the fallen snow to head home. His surname was now "White", made possible by Emma White's petition for adoption a few months earlier. The two were getting along marvelously on the 22-acre estate in Suwanee, Gwinnett County's largest private residence.

Sheriff Piersall's personal patrol car zipped by Jimmie Lee, its lights and siren activated—a rarity in Suwanee. Apparently Sheriff Piersall did not recognize the boy who was wrapped comfortably in his winter clothes. Had the lawman known it was Jimmie Lee, he would have stopped to pick him up since he was ironically headed to the White Plantation.

A few minutes later, Jimmie Lee heard another siren approaching from behind, this time discovering it was Engine No. 1 of the volunteer fire department. It, too, was traveling at a high rate of speed. Unbeknownst to the lanky youth who celebrated his sixteenth birthday less than two months earlier, the fire engine—like Sheriff Piersall—was en route to his house.

As Jimmie Lee rounded the pasture clearing to the long private road of the White Plantation, he saw the smoke. One of the property's barns was on fire, being put out by a couple of volunteer firefighters. Emma White, with a 20-gauge shotgun resting across one of her thin but healthy 65-year-old shoulders, was standing next to Sheriff Piersall. In the back seat of his patrol car were two youngsters: 13-year-old Ken Babcock and his 19-year-old eldest brother, Jack. The boys' other brother, Joseph, the same age as Jimmie Lee, was away in reform school. He had been ordered there a month earlier by County Juvenile Court Judge Peter Cei after having been found guilty of burning two crosses on the yards of a couple of Suwanee's 24 African-American residents. It now appears sibling Ken would be joining Joseph and Jack would probably wind up in jail as the duo had done the unthinkable: They were caught setting fire to the barn after spray-painting "Nigger Lover" on its doors. Emma White, who was napping in a sitting room, awoke to a barking dog, saw the boys just as they were finishing their distasteful misdeeds, and held them at the point of one of her numerous shotguns while the gardener summoned the Sheriff who notified the firehouse folks. Jimmie Lee was stunned by the hate crime. He never looked at himself as a particular color. As his biological mother had said many times over, "Colored means anything that is painted, stained, varnished or dyed. You're none of them, boy." Still, he knew racial inequality existed but not in down-home Suwanee. To him, the cross-burning incident with Joseph Babcock was an isolated display of ignorance.

After the fire was extinguished and the Babcock boys taken into custody, Emma White and Jimmie Lee seated themselves on a bench near the ten-foot statue of former U. S. President Jimmy Carter erected at Emma's direction when the Georgia peanut farmer was voted into office nearly a decade earlier.

"You know, Momma Lou-Lou, I've been thinking lately," Jimmie Lee began.

"About?" She inquired.

"Traveling," he answered.

"Who with?" She wanted to know.

"Me; just me," he replied.

"Listen, Jimmie Lee," said Emma White, "don't you let the works of those wayward boys push you from your home. This is your home now. I owe it to your honest hard-working mother to look after you."

"I know, Momma Lou-Lou, but it's not the Babcocks. It's me. I want to travel. I want to go from state to state to state. I'd like to cover all fifty states in ten years. I've never been outside of Georgia except for last year when you took me to Disney World. I just want to travel."

Emma White sighed. She was not sure, but she felt this hate crime had a lot to do with her adopted son's urge to leave. She did not want him to run off based on the stupidity of others. Nevertheless, she quietly acknowledged hearing Jimmie Lee mention traveling before. So she decided to offer a compromise.

"Listen," as she often started out her conversations, "do this for me: Go to night school—you've been out of school for five years—and get your equivalency diploma. It'll take you three or four years of attending classes a couple nights a week to bring you to where you need to be, in terms of educational skills, in order to pass the final exam. Once you have your equivalency diploma, you can travel anywhere you want and I'll give you money to set out with. But, for the sake of your real momma's soul, at least finish school. Will you do that for me, Jimmie Lee?"

The teen followed Emma White's request with a long pause. Jimmie Lee was not necessarily thinking about his answer; rather his mind had trailed off to thoughts of his mother, good ole Lilla Mae who preached that a good education could take one a long way. He remembered back when she discovered he never entered the sixth grade in the fall of 1980 and how upset she was about the discovery. The only thing that saved him from being grounded for the next month was his explanation: He did not want his mother to lose her house-cleaning accounts so he told all six of her customers that he was being home-schooled so as to quell suspicion regarding him showing up before noon to start cleaning. With Lilla Mae bed-ridden and unable to work, she surrendered to Jimmie Lee's honest help and allowed him to remain out of school, occasionally going through a few store-bought instructional books he kept with him to keep him sharp and on point.

"Well, Jimmie Lee?" It was Momma Lou-Lou awaiting an answer.

"Yes, ma'am, I'll go back to school to finish."

"Good, good. Now let's go down to the diner and get some ice cream and pie. The smell of smoke is irritating my nostrils."

Jimmie Lee produced a confused look. "Momma Lou-Lou, we have ice cream and, I think, pie here at the house."

She smiled. "Yeah, but it's always good to eat someone else's. Plus, we won't have to pay for it. I own the place, remember? It's been mine long before you were even born."

CHAPTER 5
August 1986
Portsmouth, Virginia

"And do you, Vicky Townes, take Andrew Smith to be your lawfully wedded husband, to love and to hold..." The words of Bishop Jim Dillard dug deep into 22-year-old Vicky's mental. She had been dating Andy since her birthday in late-March, having met him only five days earlier. The two worked together at McDonald's on London Boulevard at the Effingham Street intersection. It was love at first sight or so it seemed. Andy proposed marriage on Mother's Day; a pregnancy—Vicky's third—was discovered in early-July. She could only hope 19-year-old Andy was ready for all the new responsibilities he faced. "...for as long as you both shall live?"

"I do," she replied to Bishop Dillard's eternally important query.

***

The fast-moving pace of the McDonald's was unrelenting. The Veteran's Day Parade just outside the store made for good business. There were five lines of customers and the line to the drive-thru window was loaded with upwards of a dozen vehicles. Andy, promoted to Swing Manager six weeks earlier, was in charge. His wife who worked the 5 a. m. to Noon shift had already gone home.

"Twelve Regulars, Turn-Lay," Andy commanded to the primary grill team, directing it to cook a dozen fresh regular-sized all-beef patties every two minutes. "Six Quarters, Pull-Lay," was the order to the secondary grill team, prompting it to cook a half-dozen quarter-pound patties every five minutes.

The incessant ring of the fast-food joint's telephone annoyed Andy who was trained never to answer the phone during a mad rush. "They'll call back," said trainers George Trees and Donna Othello. But, it seemed, whoever was calling now—at one o'clock in the afternoon—refused to call back. They wanted to be heard—now. Finally, Andy gave up and darted to the phone, "McDonald's London Boulevard; Andy speaking."

"Andy, this is Vicky."

Andy went into a panic. His wife was only five months pregnant but complications were not a stranger to her. Although this was only her third pregnancy, incredibly, it was her sixth child and there was trouble with each previous pregnancy.

Triplets Ahmad, Ahman and Ahmar were born four years earlier—in November of 1982—and twins Darius and Darren came last December. The triplets were C-Sectioned two weeks too soon; the twins came an entire month before term. Andy wondered if there was a problem with this one, Vicky's first girl.

"Vicky," Andy said hesitantly. "The baby—"

"No, the baby's fine. Your Aunt Carolyn just called. It's your mother. She's taken ill."

Andy got the information on the hospital and room number and hung up. His shift was slated to end in three more hours and he would drive straight to Saint Vincent's Medical Center in neighboring Norfolk to check on her. He thought back three-and-a-half years when his mother, Kay, warned him that she would not always be there for him. He discovered a little over a year later that Kayla Melinda Smith, then only 41, was dying. She had a hepatic infection from years of taking prescription medications to treat her acute depression, schizophrenia and epilepsy. Her liver simply could no longer break down the various impurities commonly found in prescription meds. Now, according to Aunt Carolyn's description to Vicky, Andy's mother was entering the final stages of the infection and possessed less than a matter of weeks to live. Andy had been trying to prepare himself for the inevitable.

After work, Andy hopped into his tan 1979 Plymouth Volare family wagon and headed down Effingham Street en route to the Portsmouth-Norfolk Tunnel less than a mile away. The tunnel's traffic was unusually heavy this time of day, in spite of the holiday, so Andy was constrained to roll up his windows in order to duck the noxious fumes from the exhaust pipes of other vehicles. The tunnel led out onto Interstate 264 on which Andy traveled eastbound to reach the Interstate 64 by-pass. Once on I-64, he hit the fast lane, increased his speed somewhat, and drove the next twelve minutes at 65 miles-per-hour.

Now on Granby Street and twenty minutes into his trip, Andy again pondered what life would be like without his mother. The thought always frightened him even though he was—or so he believed—mentally and emotionally ready to deal with her passing. He'd had the last couple of years to come to grips with that which is most certain:

death. Yet he found it odd his mother seemed to have more of her faith in that which is least certain: life after death. "The Bible says," she would authoritatively begin, "'I am the resurrection and the life: he that believeth in me, though he were dead, yet shall he live.'" Then she would gracefully add, "'and whosoever liveth and believeth in me shall never die.'" Her faith—that which she knew was Truth—kept her whole. Andy's only reservation was his inability to discern the veracity of life after death since no one—aside from Jesus—ever came back to show and prove that this so-called resurrection is a fact.

Andy's Volare pulled into a side parking lot on Painter Street adjacent to the medical center. After killing the engine, he sat for awhile trying to collect his thoughts. While doing so, he lit a Newport Light cigarette, inhaling deeply with each puff, unconsciously watching the exhaled smoke as it filled the car's interior. A knock on the driver's side window startled him. He rolled down the darkly tinted window to discover an exceptionally beautiful girl who coughed and waved away escaping cigarette smoke from within the car.

"Sorry," Andy offered. "You having car trouble?"

"Yeah, sorta," she said, showing an awesome smile and perfectly shaped pearly white teeth. "I don't have one."

Andy laughed; so did she. Her laughter seemed so original, so perfect, so unique. And that smile. It intoxicated Andy.

"Are you lost?" He asked.

"No, not really," she responded, and then added, "just stranded. My sister, Zelda, was supposed to come pick me up. That was two hours ago. I think she forgot about me."

"Well," Andy began, "I'm here to visit someone—my mother actually—and I haven't been inside yet. If you want to wait in the car for me, you can. I should be out in about thirty minutes or so."

The girl looked around, then leaned forward to get closer to Andy. "It's really cold out here."

"Well," he said, "why don't you come inside with me? It's much warmer in there, I'm sure."

"Okay," she said happily. "I'm Jeanette," extending a hand as Andy got out of the automobile, "and you are—?"

"Andrew Smith but you can just call me 'Andy'."

The two began the short walk to Saint Vincent's side entrance when Jeanette unexpectedly huddled under Andy's arm as if to steal some of his body heat. "It really is cold out here," she repeated. Andy, however, disagreed. "Not so bad. Where are you from?"

"Florida," she said.

"Go figure," Andy replied. "Anything under fifty degrees is probably cold to you."

"More like seventy," she corrected with a sly smile.

Dr. Tena Elcock, a tall, broad-shouldered woman from Guyana, was Kay Smith's attending physician. Dr. Elcock was on night-duty at the medical center and happened to be in Kay's room when Andy and Jeanette arrived. She spent a few minutes outlining her patient's condition, then left.

Hey Ma," Andy greeted.

"Hi," she answered, her voice only a little less-than-normal. "And who might this attractive young lady be?"

"My name is Jeanette, Jeanette Foreman."

"The two of you work together?" Kay asked, already presuming the answer to be no since the girl wore no uniform.

"No, we just met outside," confessed Jeanette. "He offered me a ride."

"Oh really?" Kay seemed suspicious. "Did he mention he was a newlywed?"

Jeanette, feeling the piercing intrusion into her hidden nature, attempted to look innocent. "Actually, he did," she lied. "He's only offering a ride. It's pretty cold out and my sister forgot to come pick me up."

"Where do you live?" Kay asked.

"Portsmouth, in an area called Academy Park."

Kay's suspicions grew. There was something in the girl's eyes that seemed to indicate she was hiding a facet of her character—her true character—and Kay was not about to bite her tongue.

"My son married a sweet girl from Portsmouth three months ago. They have a house full of kids—excuse me, children—and she's expecting another child in the coming months. Whatever you do, don't ask him to do something that—if you were his wife—you wouldn't want another young lady to ask him to do. Do I make myself clear, Janet?"

Andy intervened, "Ma, what are you talking about?"

"Andy, let me handle this. You hear me, Janet?"

Jeanette managed a smile. "Yes, ma'am. Loud and clear. I'll wait outside." She headed out the hospital room but not before turning to politely add, "By the way, my name is Jeanette, ma'am."

Kay displayed a thumbs-up. "Gotcha."

Andy was furious. "Ma, I can't believe you did that!" He pulled up a nearby chair and positioned it at her bedside, dropping the bed rail to the lower position to hold his mother's hand despite his anger. "You don't even know her." His tone had softened.

"Boy, that young lady is a freak. A cold freak. I see it in her eyes. If you're not careful, trouble is on its way and it's coming in at a hundred miles an hour."

"Ma, you're too protective of me."

"You think?"

"Yes, I do."

"Doubtful," she flatly stated. "If that were true, I would have found a way to block your marriage to Vicky."

"But you said you liked Vicky."

"Exactly, Andy, so that goes to prove I'm not over-protective because if I were, it wouldn't matter if I liked her or not."

Changing the subject, Andy asked about her illness. "The things the doctor said, how are you holding up?"

"I'm ready to go, son. I've got a week at best. I'm ready."

"Ma, how can you be so calm?"

Kay smiled. "Because I am content. I have accepted whatever God provides for my life. The Bible says, 'Not that I speak in regard to need, for I have learned in whatever state I am, to be content.' Now you go on and take that young lady home. I just wanted to see your face and hear your voice. I'm tired."

"Okay, Ma," Andy said, rising to leave. "I love you, Ma."

"I know you do, Andy. And I love you even more."

Jeanette was sitting in the hall when Andy departed. She didn't seem to be upset. In fact, she broke into a smile upon seeing him.

"Your mom's a trip," she said with a giggle.

"Yeah, I know. Sorry 'bout that."

"It's no biggie."

"Yeah it is. She thinks you're a freak."

Jeanette burst into laughter. "What kind of freak? The weird kind or the hot-in-the-ass kind?"

Andy was taken aback by her candor. "The hot-in-the-ass kind," he acknowledged.

"Wow," said Jeanette, nodding her head as if impressed. "Your mom is one heck of a judge of character. She was right on target."

Andy stopped cold. "Say what?! You mean she was right?"

"Yep," she confessed, and then added, "but keep that between you, me, the sheets and, of course, the Isley Brothers."

***

Bishop Bob Adams, the head religious minister at Norfolk's Faith Baptist Tabernacle, stood somberly over the all-copper casket as it was being lowered into the grave and spoke his final words. "Weeping endureth for the night, but joy cometh in the morning. Most Heavenly Father God above, we offer unto you the earthen vessel of Kayla Melinda Smith, ashes to ashes and dust to dust. She is yours, dear God."

It was now the Saturday following Thanksgiving; Kay had died on Tuesday. Andy was called at home by Dr. Elcock with the sorrowful news. He broke down while still on the telephone. It was rough on him, much rougher than he had anticipated. And with five toddlers running wild throughout his and Vicky's small apartment, along with Vicky's own grossly lacking communication skills, Andy felt even more alone. He needed to get away, at least for a short time.

Following the funeral and interment, Andy's family gathered together at his Aunt Carolyn's house in the Douglas Park section of Portsmouth. Cars bearing license plates from all over—New York, Arkansas, Maryland, and the District of Columbia—graced the on-street parking spaces of Choate Street. There was food, beverages, and much socializing among the relatives of Andy, many of whom had not seen one another in quite some time. But, Andy's heart ached; he needed some consolation to fill the void in his bosom. What he needed, he realized, was a third-party who could offer comfort from a point of view that was completely unbiased. And he had just the right third-party in mind. He casually got up, went over and kissed Vicky on the forehead, telling her he needed to leave for awhile. Vicky did not pry as to where. She knew he had a lot on his mind.

Andy still remembered the little white house on Belmont Avenue where he drove Jeanette to a couple of weeks earlier. Academy Park was not far from Douglas Park and the route would be simple. Taking Choate Street to Rodman Avenue took less than a minute and from Rodman to Portsmouth Boulevard, it took only two minutes. Andy hung a left at Main, then a quick right onto DeKalb, driving the long winding street to McLean Avenue where he turned right, drove under the overpass, then took the first right onto Belmont. Jeanette's place was just a couple of blocks down on the left. Actually, all the houses were on the left because the right side was just a grassy foundation adjacent to Interstate 264 near the Victory Boulevard exit. He was barely out of the tan family wagon before the front door of the house opened and out popped a girl a few years older than Jeanette. She strongly favored Jeanette and had an awesome body like hers as well.

"Hello," she said warmly. "Who are you?"

"I'm Andy. Is Jeanette around?"

"Oh my," she said, looking him over from head to toe, "Jeanette done struck gold. I like that suit."

"Thanks," Andy said without smiling. "Is she here?'

"Oh shit," she said with an embarrassed look, "you didn't come here for me. Yeah, she's here. C'mon in, Andy."

The girl held the screen door open, allowing Andy entry into the house. As he did so, he inadvertently brushed against her large, round breasts which sat perfectly underneath her red designer Jordache sweatshirt. She smelled sweet as if she had recently showered using beauty soap. Like Jeanette, she too owned an intoxicating smile. "The two must be related," Andy said to himself.

"Have a seat," she offered. "Would you like a beer or something?"

"No, I'm okay."

"I'll go get Jeanette for you. She's in her room."

The unidentified girl disappeared into the rear of the cozy house, her hips swaying as she walked. The tight red Jordache sweatpants she wore left nothing to Andy's imagination. "Damn, she's phat," he said to himself.

Moments later, Jeanette emerged from the back, walking into the living room in a mauve silk robe that stopped barely six inches from her crotch. She looked surprised, then ashamed before producing that million-dollar smile of hers.

"What's up, Andy," she gleefully greeted as she grabbed a hold of his hand, pulling him up from the sofa and embracing him. "This is a surprise."

"Hey Jeanette. Glad to see you again."

"Yeah, same here." She had not yet released her embrace. "What brings you here out of the blue?"

"My mother died this past Tuesday. The funeral was earlier today. I—I needed to get away. You came to mind."

Jeanette's smile disappeared and her face became instantly filled with pity. "I'm sorry about your mom. Man, that's gotta be a pretty messed up feeling."

"It is," he admitted.

"Check this out," she said, finally pulling away from his body. "Sit here for a few minutes. I'll get rid of this dude I've got—"

"Oh you were on the phone?"

"No, Andy," she said with that shamed look again. "He's in my room."

"No, no, no," Andy asserted. "You don't have to do that. I was just looking for someone to talk to. I can come back."

"Andy," Jeanette said, looking him directly in the eyes, "sit your ass down. He's been here since last night. It's time for him to go anyway." She smiled again.

Ten minutes later, a guy around Andy's age appeared from the same short hallway that led to Jeanette's room. He spoke to Andy on his way out and, upon seeing the other girl in the kitchen, waved to her saying, "Take care of yourself, Zelda."

Another ten minutes passed before Jeanette came into the living room. She had showered, as evidenced by her wet hair and a huge orange towel draped about her shapely physique. "Sorry it took me so long," she said as she came over to where Andy was seated, leaning forward to kiss him on the cheek, thereafter going into the kitchen to retrieve two bottles of Private Stock from the fridge and a tray of ice from the deep-freezer. "C'mon back, Mister Andy," Jeanette expertly instructed as she headed back towards her bedroom.

One hour and four beers later, Andy—usually a light drinker—was considerably inebriated and Jeanette decided to take cold advantage of the situation. The tray of ice had long since melted. She excused herself to retrieve a fresh tray of frozen cubes. While she was gone, Andy took the time to admire her bedroom. There were no white lights. The ceiling light was yellow. The lamps on the two bronze bedside tables held two different colored bulbs—one red and the other blue—and were both on. The mixture of colors bounced perfectly off the beige walls which were adorned with passive water-color paintings—probably Norman Rockwell's—each situated a perfect yard apart. In one corner of the room, next to the open closet, was a mulch-colored leather love seat. The bed, a full-size bronze wooden-framed model by the now-defunct Louisiana furniture company, Geechie, sat dead-center. It's matching bedside tables, along with the imitation Tiffany lamps, were cluttered with the usual items: on one there was a clock, a wristwatch and blindfold, presumably for sleeping, and on the other a Princess telephone, an opened box of Lifestyles ultra-thin latex condoms, a pack of Top rolling papers and a Glad sandwich bag with a green-looking substance that resembled parsley. A 19-inch Zenith color TV sat atop the Geechie 4-drawer bureau, also bronze, and a horde of cosmetics, perfumes and typical "girl shit" were piled on the mirrored dresser directly in front of the foot of Jeanette's bed. There was no carpeting but the wooden floor was clean although no shine could be seen. Andy nodded in approval following the completion of his survey. Almost like clockwork, Jeanette returned a second or so later.

"So, Mister Andy," began Jeanette as she climbed back onto the bed with the fresh tray of ice, "now I know everything about you and you know everything about me."

"That's true," he acknowledged with slurred speech. "But I'm wondering about the ice. What's up with that?"

"Well," she said, her voice lowering to a near-whisper," that's the part I didn't tell you. I work with ice."

"Work with it?" Andy asked with a look of perplexity about his features. "How so?"

"I put it in my mouth and then put my mouth on you." She climbed up on all-fours and glided from the headboard end towards Andy who was laid out at the foot end of the bed and fixed her body over his as he lay. "Wanna see?"

The beers had stolen his ability to reason, to think about Vicky, to just say no. He never answered Jeanette, but then again, he didn't have to. Her eagerness to show him her copulation-related skills would surely override his ability to pull back from her. After all, even his mother knew Jeanette had a secret side; Jeanette herself later admitted it. Now it was time for Andy to experience it—first hand.

***

The employee break room in the London Boulevard McDonald's was silent; its only occupants being Andy and his wife Vicky who was now eight months pregnant. The two had not lived together for the past month as Andy was now staying with Jeanette and her sister, having left Vicky back in December on the premise that her five boys were too much for him to have to deal with following the death of his mother. Actually, he was whipped—pussy-whipped, that is—by Jeanette who managed to have sex with him in so many different ways that, at times, some of her antics barely seemed legal. The 23-year-old vixen was a force to be reckoned with. Her magnetism sucked him away from Vicky and his ready-made family, causing him to concoct a ridiculous excuse for leaving her high-and-dry towards the end of her pregnancy with their unborn daughter. Ironically, Vicky still loved him and she wanted him back.

"So, Andy," she said, her voice non-confrontational, soft, caring, "when are you coming home? The boys really miss you, especially the Triplets. They wonder where you are. Things can be better. Just come home so we can work them out."

Andy knew he should be home with his wife of less than six months. He had an obligation—both legal and moral—to her. Yet he found it extremely laborious to decide between lust and love. The decision is supposed to be easy—you choose that which lasts the longest, love—but for Andy, it was not so easy. Each time he entertained the thought of breaking off his extra-marital affair with Jeanette, she would simply do one more new thing to him in bed that she had not done before. After that, any thought of breaking off their link all but vanished. She took him to carnal heights that were unprecedented and there was simply no way in Hell he could pass that up for a girl like Vicky who believed the missionary position was the only acceptable form of sexual intercourse. Oral sex, to her, was repulsive. What she failed to understand, however, was that she was married to a 20-year-old guy in the prime of his sexually appetizing years. Depriving him was equivalent to pushing him out the front door.

"Andy?" Vicky called to him. "Please talk to me."

Andy began shaking his head. "I can't come back, Vicky. I'm sorry."

Vicky started crying. "The bills are piling up. I can't do this alone. The baby is due in another four or five weeks. I simply can't do this alone. Andy, you have to come home."

"I'll figure something out on the bills situation," he stated as he got up to leave, "and I'll make sure one way or the other you have money for bills. But I won't be coming back. Can't do it, Vicky." Then he added a statement which, the moment he'd said it, he immediately regretted. "Besides, you managed five children alone; six can't possibly be any different." That was probably the coldest and most unfeeling thing he could have said to his own wife; however, Andy was so addicted to Jeanette that he was simply unable to shake his irrational behavior. What he did not know was that his mother's warning about Jeanette went much deeper than he could have ever imagined. Soon, though, Andy would find out. But, by then, it would be too late. Much too late.

Later that night, after Jeanette picked Andy up from work using his car, he expressed to her his inner turmoil with not having enough money to help take care of both Vicky and the boys and Jeanette. At only $4.40 per hour, a full 40-hour week at McDonald's was simply not enough.

"Where there's a will, there's a way," stated Jeanette, citing a cliché probably more than two hundred years old. "Sometimes a man has to stand up and be more of a man than even he thinks he can be. C'mon, let's take a ride."

The two took a cruise over to Norfolk—Jeanette was driving—to its downtown business district. She parked on a street off Saint Paul's Boulevard directly facing Norfolk Circuit Court.

"You will notice," she began, "that Saint Paul's Boulevard reaches the downtown tunnel on one turn and the interstate on the other. If you go that way—pointing West in the direction of the city's juvenile court and school administration buildings—you'll hit the tunnel inside of two minutes. And if you go the other way—pointing East towards Waterside Drive—you'll be right on Interstate 264 in just over a couple of minutes."

"What does all of this mean?" Andy asked, looking about as lost as a five-year-old in Paramount's Kings Dominion theme park outside Richmond.

Jeanette leaned over and laid a passionate kiss upon his lips, following which she whispered into his ear, "What are we parked next to, Mister Andy?"

Andy looked before answering. "It's an office building."

"What kind of office building?'

He looked more closely. "A bank building."

"Correct, Mister Andy," she said, planting soft kisses on his cheek and neck. "A bank. Whatever you need is right in there, plus lots more."

Andy, unaware of Jeanette's true thoughts, assumed a more legitimate position, "Do you think they'll give me a personal loan without collateral?"

Jeanette began giggling. "I think they'll give you whatever you ask for depending on how you ask and collateral won't even come up in the short conversation."

"How do you figure that?" Andy asked.

"Because, Mister Andy, you are going to just walk in and ask for it. There are ten tellers in there. I've been watching this place for the past couple of months. It'll be quick and easy. In and out in no time."

Andy pushed Jeanette away from so close to him. "I know you're not talking about robbing a bank!"

"Shhh," she instructed, placing her index finger on his lips, "lower your voice, baby."

"Lower my voice?! No, fuck that! I'm not going to rob a bank! Are you fucking crazy?!"

"Shhh," she again instructed, unzipping his pants and casually placing her hand inside, "let's talk for a while. But first let me give you what you love: a kiss. Can I kiss you, Andy?"

"I know what you're up to, Jeanette. You're not talking about a regular kiss."

She smiled but said nothing, her warm hand by now caressing Andy's hardening penis.

"The last time you said you wanted to 'kiss' me, it wasn't on my lips and I left Vicky. I wonder what I'll do this time."

***

"Okay, let's do this," said Andy who, like the other three of the stolen car's occupants, was dressed in all black, including a long black trench coat. "Remember your jobs: Zelda's got the door, Pierre's got the floor, I've got the scoop, and Jeanette stays in the car. Everyone ready to go?"

Both Zelda, Jeanette's 26-year-old sister, and Pierre Graff answered yes in unison. Jeanette did not need to respond as she was not going inside. She convinced Andy when they first discussed robbing a bank two weeks earlier that she would best be suited to remain outside the large bank monitoring a police scanner while positioned as the getaway driver. As it turned out, the sisters were no strangers to this type of activity as both had criminal records. Pierre, on the other hand, was like Andy: a poor soul with no criminal conviction record but also no money. Pierre was also the same guy Jeanette ran out of her bedroom the day Andy showed up after his mother's funeral. Ironically, Pierre was now dating Zelda who'd called him out of the blue less than two weeks earlier.

"Okay, let's make it happen," said Andy, sounding like a pro. Jeanette had spent the last few days coaching him on sounding in control. They'd go through drills while in bed. Andy picked up quickly on the lessons. And, of course, Jeanette rewarded him after each drill. Sex was definitely her strong suit.

The trio headed inside. Zelda, armed with a small but deadly .38 caliber revolver, stopped just inside the

34

entrance as if pondering what she'd entered the bank for. Pierre headed towards the center of the banking center's main floor. Tucked in his waistband was a Mach-11 with a full conversion kit attached. Andy marched towards the row of tellers, five of which were open. He wasted no time, pulled out the 16-gauge sawed-off shotgun situated under his black London Fog trench coat, and fired off a blast into the air.

"Okay, you lousy motherfuckers! Hit the fucking floor! Now!" Andy fired a second blast into one of three security cameras while Pierre took out the other two cameras. The loud and rapid popping sounds from Pierre's fully-automatic Mac-11 were akin to a working jack-hammer tearing into concrete.

"Let's go, let's go!" Andy continued, jumping atop the long tellers' counter. "Hit the floor!" The nearly one dozen bank employees, including the tellers and four other bank personnel, complied, as well as the 27 patrons.

Andy wore a backpack with the opening on his front side as opposed to at his back. He speedily packed it with 100's and 50's, leaving the top stack of both denominations in the drawers as they were the ones that contained the dye-pack according to Jeanette. Using only his left hand to grab the loot, Andy's right hand still gripped the sawed-off shotgun. His nervousness had been consumed by the awesome flow of adrenaline through his body.

"Incoming!" Zelda yelled. That was a signal that a patron was entering the banking center. She pointed her handgun at the Asian woman and told her to lie down on the floor with everyone else. Pierre used the muzzle of his Mach-11 to guide her to the nearest open spot and then looked at his Casio watch.

"One minute in, Scoop!" Pierre hollered, keeping Andy aware of the time the trio was inside.

"Gotcha, Floor Man!" Andy responded, by now leaving the second—and heading to the third—teller's drawer.

Another minute passed and Andy was done. He grabbed the closest teller from off the floor. "Where's the goddamn server room?!"

"The what?" The horrified woman asked.

"The goddamn server room! Where is it?!"

"Right there," she said, pointing towards a plain door with a deadbolt. Andy roughly pushed her back down to the floor, ran over to the door and shot the lock through the door's inside. He kicked open the door. An obviously expensive server and mainframe were inside.

Andy used two more shells to blast both into inoperability, effectively crashing the bank's computer records system to the point it would take days to retrieve the serial numbers of the stolen cash. By then, all of the stolen cash will have been washed out. Jeanette made sure Andy remembered to disable the system.

"Three minutes in, Scoop!" Pierre, who was starting to get nervous, shouted. Zelda told him the trio would need to be in and out in less than three minutes.

"We're done, Floor Man!" Andy called out. He trotted towards the bank's entrance. "Go, go, go!" He commanded. Zelda put her gun away and stepped out. Pierre was right behind her. Andy took one last look at the helpless folks on the floor, saying, "Thank you for your cooperation, ladies and gentlemen." He smiled at the success of the heist, cuffed the sawed-off back under his coat which was by now so bulky it made him appear obese, and marched out the front door.

The four dumped the stolen car, a 1985 Chevette, a few blocks from the bank, splitting up in pairs in the parking lot of the Omni International Hotel on Waterside Drive. Zelda and Pierre jumped into her white 1967 Lincoln Continental with suicide doors—a gift from her late-grandmother—and Andy and Jeanette got into Andy's car which had been parked there the night before. The group drove in two cars to the hotel—the stolen brown Chevette and Zelda's jazzy antique—thirty minutes before the heist.

Back on Belmont Avenue in Academy Park, Jeanette counted out the money while Andy and Pierre downed shots of Canadian Club to calm their nerves. Meanwhile, Zelda was in the shower. She was having hot flashes, something she'd experienced on her previous three stick-ups.

All totaled, they got $220,000 in cash, eighty in 50's and the rest in 100's. As agreed upon, the split would be even with Andy and Pierre receiving $55,000 each, and the girls sharing the remaining $110,000. After Zelda's shower, she and Pierre left. She doubled back, however, to retrieve her handgun. She didn't say why she needed it. Andy and Jeanette celebrated with long and grueling episodes of intense sex, at the conclusion of which she gave Andy his very first rim job, practically incapacitating him for several minutes. He curled into an infant-like position and spoke in incomprehensible gibberish. It was, to say the least, a truly pathetic sight.

Later that night, Andy paid a trip to Vicky, giving her five-thousand dollars. When she asked where the money came from, Andy lied to her by telling her he won it in Atlantic City. She bought the fib.

On his way back to Academy Park, he noticed several Portsmouth and state police cars along Interstate 264, near the South Street on-ramp. They were huddled over what seemed to be a dead body. Unbeknownst to Andy, it was indeed a corpse—that of Pierre Graff's. He had been shot once in the back of the head.

***

Andy quit his McDonald's job two weeks following the bank hold-up. Jeanette insisted he give two weeks written notice. But the store still had the telephone number at Jeanette's and, on February 22, Assistant Manager Carolina Hubbard called Andy.

"It's Vicky," the longtime McDonald's employee began. "She's having the baby. Her sister called to see if we could call you to let you know."

"Thanks, Miss Hubbard. What hospital?"

"Portsmouth General. Right up the street from here."

"Thanks again." He hung up, told Jeanette, and hopped into his family wagon en route to the downtown hospital, fifteen minutes drive away. On the way, he wondered when Jeanette would let him know it was okay to buy a new car. She monitored his spending closely, making sure he did not make any mistakes. He often wondered, and even asked her, if she had done a bank robbery or something like that before. She emphatically denied it, claiming she formulated the idea from a made-for-television movie. Actually, the downtown Norfolk bank was her fourth robbery since 1984. She planned one a year, living off the take for twelve months and never engaging in lavish spending.

Marquita Smith was born at 8:56 P.M. She weighed in at a healthy weight of eight pounds even. She was as beautiful as life itself, her chocolate complexion just like her mother's. Andy was elated as he held her. However, his joy was interrupted by an unexpected—an unknown—visitor into Vicky's room.

"Good evening, folks," said the tall, well-built Anglo-Saxon dressed in a navy blue Alexander Julian two-piece suit with a fashionable Chez Roffe tie and crisp white Dover dress shirt. "I'm Detective Ted Iverson with the Portsmouth Police Department. Are you Andrew Smith?"

Andy tried not to appear alarmed. "I am."

"Could you please step into the hallway, sir?"

"Sure," said Andy, Marquita still in his arms.

"You might want to leave the infant, sir." It was more of a command than a suggestion. Andy complied. "I'll be back in a few minutes, Vicky." He gave her a light kiss on her chapped lips and planted an even lighter one on the forehead of his one-hour-and-eight-minute-old daughter before handing the precious child to her mother.

Out in the hallway stood three others, two men and a woman, all dressed in suits. They each identified themselves: Special Agents Floyd Jacobson and Louise Kemp with the Norfolk Field Office of the Federal Bureau of Investigation and Detective Thomas McLean, a robbery investigator with the Norfolk Police Department. The Portsmouth police detective was there only for jurisdictional purposes; as such, he did not hang around, leaving as soon as the two FBI agents identified themselves. The Norfolk detective spoke up first.

"Mr. Smith, we need to take you to Norfolk police headquarters to interview you regarding a bank robbery in our city last month."

"A bank robbery," exclaimed Andy. "What does that have to do with me?"

"We'll explain there, sir," Det. McLean stated. "Did you drive here?"

"Yeah." Andy replied. "My car's in the parking lot. How'd you know I was here?"

"We just left your mistress' apartment," answered McLean. "She told us where you were."

Keep your cool, Andy, he thought to himself. "She did right 'cause I don't have anything to hide. Well, let's go."

"Okay," said Det. McLean. "You can follow me in your car. These two federal agents will be right behind you."

"No problem," acknowledged Andy.

Thirty minutes later, Andy was at Norfolk police headquarters and had been advised by McLean of his Miranda rights. Det. McLean then asked Andy to get into a line-up to which he agreed. He and four others were lined up, each holding a number against their chest. On the opposite side of a two-way mirror, three persons—bank teller Edwina S'Pinall, bank customer Denise Williams and Omni hotel valet, John Ladd—each identified Subject Number Three as being connected to the bank robbery. Andy Smith was Subject Number Three.

CHAPTER 6
May 1988
Williamsburg, Virginia

Dean W. Maurice Scott, head of the School of Arts and Sciences at The College of William and Mary, intently studied Deloren Powell's transcripts over the past six years. Dee sat in silence across from the veteran educator.

"Well, Mr. Powell," started Dean Scott, "I'm concerned with your class ranking. It seems that last summer you enrolled full-time into our Summer Program. By doing so you're getting a jump on your classes but you're pulling your ranking down."

"I understand precisely what I'm doing," acknowledged Dee. "I'm pursuing a second doctorate's degree—in Education—and would like to have two doctorates in nine years instead of ten. Four summers will do it for me; I've got three more summers to go to achieve such a task."

"But your ranking, Mr. Powell—"

"Oh I don't care about that," Dee interjected. "I'm just trying to finish college in the shortest possible time while at the same time earning two doctorate's degrees. Rankings mean nothing to me."

Dean Scott sighed. "Rankings are quite important. There are only eleven percent of you all enrolled here. You all need to stay ranked as high as possible, to keep things looking good for the school, instead of cheating yourselves out of a full academic year."

"And by 'you all' you must mean psych students?" Dee inquired, knowing full well the dean was speaking of African-Americans.

"Well, no, of course," answered Dean Scott. "I'm speaking of students of color. This school prides itself in having a double-digit percentage—however low—of people of color enrolled. We want you all to do well but we want you all to graduate in the same span of time as the rest of the student body. You're circumventing that, Mr. Powell."

Dee was baffled by the lecture which he viewed as a baseless accusation that really represented a deeply rooted form of academic bias. He surmised the bias was not sanctioned by the elite university itself but was most likely confined to the aging dean seated in front of him.

"I'm getting my Master's degree in another week, Dean Scott. I have already enrolled in the 1988 Summer Program and I will attend. I'll graduate in 1990 with my Ph.D. and in 1991 with my D. Ed. You call it circumventing; I don't. Anything else, sir?"

"But you're stealing, son."

"What?!" Dee exclaimed. "Stealing? That's a bit over the edge, wouldn't you say, Dean Scott?"

"You all have to understand—"

"Cut that 'you all' crap, Dean!" Dee commanded. "That is so racist!"

"Don't get violent," the dean said, lowering his voice and standing up to move closer to his office door. "I don't want any trouble in here."

"What?!" Dee was becoming more upset by the minute. "What do you think I am?"

The dean eased towards the closed office door, opened it and called out to his secretary to call campus police. "I'll feel safer if they come escort you out."

Dee was appalled. "No need you racist bastard! I'm leaving!"

CHAPTER 7

September 1989
Suwanee

The White Plantation was bustling with townsfolk. Some were standing around chatting in small circles while others were scattered about—Sheriff Piersall was standing by the Jimmy Carter statue and the gardener, Nathan, was near the orchard patch giving the history to town resident and gossip columnist Michelle Nader. The plantation, which spanned close to two dozen acres, was hosting a celebration of sorts, a combination victory-slash-Labor Day-slash-farewell gala. The victory portion was for Jimmie Lee who'd received his GED about five weeks earlier. It was also the Saturday before Labor Day. Finally, Jimmie Lee was slated to leave Suwanee—his home for the past 19 years and 9 months—to venture out into the world. So his adoptive mother, Emma, decided to throw one big shebang.

It had been four years since his natural mother, Lilla Mae, died and Jimmie Lee still missed her every single day. His once wonderful smile had long since disappeared and only surfaced once in recent times, the day he went to Lilla Mae's gravesite with his GED to tell her what he'd accomplished. Emma went to the cemetery with Jimmie

Lee but waited in the car. It was her regular driver, David, who informed her that he could see Jimmie Lee smiling. Emma couldn't believe it; however, upon straining her aging eyes to attempt to get a good look, she discovered David was correct. To see the boy smile brought tears streaming down her cheeks. She was so happy for him.

Emma, seated on the elongated porch of the plantation's main house, admired the many guests in attendance. The manager of her café, Roberto, was seated on the porch with her. His young son, Gregory, was nearby feasting on a raw sweet potato.

"So, are you really gonna let Jimmie Lee set out on his own, Momma Lou-Lou?" Roberto inquired as he sipped from his glass of fresh lemon iced tea.

"Sure am," she said with pride. "The boy's almost twenty and he wants to venture out. No need for me to keep him cooped up here in Suwanee."

"Don't you think you're gonna get lonely without him?"

"Maybe I will, at least for a spell, but I've got the help to keep me company. There's Nathan and David who live in the servants' quarters, Alexandria comes in daily to cook the breakfast and lunch meals, and then I'll see Brian three times a week when he comes to tend the horses. That'll keep me for a spell, I suppose. Plus, I'm getting up there. Before long, I won't need any company at all."

"You've always got a plan, Momma Lou-Lou," said Roberto, amused.

"Naw," she said. "God's got the plan; I just follow it."

"Momma Lou-Lou," interrupted Roberto's son, Gregory. "Can I please have another sweet potato?"

"Sure can, boy," she answered with a loving grin. "Whatever you see, just go on and grab it—save for the liquor, of course—because there's always plenty food to go 'round here at the White Plantation."

"Thanks!" The youngster jubilantly said as he dashed off to the veggie patch to retrieve another sweet potato.

"Make sure you get Nathan to rinse it off for you, boy!" She called out after him.

"When does Jimmie Lee leave?" Roberto questioned.

"Soon, real soon," she replied. "Where is Jimmie Lee, by the way?"

"Over yonder talking with Mrs. O'Brien."

"Mrs. O'Brien? Who is she?"

"Bob O'Brien's wife."

"Bob, the farmer?" Emma asked. "I didn't know he'd married again."

"Yeah, they kept it pretty quiet. He married Sgt. Sam Moore's ex-wife, Ivanna. She goes by Ivanna Rosser O'Brien now and recently was named to head the county school board. My, my, my. She's surely one pretty woman and a heck of a dresser too."

"I wonder why they kept it quiet." Emma pondered.

"Age and maybe color," Roberto said simply. "She's 37 and he's almost 56; she's colored and he's white. Some people talk, you know."

"Listen," started Emma. "Life requires no one to choose a mate based on age—unless the gal is 13 or 14 and the fella's 60—and color is definitely out. We're in an era of time when everyone must acknowledge that no one is black or colored and no one is white but that we're all human.

"My children, both grown, learned that at very young ages. My son now lives in Pennsylvania in a place called Lancaster and is married to a lovely Costa Rican girl named Maria. My daughter lives in Virginia and her husband is a Chinaman. Indeed, a person who concerns himself with the color of a prospective mate's skin is about as ignorant as one of them ole donkeys that Bob O'Brien has on his farm.

I took Jimmie Lee into my home without any hesitation whatsoever. He had a good mother, a kind woman, honest and hard-working. Do you think for one second that I wondered what people would think? Heck no! My rich dead husband adored Lilla Mae. It didn't matter what her shade of skin was when he hired her services over 30 years ago. So when she died and left Jimmie Lee orphaned, it didn't matter to me either. I love Jimmie Lee. He's my responsibility now."

Roberto was impressed by Emma's attitude. He always knew she was a fair-minded woman; however, this was the first occasion the two of them had had such an engaging conversation on race. In the Deep South, such a subject was never an easy task but Emma White made it easy.

***

The Friday following Labor Day, the sun rose at 6:03. The morning breeze was casual. Birds chirped in unison. Not a cloud was in sight. Emma, standing on the porch, admired it all, breathing in the fresh air into her 69-year-old lungs. Today was a special day for it was the day on which her adopted son, Jimmie Lee, would fulfill his dream to travel. Emma gave him two debit cards, each with a one-thousand-dollar credit, and handed him $500 in cash. That was last night. He'd pick up his bus ticket this morning. Emma's thoughts were broken by the storm door opening. She turned to find Jimmie Lee all ready to go.

"Morning, Momma Lou-Lou," he greeted, kissing her on one of her rosy cheeks. "David up yet?" He asked, referring to the family driver.

"No, Herbie's gonna take us," she replied. David's going into Atlanta this morning. He's gotta have gallbladder surgery at one of the city's big hospitals."

"Sounds expensive," asserted Jimmie Lee.

"Yeah, it is," Emma agreed. "But I've got $8.6 million in the bank and he's been the family driver for close to 24 years so the fella's worth the cost of the surgery."

"When is Herbie coming?"

"I told him to be here at quarter-past six. Kevin Pace and his wife are visiting kinfolk down in Tupelo so I figured they wouldn't mind if I borrow their driver for a spell."

The Pace's white 1990 Lexus LS400 rounded the pasture clearing and pulled onto Emma's long private road.

"Oh my," Emma commented. "He's a bit early."

"Must be tryin' to catch the worm," Jimmie Lee added with a smile.

"You got everything, boy?" She inquired.

"Yes, ma'am," he replied. "It's only one large backpack and it's sitting just inside the front door."

"Go on and fetch it and holler back to Alexandria that we're fixin' to leave."

"Yes, ma'am."

Less than a minute later, Emma and Jimmie Lee hopped into the Pace's super-stylish luxury import from Toyota's brand new Lexus line and drove off into the morning. About fifteen minutes later, they arrived at the Trailways Bus Station in neighboring Lawrenceville. Emma couldn't bear to get out of the car, knowing her very own Jimmie Lee was setting off on his own, so she simply hugged him tightly while still in the back seat and told him how much she loved him. She reminded him to eat right, call home at least once a week and, most importantly, be careful. He exited the luxury sedan and headed into the bus station. Just as he grabbed a hold of the terminal's entrance door, he turned one last time to say farewell.

"Good-bye…Mom," he yelled, calling Emma White "mom" for the first time ever. The closest he'd ever come was "Momma Lou-Lou" which was what mostly everyone in town called her.

"Bye-bye…son," she yelled back. For Emma, it was also the very first time she'd called him "son."

A Kodak moment indeed.

CHAPTER 8
May 1990
Williamsburg, Virginia

As Deloren Powell strolled across the grassy campus of one of the country's oldest universities, he found it almost difficult to believe he had been a student for the past eight years. He made the President's and Dean's lists several semesters in a row. Unfortunately, he was ineligible for inclusion on either of the coveted lists once he started enrolling in the school's summer program. While being left off the lists did not affect his perfect 4.0 grade-point-average, it did affect his class ranking. Yet since Dee decided to use his degrees to become a writer, he never worried about job prospects. After all, he had years ago abandoned the desire to become a teaching psychologist. Seeing Professor Quartucci, a visiting scholar from Rome, broke Dee's thought. The two waved just as Dee reached his destination, Dean W. Maurice Scott's office. Dee had not seen Dean Scott in two years—with their last encounter being nasty, to say the least—and wondered what the head of the School of Arts and Sciences wanted to see him concerning. It was just a couple of weeks before graduation exercises and Dee wanted nothing to break his vibe.

After signing in at the front desk, Dee was directed to the dean's office which sat on the second floor of the 90-year-old building, refurbished less than a decade earlier. Dean Scott's secretary, Ms. Radford, bore a pleasant smile. Apparently she didn't remember the encounter between the two men back in May of 1988. She politely guided Dee to a nearby sofa and proceeded to type a white envelope already in the IBM Selectric typewriter when Dee first walked in. Within a few seconds, she was done, the envelope was out of the typewriter and on her desk, placed expertly with an unsigned letter with the dean's name in all caps embossed thereon, and Ms. Radford reached for the telephone.

"Dean Scott, Mr. Powell has arrived….Yes, sir," she said into the receiver. "Sure, sir. Right away." She replaced the receiver on its cradle as quick as she'd picked it up, looking at Dee with a sincere smile and informing him, "The dean is ready for you now, Mr. Powell."

"Thank you, ma'am," he said. "Might I add that the blouse you are wearing is exceptionally lovely." It was the biggest lie Dee had told in his entire life. The blouse was awful.

"Thank you," she excitedly responded. "It's my favorite one."

Dee stepped into the dean's spacious office. He expected to find only the dean present but much to Dee's surprise, there was one other individual, the Reverend Tyler Powell, Dee's father. The two had gradually grown apart over the last few years. Dee started making his telephone calls and home visits less frequent when he realized his father never had anything positive to say about Dee's progress in college.

As far as Rev. Powell was concerned, a psychologist and witch doctor was one-in-the-same person. He was convinced that no dedicated psychologist believed in the existence of a Higher Power. And, according to the long time clergyman, if you're not with God then you're against Him. Yet, while Dee realized the two had become distant, he still loved his father and wondered what this surprise visit was about.

"Dad," Dee began as he embraced his father who—at 54 years old—still looked great notwithstanding the heightened number of gray hairs invading his head and mustache. "What brings you all the way out here?"

"Why don't the two of you have a seat," instructed Dean Scott. "Actually, Mr.—soon to be Dr.—Powell, I called your father to tell him how proud he should be of you. Your dissertation, 'Christianity and Islam: Religions or Psychological Illusions?' was ranked as the Number One doctoral dissertation on campus. I felt your father should share in the success with you so I mailed him the dissertation a week ago and invited him here today."

Dee's doctoral dissertation—even he knew—was an insult to every Christian minister and Islamic cleric in the world. Had he written such an abominable document in an Islamic country, he would have been arrested, tried, convicted and put to death—all in a matter of a few weeks. But in America, freedom of speech and expression being fundamental rights protected by the First Amendment to the United States Constitution, Dee was safe to write such a document even though he knew full well that its content would surely offend the dedicated religious right. One other thing Dee knew: Dean Scott had read the dissertation which meant the veteran educator was well aware of the friction that its content would cause between Dee and his father, the preacher.

Almost instantaneously upon realizing he had been set up by Dean Scott, Dee entertained the rogue thought of knocking the dean flat on his ass. However, he thought, he'd be a doctor in fifteen more days and still had another year left to attend classes. No need to blow everything on a trouble-making prick like Dean Scott. Dee instead reflected on a spiritually enriching cliché he'd heard from fellow student and dorm roommate Leon Ferguson-Bey: "The best things in the hands of a fool may be turned to his destruction; and out of the worst, the wise will find means of good." With that soothing reflection in mind, Dee took a polite approach to the situation.

Standing back up, he said, "Let's go for a walk, Dad. I want to show you around campus." Rev. Powell also stood, shook hands with the dean, and exited the office a few feet behind his son who said nothing to Dean Scott. Anger is one of man's imperfections, so Dee, in an effort to do things wisely, became conscious of that imperfection and humbled himself. Dean Scott was a fool; Dee needed to avoid him.

Once outside, Dee pointed to a nearby building, introducing it as the university's law school. He started to explain its history when his father cut him off.

"You know, Deloren," the good reverend began, calling Dee by his full name, a stark reality that indeed his father was upset, "I believe I trained you, as a child, in the way that you should go in life. My goal in doing so was to ensure that when you're grown, you wouldn't depart from that training. God lovingly gave you to your mother and me over 26 years ago. We viewed you—as with all our children—as a blessing. Your mother still does but I'm not so sure anymore.

"The Bible tells me, as a father, to not provoke you to wrath, but instead bring you up in the training and admonition of the Lord—Ephesians—and by not provoking you, it will keep you from becoming discouraged—Colossians—but you, Deloren, have become somewhat of a curse to me. Your mother doesn't think so; however, I do.

"I told you a long time ago, when you were still in high school, that it is not man's job to figure out other men's problems in life. That's God's job. When you trifle with that, you trifle with God and you're, in effect, riding shotgun with the Devil. I could never stress that enough.

"But now, Deloren, you've gone one step further. You have written the most detestable, blasphemous document I have ever read in my entire life. To actually write that Christianity is a psychological illusion and not a religion is the highest form of disrespect I have ever encountered. As sad as it makes me to say what comes, I must say it anyway: I do not know who you are anymore. You are a mad scientist or something. And I no longer recognize you as my son."

Rev. Powell's words stung Dee like a swarm of killer bees. Dee was speechless; even if he was not, it made no difference because his father—at the conclusion of the one-minute lecture—simply walked away. Dee was left standing there, alone and abandoned, with no where to turn. For the very first time in his adult life, Dee acknowledged that his bond—the one he held so special and important—with his father had been severed beyond repair. He had hoped a day like this would never come. Well, it just did.

CHAPTER 9
February 1991
Burkeville, Virginia

The maximum-security Robinson Correctional Center for Males sat in the heart of Virginia's rural Nottoway County, situated just outside the small town of Burkeville, where insularity was a way of life for the locals. The correctional center, dubbed Robinson Max for short, housed 705 adult males who had been convicted of various felonious acts— including murder, robbery, rape and abduction, to name a few—and sentenced to lengths of confinement of ten or more consecutive years.

Andy Smith was one of Robinson Max's prisoners. He was there serving a mere eighteen years for an enormous 49 felonies. His bizarre case remains a conversation piece to this day, some four years after the fact. As a result, Andy enjoyed one of life's greatest pleasures: popularity among men.

Following his arrest in February of 1987, Andy was charged with five counts each of armed robbery and use of a firearm in the commission of a felony, one count each of possession of a sawed-off shotgun and grand theft auto, and 37 counts of abduction. He faced six life terms plus more than 400 years. However, Andy had an ace-in-the-hole. His wealthy aunt from the District of Columbia loved him beyond description.

Sheila Smith Sullivan, who served at that time as one of seven Under Secretaries for the U. S. Department of Agriculture, came to the rescue. Her husband, an attorney with an elite firm in D. C., went to law school with star mid-western trial attorney Jerry Spencer, and the two kept in touch over the years. Andy's Aunt Sheila scheduled a meeting between her and Spencer and a deal was forged. Spencer would take on Andy's case for $65,000 plus expenses. Unbeknownst to the seasoned and remarkably talented attorney, his fee did not all come from Under Secretary Sullivan. Andy's aunt had washed out $30,000 of the stolen bank currency, funneled it through a Japanese bank affiliate in lower Manhattan, and re-deposited the funds into one of her D.C. bank accounts. She footed Andy's remaining legal fees herself. Without doubt, Sheila Smith Sullivan truly loved her nephew.

Jerry Spencer, arguably the best trial lawyer in the country, decided to bring new color to the art of lawyering. Virginia, at that time, accepted only a handful of pleas: unconditional guilty plea, conditional guilty plea with appellate rights, conditional plea of guilty under Alford versus North Carolina (no contest), not guilty, and not guilty by reason of diminished capacity or insanity. Spencer changed all of that. In Andy's case, the brilliant attorney took the not guilty by reason of diminished capacity or insanity a step further. He entered forty-nine pleas of not guilty by reason of mental disease or defect. According to Spencer, Andy suffered from post-hypnotic nymphomania suggestion. In other words, Mistress Jeanette Foreman used her lurid and highly addictive sexual behavior to mesmerize and hook Andy to the point that he could no longer think act or exercise reason on his own. Her mouth and vagina were dangerous weapons, Spencer argued, and she used those weapons to take Andy's mind hostage and enslave him to the point that his will was so weak and vulnerable that he was in an acute state of hypnosis when he entered the bank to rob it. Spencer's effort to bring new color to the law profession worked: Andy, although convicted, was given minimum sentences—most of which were totally suspended—on all counts. He received five 5-year suspended sentences on the armed robberies and an 18-year total active sentence on the use of a firearm in the commission of felony charges; he received suspended sentences of twenty years and one year for possession of a sawed-off shotgun and grand theft auto, respectively; and he received 37 one-year suspended sentences for the multiple abductions. The only reason Andy did not walk out of the courtroom at the conclusion of the trial was because of a state law which prohibited trial judges or juries from suspending any portion of a sentence imposed for the crime of use of a firearm in the commission of a felony. Thus, Andy was required to serve active sentences on those crimes. He received one 2-year sentence and four 4-year sentences for a total of eighteen years. Since arriving at Robinson Max in October of 1987, Andy has been considered one of the most popular prisoners at the 4-building facility.

However, it was not just Andy's sensational criminal trial that catapulted him to the upper ranks. It was his heavy involvement in the prison community. He had uniquely positioned himself in various prison programs and departments to the extent that many newcomers to Robinson Max were constrained to deal with him at one point or another. Andy ran the orientation program and worked in the legal services department's law library.

When a new prisoner was received at Robinson Max, he was given an appointment to attend the two-hour New Inmate/Convict Orientation Program. Once there, the prisoner met with Andy who explained the prison's operations, including available services such as canteen, personal property, laundry, food services, medical, reading library and law library, recreation, religious and social organizations, and rehabilitative treatment. In many cases, the new guy had an appeals case pending and needed immediate access to the law library and a "jailhouse lawyer". Andy gleefully obliged him, setting up a legal appointment to meet with the prospective "client" later in the week. Andy's close association with the rehabilitative treatment staff, including the Rehabilitative Treatment Supervisor or RTS, ensured the newcomer would get at the top of the various waiting lists for rehabilitative programs. The RTS, Clayton Tabb, was a smoker—as was Andy—and the two would split the carton of cigarettes down the middle. The cigarettes served as Andy's fee to the newcomer to get the latter's name at the top of the desired waiting list. It was a fifteen-dollar fee and well worth it to any newcomer. In short, Andy learned early on that monopolizing key areas of the prison was crucial to maintaining star status, a status he delighted in.

The only area Andy had not yet penetrated was the religious realm. He hadn't located one that moved him enough to prompt him to join.

The Christian church was too religious, so to speak, and not spiritual enough. It was also too paganistic for Andy to accept.

The Islamic factions—three in all—were a different story. The orthodox community, consisting of Sunni Muslims, was so ridiculously behind time that the community actually believed that Allah, the Arabic name for God (the same God worshipped by Christians and Jews alike), left the entire world without a Prophet for the modern times. According to Sunni Muslims, Allah left a Prophet 1,400 years before to cure the ills of the world. But the Sunnis do not explain how a Prophet of 1,400 years ago can cure drug addiction, child abuse and neglect, drive-by shootings, government-sanctioned homosexuality, and other things which were not present during those ancient times. Hence, Andy could not accept the Sunni view. The Nation of Islam, the so-called Black Muslims, was what Andy believed to be a separatist organization that taught the Caucasian was the Devil. The Nation of Islam thrived on the spectacular teachings of its founder, Elijah Muhammad, a less-than-educated but truly delightful man who unconditionally loved his people and sincerely wanted to educate them on the proper way to eat and live and serve Allah. Andy did not desire to spend his time propagating separatism from, or disdain for, a particular race; however, he was extremely impressed with the Nation's elite and highly-disciplined guard, the Fruit of Islam. Still, Andy was unable to accept many of the Nation of Islam's doctrines and bypassed that faction as well. What remained was the Moorish Science Temple of America, the country's oldest official Islamic faction, founded by Noble Drew Ali in 1913. Members were referred to as "Moors" or "Asiatic Moslems" and never, ever classified the human race as Black, White, Colored, etc. Instead, the Moorish Science Temple community propagated peaceful and moving lessons of love, truth, peace, freedom and justice based upon new-era-of-time Islamic principles. This actually impressed Andy because he always believed Moslems—the English translation for Muslims—were racist hate-mongers and terrorists. The

Moorish Science Temple of America proved him wrong. Nevertheless, Andy was not yet willing to give up his vices—profanity, cigarettes, prison mash and pot—to join, although he had visited a couple Moorish Science Temple meetings in the past month or so. Accordingly, Andy decided to use a wait-and-see approach before attempting to enter the religious domain at Robinson Max.

Andy's closest associate at Robinson Max was a convicted embezzler, Scott Underwood, who held a bachelor's degree in biology/pre-med with a minor in chemistry, and a master's degree in medical logistics management. Underwood, a former Army captain, opened a medical logistics consulting firm after six years in the military. He had enlisted after his first four years of college and went into Uncle Sam's army as a non-commissioned second lieutenant. The firm he later ran held numerous contracts but Scott, greedy by birth, just couldn't get enough. He bilked accounts of $10.7 million over two years. He was caught and sentenced to ten years and seven months—courtesy of a satirical trial judge—and ended up at Robinson Max soon after. Scott was close to going home, however. He had only 16 more months left on his sentence. By law, Scott was required to serve a minimum of 5 years, 3 ½ months. Andy, on the other hand, had another six years or so left.

One day, as the two walked alone on the huge rear recreation yard, Andy brought up a rare conversation.

"Today's Valentine's Day, Scotty-Boy," he began. "Wonder what Vicky's doing?"

Scott looked aghast. "This is the first time I've ever heard you mention her directly, Andy, and I've known you for more than three years. You miss her, don't you?"

Andy retreated. "Naw, 'course not. She divorced me after the trial was over. She did right. I won't shit. No need to stick around with a guy who ain't shit."

Scott laughed. "Damn, Andy. How can you do that to yourself?"

"Truth is the light, Scotty-Boy," Andy answered matter-of-factly. "But, going back to Vicky, I was just wondering what she's doing today; that's all."

"Yeah, sure you're right." Scott's tone was unbelieving.

"No bullshit, Scotty-Boy," Andy pressed. "Just wondering."

"Okay," was Scott's reply, still unbelieving. "What's up with your college courses?" He asked, changing the subject.

Andy perked up. "Fine. As you know, I got my associate's last year from Ohio University's external degree program. I've been at the University of Nebraska-Lincoln almost a year and I'll get my bachelor's degree in another two years. Six years in all for a four-year degree."

"Yeah, but that's only because you're not on campus."

"Yeah, I know," Andy acknowledged.

"What made you pick psychology?"

"Human interaction," Andy confessed. "It'll be quite useful when I go into business for myself once I get out of this fuckin' place."

Just then, fellow prisoner Dan Vega and his prison "wife" strolled by, hand-in-hand, and exchanged greetings with Andy and Scott. Once the happy couple was out of ear-shot, Scott ridiculed the union.

"These guys are out of their minds. They're killers in the streets and fags in here."

"Dan's not a fag," Andy corrected. "He's bisexual. His 'wife', Claudia, is the fag."

"The way I see it," Scott reasoned, "if you fuck an asshole, you'll suck a dick."

"No, no, Scotty-Boy," Andy explained as he stopped walking. Scott stopped as well. "You see, Claudia's name was Claude at birth and his middle name was Sylvester. He changed his first name, and his middle name was changed to Sylvia. He wanted to be—and is—a homosexual. He needs a man to satisfy his sexual needs which consists of fucking him in his ass whenever he wants. Dan is simply passing the time by accommodating Claudia. Dan's not a fag, Scotty-Boy. Claudia's not fucking him; he's fucking her. Understand, my friend?"

"I understand that this Claudia or Sylvia character ain't no 'her'. He is a 'he' and will always be a 'he', and as long as Dan Vega is putting his penis in that sissy's asshole, he's just as much a fag as Claudia. You can say what you want. I stick to my original analogy; if you fuck a hole, you'll suck a pole. Plain and simple."

The two started walking again just as the tower guard, Officer Gus Johnson, announced the rec yard was closing in five minutes.

CHAPTER 10
May 1991
Williamsburg, Virginia

The eighteenth of May was a great day for Dee, for today he would receive his second doctorate's degree—this one in Education—from the College of William & Mary. Last May, he received his first one—in Psychology—and was still worked up from that accomplishment. The only disheartening aspect of last year's graduation was that most of his family did not show. Due to the standing controversy between Dee and his father, the latter prohibited anyone from attending. Only twin Delorna and rebel Jacob disobeyed their father's order. With a year having now passed, some of Dee's other siblings have softened to their father's prohibition. So, at this year's graduation ceremony, along with Dee's twin sister and Jacob, sisters Megan and Brianna, as well as brother Zachary, all were on hand to witness their highly educated and professionally esteemed sibling receive his due.

Now, at a vibrant age of 27, Dr. Deloren Powell will join the ranks of the few African-American males in the nation who hold not one but two doctorate degrees. He will proudly add behind his name a "Ph.D." and "D. Ed.", a stellar achievement, to say the least.

***

"Merry Christmas, Mom," greeted Dee as he handed her a large box crudely wrapped in holiday paper. "Sorry it isn't professionally gift-wrapped."

"Thank you, Dee," said Brittany Powell, a smile stretched across her face as wide as Hoover Dam. "Don't worry about the wrap, son. I'm gonna open it now anyway. It's Christmas Eve—," she chuckled, "—and no one's here but you, me, and your father. By the time everyone else gets here tomorrow, they won't be able to tell when I opened what." She chuckled again, still smiling. "What'd you get your father?"

"Nothing; he won't accept anything from me."

"You're probably right," his mother said with a long sigh. "When I told him you'd be coming back here to live after graduation, I was surprised he didn't put up a fuss. He gave me that familiar look of his and said, 'I won't deny him a roof but I still refuse to claim him as my son after what he said in that college paper.' Then he said again, 'No, I won't deny him a roof.' It does amaze me, though, how the two of you can live in the same house and eat at the same table and still never say one word to each other. That truly amazes me."

"He doesn't want to talk to me, Mom. He made that clear nineteen months ago when he disowned me. I'm not angry at him; it's the other way around. So, to keep the peace, I don't say anything."

Footsteps descending the staircase from the second floor could be heard by both Dee and his mother so she changed the subject.

"How's your book coming along, Dee?" She asked.

"Just fine, Mom," he responded as his father, speechless, walked by and on into the kitchen, still within hearing range. "I'm on the final end of the research and have started drafting the manuscript. I'm a fast and accurate typist, I intend to work on it 40 to 60 hours a week and I'm pretty much acquainted with the content so I project the one thousand to twelve hundred pages will be finished in less than four months."

"Whew!" His mother exclaimed. "A thousand or more pages?!"

"Yes, ma'am, but that's just the manuscript. The book itself will be between 500 and 600 pages, about half the size of the manuscript. It's not as long as it seems."

"And the title?" She inquired.

"The Psychological Effects of Brown versus Board of Education," answered Dee, his voice positive and proud.

His mother again changed subjects. "How about a wife?"

Dee looked puzzled, and then produced a smile. "The Psychological Effects of a Wife? Oh, that'll be my next one."

His mother chuckled again, something she'd been known to do with little or no warning or reason although this time she had one. "No, Dee, not a book, a wife. When do you think you'll start looking? You're smart, nice-looking, no babies out of wedlock and—, no bills to pay." The chuckle again; Dee joined in.

Before he answered, Dee thought a moment. Practically all of his siblings were married. Two of his three brothers had tied the knot with relatively good-looking women, although Brandon's wife was probably the most talkative woman in North America. All of his sisters were—or had been—hooked. Emily and twin Delorna were divorced,

Megan's husband died of a heart attack—at the young age of 29—a year after the nuptials, Samantha married a hard-working sugar daddy thirty years her senior, and Brianna reeled in a thug-turned-preacher whose sincere and bright smile could light up the darkest night. Only Dee and youngest brother Jacob had not yet walked down the aisle and Jacob—now in New York City sleeping with practically every woman in sight—would probably die a single man. Dee wondered if he would do the same.

Finally, he answered his mother's query. "I can't say for sure when I'll start looking for a prospective wife. I want to be a bestselling writer first. That way I'll have the means to care for her. Until that time comes—the bestseller, that is—I can't say. Heck, Mom, it could be next year or five years from now. I just don't know."

"Well," Brittany continued, "as long as you know you ought to be practicing celibacy in the meantime. So much bad mess goin' around—diseases and all—and you wouldn't want to give something fatal to your new wife. I want her to out-live me, 'cause—truth be told—I'm on my last leg as we speak. So remember to focus on celibacy, celibacy, celibacy." No chuckle followed.

Instead, Dee roared in laughter. "Mom, I've taken celibacy to a whole new level."

"Oh really?" She inquired. "How so?"

Dee stunned his mother and silently impressed his father—in the kitchen munching on a Nutty bar—with his reply.

"I am the only Powell offspring who is still a virgin."

CHAPTER II

September 1994
Chesapeake, Virginia

A single tear trickled down the cheek of the exceptionally lovely bride as prison Chaplain Will Yale said his final words: "I now pronounce you husband and wife. You may salute your bride."

Andy Smith casually leaned forward and planted a deep, passionate kiss on the lips of his new bride, their tongues probing the inside of one another's warm mouth to commemorate this most memorable occasion. Andy was sharp in his Bill Blass tuxedo with a golden bow tie and matching cummerbund. The woman he'd just married— her 4-feet-11 stature giving her the appearance of a doll baby—was just as sharp, donning a truly magnificent milky wedding gown designed by Versace. The couple's wedding rings were simple—prison rules—and were plain, stone less yellow-gold.

Andy was now housed at the Terrangi Correctional Center for Males, a medium-security facility a city over from Portsmouth, having been transferred from Robinson Max seven months earlier. At Terrangi Medium, Andy worked in the law library and—like he did at his previously assigned facility—spearheaded the New Inmate/Convict

Orientation Program. He was just getting used to the place when, four months ago, he received a surprise visitor. He nearly fainted in the visitation room when he saw Jeanette Forman, his visitor, who'd been on the run for seven years, long enough for the statute of limitation to run its course for the outstanding bank robbery warrants that awaited her here in the United States. Following stays in London, Tokyo, Frankfurt and Seoul, Jeanette returned to America in April of this year to find the warrants had been dismissed with prejudice a month before. She barged right into Andy's life and soon after asked him to marry her, to which he agreed. Today, the two made good on the agreement.

"I'm so happy," Jeanette confessed, a second tear now rolling down her cheek. "I really am."

Andy could not agree more. "Me too."

"Too bad Zelda couldn't be here," Jeanette whispered.

"Yeah, too bad."

Too bad, indeed; not to mention practically impossible. Zelda Foreman was sitting in a cell at the Hobbs Correctional Center for Females after she became the first and only woman in Virginia to be sentenced to death since capital punishment was reinstated in 1976. When Andy rolled over on her and Jeanette the night of his arrest at the hospital, the sisters were arrested. Both made bail the next day and went separate ways but Zelda was cornered at Norfolk International Airport—Jeanette had driven to the Richmond airport—when a security screener recognized her from TV news reports covering her arrest. When airport security officers attempted to detain her to ask where she was heading, she panicked and tried to flee. Officers cornered her, but she managed to wrestle away one officer's service revolver, killing two of them before engaging in a high-speed chase with Norfolk police in a car-jacked limo. Just prior to trial, physical evidence recovered from the execution-style slaying of Pierre Graff, the other male suspect in the bank hold-up, who was found shot dead along Interstate 264, linked Zelda to his murder as well. Zelda was ultimately sentenced to death for the capital murders of the law enforcement officers; she received life terms for Pierre's homicide and each of the robberies, plus 200 years for various other charges. No, it did not look like Zelda Foreman would be making it to her younger sister's wedding.

"You know, Andy," started Jeanette as the two grabbed a table towards the back of the multi-purpose room, "you've got less than three years to go before getting out." She stopped before going on. Chaplain Yale had already left; two prison guards—Senior Officer Christopher Taylor and PERT Officer Melissa Brown—remained but were too far away to hear the newlyweds' conversation. "We can spend the next two years putting together an excellent financial plan. A one-shot deal. And I'm talking seven figures."

"Seven figures is in the millions, Jeanette. You mean six figures, don't you?"

"No, Mister Andy, I meant seven like I said."

As much as Andy loved numbers, he found it unrealistic that the two of them could make millions inside of two years, especially in light of the fact that he had no substantial assets and relied upon his Aunt Sheila, now the Secretary of the U. S. Department of Agriculture, who sent him a hundred bucks once each month. Thus, he wanted to hear what Jeanette's two-year plan entailed.

"I'm all ears, Mrs. Smith," he said with a smile, reaching over to take a hold of her soft hands as he listened. "Apparently you've thought this out."

"Indeed so, Mister Andy," she gleefully acknowledged. "Here is the deal: On my way back into the country, we had a stop-over at LAX. Ironically, the Pilots Union went on strike the same day, which froze all flights. We were put up in hotels for two days. While at the hotel, a guy left behind his laptop PC on a sofa in the main lobby. My intention was to sell it but once I got it into my suite, I realized it was still on. This guy was a local architect, a designer of huge buildings, one of which happens to be the main headquarters of U. S. Bank, a 73-floor skyscraper. The main vault is only two floors from the roof. The entire make-up of the bank building—wiring, security systems, doors, vents—was programmed into the laptop PC. Instead of selling it, I ran out to buy a blank disc, copied his, and then turned in the laptop and original disc to the front desk. He showed up for it later. He has no clue I have a copy of the disc. This was back in April. I have studied the disc every single day ever since—with the exception of last night since I was so hyped up about getting married today—and can honestly say I know it by heart."

Andy, trying to figure out the specifics of the two-year plan, decided to engage in a little guesswork because he was totally clueless.

"So, let me get this straight," he surmised. "You figure if we sell the building's architectural plan to a rival architectural engineering firm, they'll pay us millions? I mean, how do you figure? I'm lost here."

Jeanette flashed a broad smile. "Mister Andy, sweetheart, sugar," she said softly, leaning over to lightly kiss him on the lips several times, "You're getting rusty, baby." She looked up front towards the guards—they were talking to each other and not minding Andy and Jeanette—before easing her hand under the table to rub Andy's thigh, the silk material of his tuxedo pants feeling sensual to her fingers. "The bank building is already up and running. It opened two weeks ago after four years of construction. We're not selling building plans, honey."

Still lost, Andy asked, "What are we doing then?"

Jeanette's hand made its way to her new husband's crotch where she squeezed the stiffness of his now-erect penis through his pants. He moaned softly. "We're gonna facilitate our financial plan by doing business with the bank on a one-shot deal," she told him.

Andy simply didn't get it. "But how?"

She kissed him again. "We're going to take out the bank vault."

"What?!! Andy cried out, causing the guards to jump upon hearing him shout.

Jeanette kept her cool—she was very good at that—by looking up front to the guards, saying aloud, "Everything's okay. He didn't know I was a virgin." The lie was convincing; Officers Taylor and Brown resumed talking. Jeanette returned her view to Andy whose mouth still lay open from the concussion of his second wife's absurd suggestion. She removed her hand from his crotch and again held both her hands in his, raising them to kiss his wedding band and each of his knuckles. "Now, my love, I know that caught you off-guard; however, just be calm and hear me out. Let's not argue 'cause it's our wedding day. Just hear me out."

Andy immediately started shaking his head, not wanting to hear another word. "No way, Jeanette. Absolutely no way. No, I'm not going to do another bank job. No way."

"Andy, just hear—"

"No," he interrupted. "I don't want to discuss it. I am not going to commit another crime. I've been in this shithole for seven-and-a-half years and still have 83 years in suspended time hanging over my head. If I so much as piss in the wind, I'm back inside with all of that suspended time to serve. I can't do it, Jeanette. I just can't."

"Andy—"

"No."

"Andy—"

"No, I said."

"Are you angry with me, Andrew?" She asked in a sensual voice.

Upon hearing the way she called his first name, Andy's frustration quickly subsided. She was so beautiful, he thought to himself. So magnificently beautiful. He remembered the night the two met in the parking lot of Saint Vincent's Medical Center in Norfolk. Her sensational looks, amazing smile, beautiful white teeth, that perfect laughter—everything about her captivated him.

"Andrew?" She said again.

"No, baby, I'm not angry with you."

"Good," she said, relieved. "Let's talk about something else; deal?"

"Sure," he responded, relieved the subject was changing. "Like?"

"There's this new armored car company in Virginia Beach—"

"Jeanette," Andy warned his tone low but firm.

She winked, then smiled, before adding, "I was only kidding, Mister Andy."

Andy appeared unconvinced, looking at her with suspicion in his gaze.

"Seriously, Andy, I was only kidding."

Andy wasn't so sure.

CHAPTER 12

October 1994
Norfolk, Virginia

The main lecture hall of the Omni International Hotel on Norfolk's Waterside Drive was standing-room-only as Dr. Deloren Powell delivered a moving speech on existing practices of indirect forms of segregation in education and how segregation continues on a relatively wide but subdued scale. The audience, over half of which was a mixture of psychology, education and law majors from area colleges and universities, listened intently as Dee articulated his message.

"In the local housing projects, there is always an elementary school, which is named after the housing project, in which Pre-K thru sixth grade curricula are taught. School officials will tell you the presence of the school is to improve attendance. Nonsense! The presence of the school is a subdued tactic to retard growth and the learning process. The instructors are often overworked, stuck with classrooms jammed well over the suggested student-to-instructor ratio, and the books are often old and out-dated, practically useless. The key to the school officials' success is to ensure that project students stay in project schools with other project students. Hence, the only growth these young minds receive is growing in the understanding of project life. The only learning process they enjoy is learning the essence of life in the housing project. Placing elementary schools in our housing projects, naming them after the particular project, and holding juveniles hostage for the first crucial years of their at-risk lives is psychologically traumatizing, educationally irresponsible and legally challengeable under the U. S. Supreme Court opinion in Brown versus Board of Education."

The lecture hall's attendees applauded ferociously upon hearing Dee's position which was first pronounced in his 501-page book, The Psychological Effects of Brown versus Board of Education, published two years earlier. To date, the book has sold 60,000 copies. It was a far cry from a national bestseller, as Dee had hoped for, but sales have provided Dee with a steady income since the book was released, allowing him to collect $114,000 in gross royalty payments. He used his first royalty check, which came two months after the text's release, to spice up his wardrobe. The second check, arriving that October, allowed him to move into his own place: a $460-a-month two-bedroom, one-bathroom rented townhouse in Portsmouth's Yorkshire Square. His car, a ruby-red 1989 Mercedes-Benz 190E, came in December, rounding out 1992 with all of his primary needs met. By March, Dee was ready to enter the lecture circuit to promote his first book and today his audience was seemingly the largest—and most involved—he had thus far addressed.

"In other elementary schools," Dee went on, "instructors use what are known as 'clusters' to bunch together students in small groups according to their learning progress. By clumping these children together, school officials justify the instructors' actions by claiming that it allows instructors to allow students to learn from other students who are near or at the same level. Sounds good, doesn't it? Know what? It's segregation as well. Most notably, clusters, by and large, are racially segregated. White students are grouped with other white students and black students are grouped with other black students. It is school segregation at its best: You are over there, we are over here. You learn your way, we learn our way. In sum, if the child lives in a housing project, he doesn't have to worry about clusters because the whole damn school is a cluster!"

The audience erupted in a mixture of laughter and applause. "And if the child lives elsewhere and has to attend the school uptown with the better budget, better books and a 'lighter' student enrollment, he gets thrown into a cluster to make sure he learns no more than that which he would have learned in the elementary school situated in the housing project downtown!" The applause grew ferocious again, culminating into a standing ovation, to which Dee was well pleased.

Shortly thereafter, Dee's speech ended. He signed a dozen or so books and handed out his professional card. While conversing with some of the attendees, his Motorola cellular phone hummed—he had it set on silent-ring mode—and he excused himself to answer. Since it was his personal cell phone, only his parents, brothers and sisters had the number, he knew it was one of his family members calling. The phone's Caller-ID read-out revealed his parents' vast home off Rotunda Drive so Dee assumed it was his mother. It wasn't.

"Dee, it's me, your father."

Dee was stunned, unable to say anything beyond the "hello" he answered with.

"You need to come to the house right away." With that, his father hung up without awaiting confirmation.

***

Dee never imagined he would spend a birthday alone. Even while in college, he would at least celebrate with his dorm roommate. Today, March 28, 1995, he turned 31 years old and here he was, at home, alone with nothing to do. His twin sister re-married last summer and she and her new husband, xylophone player Jeremy Zimmerman, were on vacation in Chicago for her birthday. Delorna did, however, call Dee early this morning to wish him a Happy Birthday. No one else called. Not a soul.

The townhouse within which he lived was dead silent. He played no music, nor was the television on. Dee was peacefully seated on the Ethan Allen sofa, its plain black leather going well with the shag carpet which was white. The matching love seat took up a corner towards the rear of the living room where Dee sat. His 30-inch Sony color TV sat atop an inky, shiny entertainment center case fully equipped with a receiver, turntable, CD player, reel-to-reel, cassette tape deck and four powerful speakers, a $2,000-system well worth the expense, though one wouldn't think so since Dee seldom turned the damn thing on.

The sense of overwhelming sadness Dee experienced on special days like a birthday—days that reminded him of his mother or youngest brother, Jacob—was so great, he was constrained to seek counseling. Virginia Beach psychiatrist Lee Kim Xanapeth prescribed anti-depressants. Dee was thankful that, in spite of suffering from depression, he—like millions of other Americans—could still lead a normal life with the proper counseling and medication. His depression was pretty much under control. But, the special days—they hurt so much.

Many nights have passed, over the preceding five months, where Dee was awakened to the same dream: Rev. Doug Byrd, Dee's father's lifelong closest friend and fellow clergyman, standing over the caskets of Dee's mother and brother in their double-funeral, saying, 'Ashes to ashes, dust to dust'. It was a memory Dee simply could not rid himself of and its presence bothered him immensely.

Brittany and Jacob Powell were killed when their plum-colored 1979 Cadillac Eldorado was struck head-on along a span of Frederick Boulevard in Portsmouth. The driver of the other vehicle, a widowed father trying to prevent his sons in the rear seat from fighting with one another, lost control of the older-model Toyota Corolla. Both vehicles held full tanks of gas, causing two fiery explosions. Only the small boys, one 4 and the other 10, survived.

There was a knock at Dee's front door, bringing him out of his slumber. He answered to find Mrs. Carrington, Yorkshire Square's rental office manager, who carried in her hand a single chocolate cupcake with a lit candle placed in the center.

"Happy Birthday, Dr. Powell," she greeted with a warm smile. "Glad to have caught you home. I can't stay. I just wanted to let you know that we here at Yorkshire believe in keeping up with our residents' birthdays, so here you go." She handed him the cupcake. "Hope you have an absolutely, wonderful thirty-first birthday!"

"Thank you so very much," Dee said, forcing a smile. "You're very kind."

"No problem, Doctor," she replied. "Have a great day!" She added as she turned to leave.

Dee closed and locked the door, blew out the candle, walked into the kitchen and tossed the cupcake in the garbage can.

***

The Dell Computer P75T booted up to the usual group of icons. Dee, sitting there with a plain look on his face, waited momentarily. Then he clicked on the "Microsoft Write" icon, opening a blank screen with a sallow background and coal-black border. In this word-processing program, Dee would begin his second book today, October 23, 1995, exactly one year after his mother and youngest brother were killed. The title of the book would be consistent with why Dee decided to begin writing today. So he skillfully began typing, stopping once he'd completed the title, displaying a dry grin. It read, "The Psychological Implications of Promoting a Non-Existent God."

The telephone rang. Dee picked it up two inches from the cradle and hung it back up. He started typing again, this time completing the by-line; "By Deloren Powell, Ph.D., D.Ed." The telephone rang again. Dee cursed under his breath. Instead of disconnecting the caller a second time, Dee answered it.

"Hello," he greeted.

"Dee?" It was his father. The two had begun having occasional conversations after the tragic car crash a year ago. "I think something is wrong with your phone."

"Hi Dad," Dee said, looking at the few lines he'd just typed, producing an evil smile. "Funny thing you called."

CHAPTER 13
March 1996
Victoria, Virginia

The six children were vibrant and happy as they ran in small circles on the vast outdoor prison visitation yard, oblivious of the fact that the hundred or so men on the yard with them were considered society's rejects, convicted felons thrown into prison for various acts of criminal misdeeds. One of those men, all of whom were easily identified as prisoners by their cerulean hospital scrubs, was intimately connected to the six youngsters: To five of them, he was their step-father; to the sixth, her natural father.

Andy had been through a great deal lately—some things good and some bad—and seemed to just begin to bounce back into the swing of things. He was back with Vicky, in spite of the fact that they had been divorced for several years, and his second wife, Jeanette, lost her life in August of 1995. Vicky started visiting early last fall; the triplets, twin boys and daughter Marquita tag along each time. Visits with Vicky and the children, along with his transfer to a minimum-security prison, were the good things that helped Andy bounce back. The bad things— which focused solely upon Jeanette—were unrelenting. Larsen Mini, as the Larsen Correctional Center for Males was known, sat close to the Virginia-North Carolina border. The 480-man facility was nestled in rural Lunenburg County's smallest town, Victoria, which—like the residential area surrounding Robinson Max where Andy served time several years earlier—was loaded with insular locals who spat chewing tobacco juice as a common pastime. Andy was transferred here several months ago following years of stable disciplinary behavior but mainly due to the corrections department's desire to quell the media circus surrounding the surreal and violent incident involving his second wife and her condemned sister. With Terrangi Medium, Andy's previous assignment, so near the city, it became a regular for area reporters. Yet with Larsen Mini so far away, the opposite became the case. The transfer was a win-win situation for both Andy and state corrections officials.

Jeanette Smith and two men—one from New York City and the other from D. C.—carried out a truly daring armed robbery in broad daylight when the heavily-armed trio commandeered an armored car on a side road in Virginia Beach's Pungo section. The group had earlier set up Detour signs to divert the money-packed vehicle's usual route and then used armor-piercing weapons to snipe the driver and his front-riding partner. A four-ounce cube of C-4 plastic explosive quickly blew off the cash door, inviting the rear-riding guard to try on his Hero Shoes by emerging with a blasting Remington pump-action shotgun. Jeanette wanted him for herself, bringing him down with two—the third missed—Black Talons. Unfortunately for Jeanette, the hero's shotgun blasts weren't all in vain—one of her guys was wounded at the scene—and only she and one other, the New Yorker, were able to get away. When the dust finally settled, all three armored car guards lay dead, a suspect was mortally wounded, $1.44 million was unaccounted for, and Jeanette Smith was no where to be found. The one comrade, who escaped with her, Les Vinson of Queens, was killed in a shoot-out with Chicago police and FBI agents a month following the deadly heist. Jeanette had vanished.

Five months later, on August 18, two days before Zelda Foreman was scheduled to die in Virginia's electric chair, Jeanette emerged from her hide-out in Atlanta with a sophisticated plan to facilitate what she construed as the second-most bizarre Death Row escape in Virginia history. She and Noah Lee Faulk, Jr., the son of a prominent Atlanta-area humanitarian, would pluck Zelda from the Death House at the maximum-security Garraghty Correctional Center for Males in Jarratt. Zelda had been moved there a week earlier from the state's only prison for females. Jeanette and Noah Jr., an explosives and weapons buff were slated to meet Alfred Carter, a former Army helicopter pilot from Dallas, at the Richmond International Airport. The group's plane arrivals were scheduled within nine minutes of each other. The three greeted one another in the airport terminal, then immediately left together, climbing into a coppery 1996 Mercedes-Benz 300E with smoked windows and driven by Jenny Kennedy, a trusted lesbian Jeanette slept with from time-to-time after she married Andy in prison—Jeanette's way of staying faithful to her hubby by not sleeping with another man. Jenny made a half-dozen trips between her home in Henrico County and Jeanette's safe-house in Atlanta's North End since the armored car stick-up. That night, the two enjoyed intimate moments in the colossal master bedroom of Jenny's brick townhouse on Cambridge Court, while Noah Jr. and Alfred took up the guest bedroom and living room couch, respectively.

Four o'clock the next morning, a Saturday, Jenny ushered the group of who would become known as the "Garraghty Max Three" to a small private airfield in nearby Hanover County where a contact named Myler—no one knew his first name—awaited the group's arrival. Myler stood next to a small cache of weapons, including two .60 caliber fully-automatic rifles complete with shoulder supports but less the tripods and two M72A1 LAW rockets, commonly referred to by a shorter name, "LAW", which stood for light, anti-tank weapon. Approximately forty-five to fifty yards away sat a pea-green Huey chopper. Finding everything in order, Jeanette paid Myler his $480,000 in cash, of course, having mailed Jenny the money months earlier to hold pending the transactions taking place now. Jeanette and Noah Jr. locked, loaded and donned the weighty .60 calibers. Noah Jr. also took possession of one LAW, arming it right on the spot, leaving the second one unarmed as it served only as a back-up and arming it would only take about two seconds. With that, the trio headed to the Huey, leaving Jenny standing next to Myler. With Alfred at the chopper's controls, the Garraghty Max Three-to-be soon after disappeared into the early-morning sky flying well below radar. It was 4:45 a.m.

At exactly 5:08 a.m., Garraghty Max's Tower 2 Officer, an older man with sleep in his eyes and wearing a name tag that read "Turner" heard helicopter blades in the immediate area. Turner looked east and west—the prison was north—but saw nothing. Just as he turned to look south, the Huey appeared above a line of trees. Turner, figuring the military aircraft was in the area conducting some form of pre-dawn training exercise, briefly wondered why it was flying so low but fatigue from having completed eleven of a twelve-hour shift dissuaded him from stressing himself on the thought. As he turned back around, facing north, the Huey headed his way. Roughly 15 seconds later, Turner, realizing the Huey was much closer, turned again to the south, only to find he was in the line of fire of a man with an extremely large weapon. The man, leaning from the noisy helicopter, smiled as he pulled the trigger, pounding the guard tower's glass panes—and Officer Turner's body—with a dozen rounds. The jailbreak was underway.

Garraghty Max had five guard towers, one each to the south of the prison's four housing units: Alpha, Bravo, Charlie and Delta, and another to the front of the prison's entrance. The Death House was a part of Delta Unit which Tower 2 overlooked. The Huey quickly landed; Jeanette and Noah Jr. disembarked. While Jeanette covered him, Noah Jr. aimed a LAW towards the emergency exit door to Delta Unit and fired. The short-range surface-to-surface missile tore the steel-gray door and practically its entire frame into bits of metal fragments, making entry easy. Since there were no guns inside the security perimeter of Garraghty Max, the dangerous duo's job would be relatively simple.

Meanwhile, Officer Wiggins, assigned to Tower 3 which overlooked Charlie Unit, was in the only guard tower wherein one could visually see Tower 2; however, Wiggins, donning headphones that led to a Sony Walkman by her side, was kicked back—with eyes closed and both feet propped up—listening to one of Luther Vandross' sensational hits, "Power of Love." While Wiggins chilled to the moving lyrics, she was totally unaware the Death House was under siege.

Death House Control Booth Officer Leticia Branch hopped in fright at the sound of the nearby explosion. The security camera monitoring the side hallway, where smoke billowed in from, went dead within seconds of the blast. Officer Branch radioed to the Death House's floor officer, "Officer Collier, Officer Collier, report to the control bubble! There's thick smoke coming down the side hallway!"

Melvin Collier, an 11-year employee of the Department of Corrections, was already en route. He too heard the enormous roar from the explosion; however, Officer Collier did not seem the least bit alarmed, casually walking from the Death House floor to the control booth, signaling to Officer Branch to let him inside. Just as Branch buzzed him inside, two armed individuals appeared from the smoke-filled hallway. Branch screamed; Collier grabbed her by the throat and began strangling her. Meanwhile, Jeanette and Noah Jr. headed straight onto the floor of the Death House. As the two ascended the 18 steps to the upper tier, Leticia Branch's lifeless body slipped from Collier's grasp. He reached over to the control booth master panel and pressed the "D-15" button. Its bulb went from Red, the locked and secure mode, to Green, the unlocked mode. Zelda Foreman's sea-green cell door slid open with Zelda stepping out to meet her sister. There were no hugs or celebrations, just a direct command from Jeanette, of course, "Let's go!" The trio headed down the steps to exit while the forty-five other condemned prisoners—all males—shouted them on through the six-inch-by-six-inch window on each cell door. Once off the Death House's main floor and back to the hallway next to the control booth, the three encountered Officer Collier who was patiently waiting. "Nice work, Mel," stated Zelda, leaning up to kiss the 6-foot-10 field training officer who'd fallen in love with her. "You ready for the bullet?"

Collier nodded, closing his eyes and clinching his teeth. He had agreed to take a single shot to the abdomen, but Jeanette had other plans. She raised the .60 caliber chest-level and pumped six rounds in two seconds into the body of the corrupt guard. Zelda was unfazed, understanding that it was better to have a dead witness to a murder than a live witness to a prison break.

Noah Jr. headed out first, covering the sisters as they darted to the awaiting Huey. The chopper lifted off a half-second after Noah Jr. climbed aboard. At that precise moment, prison guards from Charlie Unit—upon hearing Delta Unit's Control Booth Officer radioing something about smoke—were attempting to get inside Delta Unit. Unbeknownst to them, the guards inside were both dead, making the responding guards' entry impossible. The Huey's pilot, Alfred Carter, quickly looked at his Timex just as he lifted off. It was 5:15 a.m. The entire plan had gone off flawlessly, or so it appeared.

Master Trooper Dennis Howell with the Virginia State Police was pulling onto Rehabilitation Parkway when he noticed a military helicopter leaving from one of the prison's yards. He immediately became suspicious, calling in the observation to Central Dispatch.

"Unit 1-5-3 to Central," radioed Trooper Howell.

"Go ahead, 1-5-3," answered the female dispatcher.

"Central, my 10-20 is Rehabilitation Parkway; was 10-17 to Garraghty Max to investigate suicide in Bravo Unit; currently observing military craft—a Huey, it looks like—lifting off and away from interior perimeter of prison; request that you place Incident Response on stand-by while I'm 10-6 investigating; include Air-Support; copy that?"

"10-4, Unit 1-5-3; Central clear at Zero-Five-Sixteen hours."

At 5:43 a.m., the pea-green Huey, stolen from the Fentress Naval Air Station the day before, landed in the same Hanover County airfield from which it departed just under an hour earlier. Myler was long gone; Jenny was snoozing behind the wheel of the coppery Mercedes-Benz. She awoke to the noisy chopper as it touched down. Alfred, the pilot, powered down the big bird as the three other occupants disembarked. Bringing along their weaponry and stuffing them into the trunk of the Mercedes, the trio climbed into the well-maintained import with Jeanette in the front seat with Jenny and Zelda and Noah Jr. in the rear. Alfred was only several yards behind them, joining the rear seat riders a half-minute later.

Thirty minutes after that, they were back on Cambridge Court in Henrico, toasting one another with gin-and-juice cocktails and delighting in Moroccan hashish mixed with Acapulco gold. By mid-morning, Jeanette and Jenny were off making love in the latter's bedroom while Zelda made up for lost time by engaging in a no-holds-barred fuck session with both Noah Jr. and Alfred in the guest bedroom. But by early-afternoon, with the group of outlaws fast asleep, a horde of law enforcement officers and specially trained corrections guards—known as PERT Members—converged on the townhouse. Members of the Virginia State Police, FBI special agents from Richmond, Henrico County police and Garraghty Max's elite Prison Emergency Response Team comprised the 47-man apprehension assemblage. A tipster, the owner of a Richmond-based bail-bond company, alerted police after seeing Zelda Foreman's picture on a special news report. The tipster, a woman, was retrieving the morning newspaper when Jenny's car returned that morning. She noticed the girl in the flame-colored jumpsuit and jokingly said to herself that the girl favored the one scheduled for execution Sunday night. The tipster was horrified when she saw the same girl on Channel 6's special report. Now, with the liquor, hashish and marijuana, and intense sex having drained the outlaws of their energy, they were about to come to grips with the true meaning of a rude awakening.

The apprehension assemblage assumed the Garraghty Max Three, as well as Zelda Foreman and house owner Jenny Kennedy, was all heavily armed. Actually, nothing could have been further from the truth. Noah Jr. never brought the weapons from the trunk into the house. All of them were unarmed. Nevertheless, the law enforcement and corrections personnel were oblivious to this crucial bit of information. As a result, 30 of the 47 lawmen stormed the townhouse in a blaze of incessant gunfire. When the smoke cleared, everyone inside was killed, and two others—FBI Special Agent Kariem Salaam and Henrico policeman Anthony Faltz—lost their lives to friendly fire. In all, 157 shots were fired.

The funerals of Jeanette Smith and Zelda Foreman were attended by more media personnel than family and friends and Terrangi Medium was bombarded with requests for interviews with Andy, all of which he declined. His aunt, Sheila Smith Sullivan, visited with him several times immediately following Jeanette's burial, finding him withdrawn and depressed. The stress was taking its toll on him and he spoke of Jeanette's funeral—which he was allowed to attend with two armed prison guards—during practically every visit with Aunt Sheila. She loved her favorite nephew and needed to do something to help keep him afloat. Ultimately she convinced Vicky to contact him and reconnect their ties.

Today, some several months after Vicky and the children had been back in Andy's life, he enjoyed the glee of a visit from them. He sat silently on a hard-plastic cream-colored chair; Vicky sat across from him on a similarly colored chair—hers more of a xanthic shade—eating a bag of Lay's sour cream-and-onion potato chips. She was still quite charming—32 years old with an excellent grade of jet-black hair to go along with her pitchy hue—and still managed to dazzle Andy like she did when he first met her in 1986. He smiled at her loveliness, causing her to stop chewing on a potato chip she'd just bit into to inquire of him.

"What you grinning for?" She asked in that serene, nonchalant tone she'd had since childhood.

"Just admiring your beauty, Vicky," he answered.

"Oh," she said, going back to chewing. "Thanks, I guess." She wasn't a genius or anything remotely close; however, she wasn't totally illiterate either. And while she used less-than-perfect English and possessed an attitude of utter simplicity, Andy did not complain. He loved her for her; nothing more.

"I'm ready to go home, Vicky," he volunteered. "I really am ready and just can't wait." He paused a moment. "I want to open a credit information consulting firm. I'll hold seminars showing people how to get out of debt while at the same time save sufficient monies for retirement."

"Can you do that with a record?" Vicky wanted to know.

"Yep," he said matter-of-factly. "You can't consider or call yourself a financial planner. You have to be licensed to be one of those."

"What does this credit whatever-you-called-it firm consist of?" She inquired.

"Credit information consulting firm; it will consist of—" he stopped to break into a wide grin "—financial planning."

"But you just said—"

He lifted up a hand, the palm facing Vicky. "Wait, Vicky. I said I cannot consider myself or call myself a financial planner. I'm not. I will be considered and called a 'credit information consultant' which is perfectly legal. I've researched it."

Forever the skeptic, Vicky pressed on, "Are you sure, Andy? Because I don't want you to end up in trouble again."

"It's perfectly legal," he reinforced. "Trust me."

"My momma said to never trust a man who says trust him," she said with a cute grin.

"That was only confined to sex," he countered, breaking into a grin as well, then leaning forward—stretching himself a bit—to plant a kiss on her juicy lips, tasting the salt from the potato chips. Their moment, however, was interrupted by Officer Flowers, one of few guards permanently assigned to the visitation yard, who came to inform Andy that his three hours of visitation had expired. Prison rules required the prisoner and his visitors to terminate the visit within five minutes of being told of the expiration. Vicky summoned forth the children: triplets Ahmad, Ahman and Ahmar, twins Darius and Darren, and Andy's daughter, Marquita, all of whom hugged Andy as they departed. After they'd each had their turn, Vicky stepped forward for hers; embracing Andy with all the strength she had, as if attempting to take some of him back home with her.

They kissed with indescribable passion before letting one another go.

"Before long," Vicky said at the yard's exit gate, "you'll be home."

"I can't wait," stated Andy, his tone serious, straightforward.

"Me neither," Vicky added as she turned to leave.

CHAPTER 14
February 1997
Athens, Greece

"Did you enjoy your stay in Athens, sir?" The lovely flight attendant asked the American gentleman as she adjusted his headrest.

"Sure did," the man said with an honest smile, then added, "and all of Greece, for that matter."

"Will you visit again soon?" She wanted to know. Her English was perfect.

"Not likely," he replied. "I was here doing research for a book—my second one."

"Oh, a writer; how nice."

"Thank you," he said as he reached into his jacket to retrieve his card. "Here you are. I'm Deloren Powell, Dr. Deloren Powell." His smile widened. "If you're ever in the United States, call me."

"You're very kind," she said pleasantly, accepting the card. "We will be taking off very shortly. Enjoy your flight."

"Thanks," he stated, watching the sway of the flight attendant's hips as she moved into the coach-class area.

Dee was the only passenger in first-class; the other seven seats were empty.

Dee took a moment to reflect on his travels. He had spent the last ten months in India, Africa and Europe, staying in India for three months and three-and-a-half months each in both Africa and Europe. Having collected a plethora of data and notes, as well as photographs of archaic sites, Dee would finish his book well ahead of schedule—by May. The Psychological Implications of Promoting a Non-Existent God would hit book stores by September, he surmised. As Dee collected his research results, he worked on the manuscript each night and now had over 900 pages completed. He projected a final manuscript of just over a thousand pages, a little longer than his first book which encompassed an even one thousand pages in final manuscript form.

The good-looking flight attendant returned, offering Dee a choice of various liquors. "Let's see," he said as he decided. "Well, give me a Scotch and water with ice, please," he chose, smiling. Little did she know why he was really smiling. Dee was silently amusing himself from his earlier flirtation when he told her to call him if she ever visited the U. S. He knew it would never happen. Actually, that was precisely the reason he made the offer. Dee was a loner and knew it. Most importantly, he accepted it. He was 33, single, no children—probably one of very few non-religious male virgins over 30 years old left in Virginia—and no family. His entire family had by now disowned him with the sole exception of twin Delorna and a niece—his sister Samantha's 11-year-old —named Ashley following the family's discovery of his second book's subject matter. His father happened to have called Dee the day he started the book. When Dee volunteered the title of the book, his father did something Dee had never thought possible: Rev. Tyler Powell cursed, telling his son, "You're hopeless, you sick bastard! Your ass is going to burst Hell wide open!" Before Dee could respond, his father slammed the phone in his ear. That was 16 months ago. The two have not spoken since.

"Thanks," Dee said to the flight attendant as he accepted the Scotch-and-water on the rocks. "By the way, what is your name?"

"Nikita," she said, adding, "And I'm single."

"As am I," Dee chimed in.

***

Fifteen hours and two other planes later, Dee touched down at Norfolk International Airport, having gone through the Frankfurt main airport in Germany and John F. Kennedy International in New York City. The night had fallen over this major Virginia City and Dee was ready to get back to his place in Yorkshire Square in Portsmouth. He covered everything with sheets before leaving the country last April, threw out all perishable foods and turned off or unplugged everything in the house, save the refrigerator—which housed only two open boxes of Arm & Hammer baking soda—and the ADT alarm system. Prior to leaving, he forwarded the electric and gas companies checks for a hundred bucks each just to cover minor monthly surcharges. As for his telephone lines, both were forwarded to his cell phone. His rent, now $510 per month, was electronically deducted by his bank and transferred to the rental office's bank on the first of each month. Money was no problem, as sales from his first book, a $19.00 hardback, were approaching 100,000 copies over the past four-and-a-half years, putting more than $180,000 in Dee's pockets. Still, he led a simple life,

94

replacing only his 1989 Mercedes after driving it for three years. In its place came a blood-red 1995 Mercedes-Benz 300E, becoming Dee's first-ever brand new car, serving as his Kwanzaa gift to himself.

He flagged an oncoming Yellow Cab Company taxi in front of the airport terminal. The driver, a woman in her thirties with a sooty but unblemished face, got out to help him load his luggage into the trunk which made an awful squeak when it was opened. Dee climbed inside and gave instructions once the driver was behind the wheel. "I'm going to Portsmouth. Stay on I-264 when you exit the Downtown Tunnel and go down four exits to the Victory Boulevard one. I'll guide you from there."

A half-hour later, Dee was home, dropping the taxi driver twenty dollars to cover the fifteen-dollar fare and two-dollar trunk storage fee plus a few extra as a tip. The polite driver, whose cab permit identified her as "Dena Hockaday", also helped Dee take the luggage—three bags in all—to the townhouse's front door. "I'll take it from here," he advised.

***

"Happy Birthday, Uncle Dee," a smiling Ashley said as she handed Dee a crudely wrapped gift. "I picked them out myself."

"And I take it you did the wrapping as well?" Dee asked with a wink.

"Yep," replied Ashley.

Delorna wanted to make her and her twin's birthday as pleasant as possible so she'd decided to spend the entire day with Dee, bringing along Ashley who adored her uncle much to the child's mother's dismay. But Delorna convinced Samantha not to do anything to turn the child, an innocent, against her favorite uncle.

"This is wonderful, Ashley," exclaimed Dee upon opening the 14-inch-long by 10-inch-wide present and finding a dozen Mead legal pads and two dozen blue Paper Mate medium-point ink pens. "For my writing, I presume?"

"Yep," she acknowledged with glee.

"Thank you so much, sugar pie," Dee said, leaning to kiss the child's forehead. He wouldn't dare spoil her kind gesture by informing her that all his writing was done on computer. "This is really wonderful," he reinforced.

Dee was very near to completing his book. He had only two chapters and the closing comments remaining to be done and really felt good he would be wrapping up everything in another four or five weeks. Excerpts had already been released by his agent, Krystle Gray Hill with the licensed professional managing agent firm of Gray, Langston & Moseley in Richmond. Reviews were split down the middle: scientists and psychology buffs and, of course, professed atheists all anticipated the book's upcoming release while the religious right sharply ridiculed and condemned it. One person unknown to Dee had been sending him threatening e-mails, claiming Dee was the Anti-Christ and vowed to dethrone him, but he shrugged the sender off as some religious fanatic trying to intimidate him. He had no plans of changing his living habits, including the $1,800-speech fee he was offered by Norfolk State University to address first-and second-year psychology students enrolling in the upcoming Summer Program at the 62-year-old university. What impressed Dee most about the offer was that he was asked to speak well before his book was to be released, an absolute rarity, especially at a historically African-American school. It was no secret that African-Americans are typically hard to please. They generally embrace a Missouri native's attitude—"show me what you're working with"—before inviting authors to speak to them regarding that which they have neither seen or can tangibly take a hold of. Such an attitude, however bizarre to others, was typical of a people who had been trampled upon, lied to, oppressed and enslaved—both mentally and physically—for hundreds of years. Hence, Norfolk State's offer to have Dee speak there was quite impressive, to say the least, and he jumped at the opportunity.

***

"I would ask you how was your Easter, but I suppose you don't celebrate the crucifixion of a prophet that, according to you, is fatherless." The verbal observation of Krystle Gray Hill, a principal at the largest managing agent firm in Virginia, caused Dee to laugh.

"I suppose you're right," Dee said, laughing again. "But I did do something spectacular: My income tax returns were mailed prior to the national deadline."

"How was that so spectacular?" The 66-year-old Englishwoman asked.

"Because I've always mailed them on or after April 15th," Dee almost whispered. "I think I'm getting better."

"Maybe so," she said, and then changed the conversation. "So, where are you with the book?"

"Last chapter," Dee said in a matter-of-fact voice. "After that, I do the closing comments and it's a done deal."

"Good," she said. "We want to have it released in August, just before the colleges start their academic years."

She reached down to retrieve her briefcase. "I have some docs to go over with you, Deloren."

"Can't they wait until we finish lunch?" Dee questioned. "I mean, really, I don't get out here to Richmond that often—it's a change of pace for me—and I don't necessarily like to rush to get back to Portsmouth."

"I guess not," she said, a bit sarcastically. "With no wife and all, no need to rush, huh?"

"Let's not get into that again, Ms. Hill," Dee told her, a little irritated. "Having a wife will not make me look any better to the reading public than any other writer."

"Listen to me, Deloren," she said, reaching across the table and grabbing Dee's wrist and holding it. "Without a wedding band on this hand, you will still be thought of by many as an unstable, loose cannon-of-a-writer who loves religion-bashing. A wife gives an appearance of stability; children add credence to that appearance. With a missus and one or two crumb snatchers, it'll soften your image a bit and show you more as an educated man with profound ideas that just happen to spark controversy. Trust me on this; I've got forty years' experience." She released Dee's wrist.

"I don't want a wife right now," he declared, his irritation now more pronounced. "Once I get a national bestseller, then I'll start looking. Until then, let the subject go."

"A little touchy, eh?" She observed. "Well at least get a girlfriend."

"For what purpose?" Dee inquired.

"It eases stress," the Englishwoman reasoned. "Whenever you're uptight, you call her over, the two of you have a one-hour hump session, she goes home, and you go to bed."

"That's not a girlfriend, Ms. Hill," he snapped. "They call that an escort. Your description simply left out the $100 fee."

"Actually, the fees run $150 to $200," she corrected. "But you can broker a package deal for $300 for three hours if you're a repeat customer."

"I'm scared to even ask how you know that," stated Dee.

A few minutes later, Krystle Gray Hill asked their server for the check, which amounted to $65 counting the gratuity, paying for it with an American Express-Platinum. Her Sprint cell phone rang as she handed the server the credit card.

"Talk to me," she answered in her usual unorthodox fashion. "Hi there…Sure…That's good…Okay, sure… That's fine. Bye." She disconnected the caller and tucked the French-gray cell phone in her xanthous Donna Karan summer jacket. "Wanna follow me somewhere? Then we'll go back to my office to sign the docs."

"Where we heading?" Dee wanted to know.

"Virginia Parole Board over on Atmore Drive."

"What's there, if you don't mind me asking?"

"I don't; they post prisoner releases six weeks in advance. I need to find out when this guy is being released. Word is, he's on the June list but one has to go there personally to get the exact release date. The parole board's release posting only gives the month."

"Wouldn't it be simpler to count six weeks from today, April 18th, and figure the date out yourself?"

"Not that simple, old chap," she replied. "The six weeks are not always exact. One has to ask."

"One other question—and yes, I'll follow you—I have: Is this prisoner writing a book or something?"

"No, he isn't," she admitted, smiling at the server who'd returned with the credit card receipt which the Englishwoman signed after sliding the American Express off the small, bottle-green check tray and into her yellow leather purse. "One of my clients has been trying to interview this guy for over a year-and-a-half. He wouldn't give any interviews while inside; we're hoping he'll change his mind once he's free. My client's book is almost done; however, she needs to interview the guy to insert certain information in various parts of the book."

Dee was curious. "Is the guy coming off Death Row or something?"

"No, but close. His wife was killed in a house out in Henrico after breaking her sister out of prison. The sister was on Death Row."

Dee's eyes widened. "Hey, I remember that! That was national news. The cops killed the whole house, including a couple of their own, and an investigation later revealed the escapee and her liberators were unarmed."

"That's the one," she said with a wink. "Now, if you were writing that one, you'd have two wives and twelve crumb snatchers."

Dee appeared baffled. "I don't understand."

"Bestseller, Deloren," she explained. "You said you'd marry if you get a bestseller. That book would be not just a national—but an international—bestseller. You could indulge yourself by taking two wives and pump lots of crumb snatchers in them both."

"Yeah," he said, grinning, "and my next book after that

one would be from my own prison cell. It'll be called, 'Life of a Bigamist'." The comment sent them both into bursts of uncontrollable laughter.

"Let's go, Deloren," she said through tears.

CHAPTER 15
April 1997
Victoria, Virginia

"They gave me my release date yesterday," Andy announced to Vicky who'd just sat down only five minutes before. "I go home on Tuesday, June the third—38 days from now. It was posted by the Board on April the 18ᵗʰ and sent here a week later."

"Oh, Andy, I'm so excited," she cheered, getting back up to hug and kiss Andy again. "I'll bring all the kids up tomorrow after church so we can tell them together."

Andy was ready to get out of the joint. Even though Larsen Mini had no fences or guns, it was still prison and Andy made sure he never forgot that. All things considered, Andy had done quite well for himself while in prison. He went back to school to get his GED, and then enrolled in college, attending for six years and earning a B.S. degree. He was quite adept in Virginia law and American jurisprudence in general. And he had become somewhat of a business buff, studying the Money section of USA Today as often as possible and managing to get a hold of a Wall Street Journal from time to time. Money left to him by Jeanette before she was killed and the set-aside funds from Aunt Sheila totaled $9,020.97 and $1,002.33, respectively, both of which he had dipped in on occasion, taking just under $980 from Jeanette's money and close to a thousand from his aunt's. Indeed, Andy was ready—mentally, educationally and financially—to get out.

After Vicky re-took her seat, she looked Andy square in the eyes to ask, "Are we gonna get married again?"

The question was a tough one, one that Andy had not even entertained. He thought of Jeanette often and missed her beyond description. Yet, he knew he loved Vicky—all over again. He found his answer and rendered it.

"That is a very strong possibility, Vicky."

CHAPTER 16
May 1997
Portsmouth, Virginia

The blood-red Mercedes pulled into the parking lot of the McDonald's on Airline Blvd which sat next to a hi-volume Shell-Miller Mart gas station and convenience store. The Mercedes' driver parked and emerged from the car. Out came Dee, decked out in an ashen Botany 500 two-piece suit, a crisp chalky Pierre Cardin dress shirt, beet-red Elizabeth Arden tie with matching pocket tuck, and a pair of silvery Bostonian dress shoes. He strolled across the short lot and stepped inside. The fast-food establishment was one of Dee's favorite places to eat and he dined there often. Today the customer traffic was somewhat light, a surprise to Dee who'd expected long lines since it was Memorial Day. He ordered a quarter-pounder with cheese, extra-large fries, large banana milkshake and two hot apple pies. He informed the cashier that he would eat-in. Just as he handed the teenaged cashier a ten-dollar bill for the $6.82 tab, a creamy 80's-model Cadillac Seville pulled into the parking lot and took the space next to Dee's 300E. The driver never got out.

Dee lounged in the non-smoking section of the restaurant, grabbing a booth next to a window facing the portion of the lot where his car sat. Across from him in the next booth was an elderly couple who looked to be well into their seventies. They were sharing a bucket of French fires and each had a cup of coffee. Dee figured the two probably had been married for at least a half-century. He smiled silently, biting into the hot and delicious burger as he did so. While he ate, he also ran over in his mind the couple things he needed to take care of today—drop by to visit his twin sister and take his Benz to the automatic carwash. The latter thought prompted him to peer out at his auto, noticing the slick Cadillac to the left of it. Dee went back to eating.

Fifteen minutes later, Dee finished up, leaving only a few cold fries and less than half of his second apple pie. A "clean freak" by nature, he took one of his napkins emblazoned with the McDonald's logo and wiped the booth's smooth table surface, saving the lot-and-lobby employee a little work. Dumping the foodstuff wrappings into a nearby trash receptacle and placing the pearly plastic eat-in tray atop the receptacle in its designated slot, Dee headed out the same door he'd entered, waving to the minimum-wage workers as he left.

Dee climbed behind the wheel, started the engine, threw the four-door import in Reverse and backed out, taking a mental note that the clean-cut Cadillac had not moved and its driver—a woman—was still inside. Must be waiting to pick up one of the McDonald's employees, Dee presumed. He took a left onto Airline Blvd., driving down past Alexander's Corner and on towards the trisection of Airline, Rodman, and Dartmouth. A block before reaching the trisection, home to Portsmouth's hottest chicken joint, Dee turned left at Arlington Place, reaching the familiar two-story brick house at 4224 in less than a minute. Out front sat two vehicles, a dove-gray 1984 Ford Thunderbird and a black 1986 Dodge Caravan, both of which belonged to his sister, Delorna, who—as Dee could never understand—managed to hold onto and maintain the only vehicles she'd ever owned. The T-Bird, bought new in late-1983, was her regular car and had an astounding 184,000 miles on it. The Dodge, which she scooped in early-1987 after it was repossessed from its earlier owner of about 15 months, was her leisure-slash-weekend-slash-travel vehicle and had only a little over 91,000 miles logged. Dee parked on the street as opposed to pulling up into the driveway. His favorite niece, Ashley who spent each and every weekend with Delorna—childless and separated from Hubby No. 2—was expecting her Uncle Dee and had been loyally perched at the living room's bay window awaiting his arrival. The moment she spotted the Mercedes, she bolted through the front door and ran out to the curbside to meet him.

"Uncle Dee! Uncle Dee! Uncle Dee!" The jubilant child chanted. "I've been right there waiting on you the whole time," she added, pointing to the bay window.

"Well, hello there," greeted Dee, scooping her up into his arms. "Good gracious, girl! You are getting heavy in your old age."

She giggled. "I'm not old yet, Uncle Dee." She lowered her voice to a whisper. "But my step daddy is," she added, giggling again.

"Now, now," Dee warmly admonished. "That's not nice. Besides, you're only as old as you feel." Letting her back down again, Dee and Ashley headed into the house. He did not notice the Cadillac Seville parked up the street. It had followed him.

***

Following a three-hour, five-minute visit with his sister
and niece, Dee was on his way again. He honked the horn
of his 300E as he pulled off, leaving Delorna and Ashley
waving to him from the porch. Dee saw the Cadillac as
he drove down Arlington Place. Isn't that the same car
from earlier, he wondered, but then dismissed the thought
on the rationale that there is definitely more than one
creamy Cadillac Seville in the entire city of Portsmouth.
He turned right at Airline; drove down to Alexander's
Corner and veered onto Portsmouth Blvd. He followed
the long road for nearly two miles before reaching City
Park Avenue where he turned right. A block down sat
Rodney's 24-Hour Automatic Carwash, which specialized
in touch less car washings with high-powered spray guns.
The five bucks was worth it.

Dee pulled up to the first available bay, passing a fresh-
looking brick-red 1997 Mazda MPV Sport with plush,
stylish, off-white all-leather interior and 22-inch chrome
rims. The owner of the custom-designed multi-purpose
vehicle, an expensively dressed man in his early-thirties,
was in the company of an extremely well-developed girl
about 19 or 20 and a young child—also a girl—who looked
no more than three years old. As Dee stopped to slide
a five-dollar bill into the computerized payment system,
he noticed the youngster wore a T-shirt that read on the
front, "My name is Amber…" When the child moved to
head towards the older girl, probably the child's mother,
Dee saw the wording on the back: "… and my daddy's
name is Lil' Paul, a real O.G." Dee, sheltered for most of
his life, raised in a good familial setting and attending one of
the finer universities in the country, had absolutely no idea
that "O.G." meant Original Gangster, nor did he know the
man at the sporty van was Paul "Lil' Paul" Mills, allegedly
one of the city's most notorious syndicate men and one of

very few reputed African-American mobsters so feared by the majority that he reportedly never even traveled with bodyguards. Unable to decipher the two-letter acronym, Dee carried on, driving at a snail's pace into the bay. Once inside, an electronic eye activated the spray guns. Nine minutes thereafter, Dee exited. Usually, most people wipe-their vehicles dry. Dee abhorred manual labor, save his townhouse's regular cleanings, and chose instead to let the Mercedes air-dry as he headed home.

***

The next morning, a Tuesday, Dee was slated to meet with Dr. Newby, an assistant dean at Norfolk State, to iron out any last-minute details for his speech a week later. The two scholarly gentlemen were to meet at nine o'clock sharp. Dee was up at six-thirty, took his usual one hour to get showered, shaved and dressed, thereafter heading downstairs to fix himself a hearty breakfast. He feasted on a half-dozen miniature waffles and an equal number of breakfast sausage patties, along with three slices of buttered toast and a tall glass of chilled apple juice. At eight-fifteen, following a call from his agent in Richmond to let him know she had just finished reading the manuscript of his second book and was more than pleased, Dee turned on the townhouse's security system and ambled out the front door. What he met stunned him out of his senses: A woman dressed in all white was kneeling on the walkway leading to his townhouse. She was surrounded by long white wax candles lit and set in gold-toned candlesticks. In her hand was a large book, which appeared to Dee to be the Holy Bible, from which she was reading.

"And I stood upon the sand of the sea," she read barely above a whisper, almost chanting, "and saw a beast rise up out of the sea, having seven heads and ten horns, and upon his horns ten crowns, and upon his heads the name of blasphemy."

Dee did not know the woman who happened to be quite decent-looking and he wondered if the obviously deranged woman realized she'd set up her whatever-this-thing-she-was-doing on his walkway believing it to be someone else's walkway. He slowly approached her. She never looked up; just read.

"And the beast which I saw," she continued, "was like unto a leopard, and his feet were as the feet of a bear, and his mouth as the mouth of a lion: and the dragon gave him his power, and his seat, and great authority."

"Excuse me, ma'am," Dee attempted to interrupt.

But the unknown visitor ignored him. "And I saw one of his heads," she persisted, "as it were wounded to death; and his deadly wound was healed; and all the world wondered after the beast."

Again Dee tried to cut in, keeping his tone normal and non-confrontational, "Ma'am, if you'll stop a moment—"

"And they worshipped the dragon which gave power unto the beast: and they worshipped the beast, saying, 'Who is like unto the beast?'" She paused for less than a second, and then went on. 'Who is able to make war with him?'" She paused again, looking up at Dee who stood about six feet away, then returned her view to the large book—which Dee confirmed was a Bible—to keep reading. "And there was given unto him a mouth speaking great things and blasphemies; and power was given unto him to continue forty and two months."

Dee looked around. There were no other Yorkshire Square residents in sight. Then he noticed it: The creamy

Cadillac Seville—the one he saw the day before, first at the McDonald's, then again as he left his twin sister's Westhaven home on Arlington Place—was parked long-ways, blocking his Mercedes in its reserved parking space. His car seemed to be sitting lower than usual. A closer look revealed that all four tires were flat. A sudden sense of fear gripped Dee, prompting him to step back a few feet as he once again focused his attention on the unidentified woman surrounded by the lit candles.

"Who are you?" He asked. "Did you flatten—?"

A rise in her voice, while reading, made Dee pause without completing his inquiry. "And he opened his mouth in blasphemy against God," she carried on, "to blaspheme his name and his tabernacle and them that dwell in heaven."

Dee's mouth dropped open upon realizing from where the woman was reading—it was the Book of the Revelation of Saint John the Divine—and further realized she was orating on the so-called Anti-Christ. According to Dee's studies, the Anti-Christ, strictly speaking, is considered to be the great antagonist of Prophet Jesus, the Anointed One. Studies suggest the Anti-Christ is expected to spread evil before the Second Advent but is finally to be conquered at Prophet Jesus' return. Now Dee knew for sure the woman was seriously deranged and wondered how she confused his residence with her intended target wherever that may have been. Then a thought bolted into Dee's mental, one he tried to immediately dismiss but could not. He wondered what if she doesn't have the wrong house. The thought sickened him. Nevertheless, things began to piece themselves together: the threatening e-mails calling him the Anti-Christ, his sightings of the Seville yesterday in the exact same places he were, the car now blocking 'the exit path of his own vehicle, the four flat tires, the woman here on his walkway. Oh shit, Dee considered, she could be reading that to me! He took another few steps backward. The unfazed woman maintained her reading.

"And it was given unto him to make war with the saints and to overcome them: and power was given him over all kindred and tongues and nations." She ceased long enough to pull a small bottle from inside her all-white outfit. The clear bottle, which looked roughly the size of an airplane liquor bottle but with a much shorter neck, held some type of liquid; Dee had no idea as to what type. Still holding the open Bible with one hand, she used two fingers of her other hand to unscrew the bottle's cap and Dee watched the light-weight aluminum cap fall to the paved walkway. Her reading continued. "And all that dwell upon the earth shall worship him, whose names are not written in the book of life of the Lamb slain from the foundation of the world." The personable woman's voice raised another notch. "If any man has an ear, let him hear." Her voice grew higher. "He that leadeth into captivity shall go into captivity: he that killeth with the sword must be killed with the sword. Here is the patience and the faith of the saints." Another notch up, her voice climbed. "And I beheld another beast coming up out of the earth; and he had two horns like a lamb, and he spake as a dragon." Louder. "And he exercised all the power of the first beast before him and causeth the earth and them that dwell therein to worship the first beast whose deadly wound was healed." Louder, now almost yelling. "And he doeth great wonders so that he maketh fire come down from heaven on the earth in the sight of men." She glanced up at Dee, her look blank and unreadable. "And deceiveth them that dwell on the earth by the means of those miracles which he had power to do in the sight of the beast; saying

111

to them that dwell on the earth, that they should make an image to the beast which had the wound by a sword and did live." Dee was now trembling in fear, unable to speak, incapable of discerning the religiously fanatical woman's true intent. He backed up more, feeling the hard brass handle of his Window Wizard brand storm door in the small of his back. "And he had power to give life unto the image of the beast that the image of the beast should both speak and cause that as many as would not worship the image of the beast should be killed!" No doubt, she was now yelling. "And he causeth all, both small and great, rich and poor, free and bond, to receive a mark in their right hand or in their foreheads!" She abruptly stood; Dee spun around to seek refuge in the townhouse. He dropped his keys. "And that no man might buy or sell, save he had the mark or the name of the beast or the number of his name!" Dee got a hold of his keys and went for the door, his hand shaking miserably and causing him to miss the key hole—twice—before dropping the key ring again. The insane female visitor started creeping towards him, still reading in a loud and powerful voice, holding up the small bottle just a foot above her head. "Here is wisdom! Let him that hath understanding—" Dee had the keys once again "—count the number of the beast: for it is —" She moved closer and closer "—the number of a man; and his number—"Dee got the key inside the lock and turned "—is Six hundred—"As he got the door open, she by now was right at his back, just inches away "—threescore and six!" The Bible fell from her hand; she grabbed a hold of Dee from the back of his neck. He struggled to get inside but her grip was unbelievable. Control the head and you control the body, he realized. She then doused the liquid from the small bottle onto Dee's head and left shoulder. He yelled out in fear, stumbled and fell just inside the doorway. She doused more liquid onto his back, saying absolutely nothing. Her silence petrified Dee who again struggled to get away. She shoved her right foot into his back as he lay helpless on his face and finished pouring the remaining contents of the bottle onto him. Then she spoke directly to him, saying in a loud, haunting voice, "Dr. Deloren Powell, you are the Anti-Christ and you must die! You are the Anti-Christ and you must die! You are the Anti-Christ, and you—"

"Freeze!" A male voice screamed from very close-by. "Police! Get your fuckin' hands up, lady! Now!"

Dee was overjoyed to hear the word "police" and began crying in relief. Just as he rolled over onto his back, he watched one of two Portsmouth police officers, both with guns drawn, roughly jerk the woman from the doorway and viciously toss her to the ground. He replaced his gun to cuff her. The other officer still gripped his weapon, pointing the nickel-plated 9-mm at the aloof woman. Once his partner secured her in handcuffs, he too replaced his sidearm, looking to Dee and asking, "You okay, sir?" Dee-wiping tears, could only stare in utter shock. Then, his ADT alarm system sounded off. In his haste to get inside the townhouse, the system, which had been activated when he departed earlier, allotted him 90 seconds once he'd re-opened the front door to de-activate it. Because he did not, it triggered. He clumsily scrambled to his feet to disarm the piercing siren. Moments later, the telephone rang—the ADT Home Monitoring Center calling to follow up on the matter. They were so good at that.

It turned out the woman's name was Jowanda O'Laughlin, an Irish Nigerian—amalgamation at its best—from Fresno, who'd moved to Virginia following her 1994 release from a California state mental hospital. She was arrested and charged with trespassing, destruction of private property, assault and battery, and threatening bodily harm. It also turned out the small bottle of liquid she doused on Dee was olive oil, her own "holy water" and quite harmless.

The police officers, both Yorkshire Square residents, had just ended their midnight-to-eight patrol and were heading home. They saw the commotion from their cruiser which the police department allowed them to take home as they passed Dee's place. Dee thanked them repeatedly after another cruiser showed up to cart Jowanda O'Laughlin off to jail. Dee cancelled the appointment with Dr. Newby and rescheduled it for the next day. Later, on the 12-noon news, Dee discovered the woman was being held on an $11,000 bond, cash or surety. He was relieved she was behind bars. How long she would be there was something he did not know. Unfortunately for—and unbeknownst to—him, he would again see the severely troubled woman and the reunion would be nothing remotely close to pleasant.

CHAPTER 17
June 3, 1997
Portsmouth, Virginia

Ten years three-and-a-half months after a Norfolk police detective and two FBI agents escorted Andy into custody from a Portsmouth hospital, he was again a free man, arriving in Portsmouth via a limousine. He felt he deserved the luxurious two-and-a-half hour drive from Victoria and had it set up a few weeks prior to his release. The slaty Lexus stretch limo pulled up to Vicky's Holly Hill Lane condo at precisely eleven o'clock in the morning. She was waiting patiently at the front door; the children were still in school.

The first thing Andy did—however bizarre it may have seemed to Vicky—was light a fire in the condo's austere fireplace. Once it was at a steady burn, Andy shed his prison garbs and tossed everything, including the brown state-issued boots, into the flames. Then he walked stark naked into the bathroom in the hallway leading to the bedrooms and ran himself a full tub of hot bath water. Vicky could only watch in amazement. He climbed in the tub, wincing from the high temperature of the water, and submerged his entire body. After ten seconds or so, he came up, letting out a loud "Yes!" The tub bath, he explained, was a longstanding tradition of parolees in order to get the stench of prison off their bodies. Since there were no tubs inside, one could never truly get clean unless and until he hit the tub once home. Following the bath, Andy and Vicky retreated to the master bedroom to make love. He ejaculated a little more than two minutes into the sex; however, his second round carried him nearly twenty minutes. Afterwards, he was exhausted. Vicky offered him a glass of ice water, to which he vehemently objected, reasoning, "It'll burst my heart open." Another prison thing. Instead, he curled into a ball and fell off to sleep. It was 12:30 p.m.

Two hours and fifteen minutes later, Andy was awakened by a pleasant sight—the Triplets had arrived home from school. Ahmad, Ahman and Ahmar stood over Andy looking like a group of Catholic priests issuing a dying parishioner's Last Rites. When the grogginess cleared him, the boys broke into simultaneous smiles, each 14-year-old greeting Andy with a mighty hug. Twins Darius and Darren showed up 45 minutes later; Marquita was home at 3:45. The eight of them later piled into Vicky's blue Ford Explorer and enjoyed dinner at the Old Country Buffet on Portsmouth Blvd one city over. They promptly returned home to spend the rest of the evening conversing and making up for lost time. Andy was so very happy to finally be home.

CHAPTER 18
June 3, 1997
Norfolk, Virginia

The speech given by Dee at Norfolk State University went perfectly. Afterwards, he drove to Chesapeake for dinner at a popular restaurant, Old Country Buffet, located one-half mile from the imposing Chesapeake Square Mall on Portsmouth Blvd. He sat next to a large family made up of a set of triplets, twins and a solo daughter. Once done, Dee made his way home back to neighboring Portsmouth. It was 6:45 p.m. when he pulled onto Lancer Drive. And, unfortunately, he did not see the creamy Cadillac tucked away next to the rental office. But its driver, Jowanda O'Laughlin, saw Dee. She quickly started her engine, tossed the auto into Drive, and pulled out behind Dee, only several yards separating them. Dee pulled into his reserved parking space, oblivious of the car behind him, cut the engine and started to exit. He heard a car door open, he heard the fast approach of a set of feet, but just when he turned to investigate, all he saw was a large knife as it came down upon him. He had only enough time to bring both of his own hands up to protect his face. Just as he heard and felt the sickening tear of his flesh from Jowanda's ten-inch knife, seven inches of which was surgically sharpened steel, there was a thunderous roar. It was a gunshot and down went his attacker. Behind her, dressed in a tank-top, shorts and flip-flops, was one of the police officers who'd arrested her a month earlier. As Dee began to faint at the sight of his gushing blood, all he could think of was how perfect his speech went. Oh so perfect. Then, everything went blank.

CHAPTER 19
Christmas Eve, 1997
Suwanee

Old Man Winter had practically crippled all of Gwinnett County and the surrounding areas. Temperatures lingered below freezing for days at a time. Harsh winds caused the wind-chill factor to take a seemingly permanent seat in the negative-zero range. But nothing, absolutely nothing, prevented Jimmie Lee White from coming home each year, usually arriving a couple of days before Christmas and not departing until the day after New Year's. This year's return, like the eight before it, was no exception.

The Trailways bus station in Lawrenceville was packed yesterday as Jimmie Lee arrived. William, the White Plantation's driver of the past eight years, was already there waiting when Jimmie Lee's bus pulled into the terminal.

"Howdy, Master James," greeted William with a smile. "Glad to have ya home again, sir."

"Glad to be back," Jimmie Lee gratefully said.

William replaced the family's former driver, David, in the fall of 1989. David died of complications during gall bladder surgery. Emma Lou was devastated by the loss as David had been her driver for nearly a quarter-century.

But William quickly blended in, becoming the gardener's new roommate in the servants' quarters. He and Nathan got along exceptionally well.

"Watch your fingers, Master James," William said as he closed the right rear passenger door. "We'll be there in just fourteen minutes." Jimmie Lee was always impressed with the driver's preciseness. And, just as he'd said, William pulled the gray 1994 Cadillac Fleetwood onto the estate exactly fourteen minutes later.

"Looka here, looka here, looka here," Emma Lou said from the porch. "C'mon inside boy and get warmed up."

"You're gonna catch cold, Momma Lou-Lou," Jimmie Lee warned. "You're seventy-eight years old."

"No, I'm not," Emma said as they walked inside. "I'm only seventy-seven." She let out a "whew" as she slammed the door. "Don't put nuthin' extra on me, boy," she added warmly.

The two greeted each other with a firm hug and kisses before perching down by the massive fireplace to conduct their usual year-in-review chitchat. A few hours and several mugs of hot cocoa later, Jimmie Lee was ready to retire to his old bedroom on the second floor to enjoy his first night of rest at home.

Today, just one day before Christmas, the temperature remained the same—twenty degrees—with a wind-chill factor of minus 9 degrees, prompting Jimmie Lee to stay inside. But before he headed upstairs, company came calling. A few townsfolk dropped by, including Michelle Nader, the local gossip columnist, who wanted to know how many states had Jimmie Lee thus far covered.

"Twenty," he responded, adding, "Which is a far cry off from where I'd like to be." Explaining further, he said, "You see, Ms. Nader, I wanted to cover all fifty states in ten years but I've been covering only two or three a year."

"Why so?" She asked, her eyes fixed on his as if he was set to reveal next week's winning lottery numbers.

"'Cause I get in a new state and really like it; gets hard to leave. So I kinda end up staying between four and six months as opposed to the two-and-a-half-month maximum time I'm supposed to stay. In order to hit all fifty in a decade, like I set out, I would need to do at least five states a year. I'm way off from that."

"Are you meeting any women, Jimmie Lee?" She asked staring at him like his answer would qualify for a Nobel Prize.

"Noooo," he said with a sign. "I'm really not looking 'cause I wanna stay focused on my traveling goals."

"Do you think love'll come your way, Jimmie Lee?"

"One day," he stated, offering a smile.

CHAPTER 20

January 1998
Virginia Beach, Virginia

The offices were small and a bit cramped but the people who worked in them paid little attention to size; rather, each was focused full-force ahead, the exact image of their respected leader, a 31-year-old named Andrew Smith. He preached positive mental attitude, he preached success, and he preached money.

TSE, the acronym for Townes-Smith Enterprises, was a credit information consulting firm of which Vicky Townes, Andy's first wife, owned a 55% stake. Andy owned the other 45%. TSE specialized in seminars that taught people how to get out of debt while at the exact same time saving for retirement and accomplishing both without going into the poor house. A clever hook indeed! Needless to say, business was booming: seminar seats, a total of 160 per weekend, were booked out 4-5 weeks in advance. There seemed to be no end to the in-flow of revenue and Andy loved every minute of it. Indeed, he had planned the business concept well in advance of his release and had vowed not to let anything or anyone stop him.

"I need you to sign these docs, Miss P.," said Rhonda Stringfield, the office's official administrative assistant.

She was talking to Shardae Pearson, the business' Senior Vice President and Chief Financial Officer. Shardae, an accounting finance major from Norfolk State University, was hired four months out of college. She was very competent, articulate and good-looking. Andy loved her and brought her on board. Back then, which was only four months ago, the office staff consisted of just Andy and Shardae.

"Here you are, Rhonda," said Shardae after a quick perusal and signing of the documents. "I'm going to lunch now."

"See ya in an hour, Miss P," yelled out Rhonda who was already walking away after getting the signature. The pace of the daily operations warranted no idling about.

Vicky Townes was President and Chief Executive Officer of the business by virtue of her relationship with Andy. She had no business experience and appeared only on the official stationary. She didn't even have an office. Andy, however, wanted her to feel as if she was an integral facet of his dreams for the future, hence the "ghost" titles.

TSE was located on Virginia Beach Boulevard not far from the city's Resort Strip. Situated in a brick office building across the street from a 7-11, the company recently began leasing all seven suites on the second floor of the Coldwell/Banker-owned building. Formerly they leased only four.

Andy was listed as Executive Vice President and Chief Operating Officer—even though everyone treated him like the chief executive—and had his own office. Shardae had the office next to his. Rhonda, the Administrative Assistant, worked from the third office. Three other offices faced theirs: two were seminar rooms and the third was where the Office Services Technicians toiled. Holding those posts were 16-year-old Latoria Taylor of Portsmouth and Branchville native Krista Wynn who, at 22, was working at TSE just to pass time until her college graduation in May. The seventh office was a small conference room with seating for a half-dozen.

"Tori," Andy yelled from his office as he viewed recruiting numbers from the monitor of his desktop PC. "Let me look at ya!"

"Comin'," she responded, grabbing a Mead notepad as she sprinted out. She was quite a young lady. She had just given birth only a few months before—to a baby girl she named Moeesha—and was constrained to enter the work force. Andy hired her two months ago, a few days after she turned sixteen. She works Monday thru Friday from 3:30 each afternoon until 10 at night. On Tuesday, Wednesday and Thursday nights, she catches a ride with Andy since they are the only office people from Portsmouth. The other two nights—Monday and Friday—she catches the city bus.

"Yes sir?" She inquired as she stepped inside his cozy office, decked out in a Roland Movret top and a striking Heikejarick skirt. Both were green and looked stunning on the personable young vixen.

"Call all the Home Teleworkers and tell them I've got a yard for the first one to hit a dime-piece this evening. You got it?"

"Yes sir," she answered, then confirmed, "Call all thirty of our phone people in Norfolk, Portsmouth, Virginia Beach, Chesapeake and Suffolk, and tell them a one-hundred-dollar bonus goes to the first person to hit ten confirmed recruits this evening."

"That's right," he said without looking up. "Go, go, go," he pressed, still fixated on the monitor.

As Latoria darted out of the office, she nearly knocked down Krista who was heading in.

"Mr. Smith?" She said softly as she peered inside.

"Come, come," he said as if he already knew what she wanted. "I'm listening."

Krista was also well-dressed, sporting an entire Zepi of New York City outfit. The Lifestyle Clothing Company owned the Zepi name and prided itself in one day becoming another Enyce or Fubu. Krista wore a red, collarless top and very tight roseate jeans. Her light-weight jacket was white and the slick-looking hat, tilted slightly downward with a gangster's touch, was oyster-white. She looked marvelously delightful.

"A girl just called," she began. "She's inquiring about an OST job. I told her we didn't have any openings but took her name anyway." She slid an orange sticky note onto Andy's desk.

Andy looked up briefly. "What's the girl's name?"

"Ronica, Ronica Little."

"I'll remember that," he assured, looking back at the monitor and keying in figures. "Go help Tori make those calls."

"What calls?" Krista wanted to know.

"Go ask her," he said, never looking up. "By the way, slick outfit you got there." He paused his typing, looked up with a warm smile, winked, then inaudibly mouthed, "Go, go, go" before going back to his own work.

"Miss P!" He shouted at the top of his lungs just as Krista departed, causing her to jump, startled. "Let me look at ya!"

Krista turned back toward the open office door to inform him, "She's gone to lunch, sir."

"Rhonda! Call Miss P's cell phone, then send the call back here to me!"

***

That night, as Andy pulled up in front of Latoria's Ann Street apartment in Portsmouth's Park View subdivision, the car's mobile phone chimed. "That's Vicky," he guessed aloud.

"Andy Smith," he answered.

"It's eleven o'clock, Andy," Vicky's voice said without greeting him. "You're fifteen minutes late, hon."

"I know," he began, "but you know I drop off one of my people three nights a week."

"Yeah, but you're still here by ten-forty-five. Are you running your mouth, Andy?"

"Naw," he said, waving a silent goodbye to Latoria as the nubile teen exited the car. "I'll be there in about fifteen more minutes, Vicky. We didn't get out of the office until a quarter-past ten."

"Well," she sighed, "your supper will be in the microwave. Just heat it up and enjoy. I'm heading to bed."

"Okay, Vicky, I'll see you after while."

"Andy?" She called out, sounding serious. "We need to have another talk."

Another, he caught. "Sure," he said. "I'll see you soon."

As Andy drove down Ann Street, taking a left onto Elm Avenue, his mind wandered to Vicky. He knew she wanted to either talk about marriage or his long hours, both of which had come up before. Andy felt his work schedule was—although long—necessary to make the huge amount of money the company was pulling in. Even still, his schedule did at least leave a few hours with his family. He was off all day every Monday—except the first Monday of the month—and he left work early—at 7 P.M.—every Friday. His normal arrival time each day— ten o'clock sharp—was even considered late for most company heads. The only downside was that Andy did his own seminars which meant he was also away from home both Saturday and Sunday for upwards of fifteen hours each day. So now, he figured, Vicky may be again feeling neglected. He pondered how to approach the situation, turning right onto South Street as he did so, determining he'd probably need a better angle than the baby-I'm-just-trying-to-make-some-money line which was growing old.

As he turned left at Des Moines Avenue, viewing the notorious Swanson Homes housing project in his rear-view mirror, he took the almost immediate right onto Deep Creek Boulevard. Andy also entertained the thought that the talk could be of marriage. Realistically, he had no desire to marry the same girl twice. It made him feel like a male version of Elizabeth Taylor. But never in a million years would he tell Vicky his true feelings. No fucking way.

Soon, Holly Hill Lane was in sight onto which Andy made his final turn, pulling up onto the two-car elevated driveway next to Vicky's Ford Explorer. A minute later, he walked through the front door.

***

127

"Okay, Miss P," Andy said as he sat at the conference room table, "time for our daily rap session."

It was customary for Shardae and Andy to have a sit-down each day he worked, usually from about 1:30 'til 2:30 or 3. Rhonda also sat in, taking notes. Since Shardae worked one o'clock to ten, Andy liked to get with her before she got too engrossed in her day. The rap sessions centered on daily recruiting numbers goals as well as confirmed, that is, prepaid, recruits. From time to time, as a motivation tool, Andy would teleconference in his two top Teleworkers as if their input were crucial.

"Before I go over the numbers," she began, rising to head over to the purple chalk board, "I want to run something else by you."

"Sure," Andy said, looking at her. Her attire was superb: a yellow blouse by Angelo Lameroy of New York, golden slacks from Fendi with matching sallow Fendi flats. Shardae was fairly short—only 5'2"—and a far cry from her six-footer mom, a longtime collections manager with Norfolk-based Future Finance Company, a subsidiary of Charlie Falk Auto Wholesalers Inc. The mom, a full-blooded Anglo-Saxon, fell in love with a reformed city slicker with a small-time criminal record and a desire to hook up with a girl of the Caucasian persuasion. The African-American roofer eventually met and married Shardae's mom, impregnating her the same year. Shardae's biracialism made for a sensational hue, striking gray eyes, and hair that looked to have been made for a doll baby. She was so delicious-looking that the first thought that crossed a man's mind at sight of her was typically "Wow! I bet she'd make a pretty baby."

"Why are you staring at me like that, Mr. Smith?"

Shardae's question brought Andy out of his moment of reflection. "Just waiting on you to start talking, I guess."

"I believe we are in a position to expand into the Newport News and Hampton areas," she started, her voice serious.

"The Peninsula?" Andy asked with raised eyes. "How many people do you think we'll need?"

"We can do it with just twelve more Home Teleworkers. Take a look." She began scrawling figures on the chalkboard, drawing arrows from figures to named cities, and explaining herself as she went. Once complete, she turned her attention back to her boss, replaced the piece of chalk and brushed her hands together to remove any dust. "That's it," she concluded.

Andy sat in silence, rethinking his top deputy's plans. After nearly two minutes of looking at the chalk board, gazing into empty space, spinning around in his chair, and rapping on the desk from time to time with a Paper Mate American No. 2 pencil, he finally spoke up. "Okay, I'll go with it. Draw up a written financial proposal, have it on my desk in twenty-four hours, and by next week we will be in the implementation mode.

Shardae raised a jubilant fist. "Yes!" She cheered.

Thereafter, the trio—counting Rhonda—went over the numbers for the day.

***

By Valentine's Day, the Peninsula operations were up and running. A dozen new Home Teleworkers were hired. Like their counterparts in Hampton Roads, they'd work from the privacy of their own residences Monday thru Friday from 3 p.m. to 9 p.m. They had a choice with regard to how they reported their daily recruiting totals: they could call the Virginia Beach office every thirty minutes or they could wait until the end of the night. Each home worker was paid by commission, earning twenty percent of the seminar fee of $49.95 for each successful recruit. Latoria and Krista, meanwhile, did the confirmation call-backs. Both worked 3:30 p.m. to ten at night. Peninsula operations revenue, combined with Hampton Road's, pushed total revenues past the $100,000 mark at the end of the fiscal second quarter, the last week of February. Andy was most definitely pleased.

***

Although Andy usually took Mondays off, he felt like working today so he decided to make Easter Monday a day of toil. Just as he pulled up in his new 1998 BMW 740i, he noticed a relatively young girl step from an older model Honda Accord LX. It was black like Andy's import. Then he looked closer into her face—his heart stopped. The girl was about 20—maybe 21—and was a dead-ringer for Jeanette, his gun-toting, jail-breaking second wife. He was speechless as he parked his car next to hers, wasting no time in getting out to greet her.

"Hi," he said nervously. Are you lost or something? Do you need directions?" Work suddenly left his mind.

"No," she said. Her sweet voice was mesmerizing. She even sounded like Jeanette or so it seemed. "I'm waiting on the TSE people."

Andy was taken aback. "That's me! I'm in charge of TSE. I'm Andy, Andy Smith, Chief Operating Officer. And you are?"

"Ronica Little," she began, offering him her hand. But instead of shaking it, Andy placed his trembling lips on the

130

back of it and planted a kiss. She looked a bit surprised but continued on:

"I wanted to follow up on a job application I put in three months ago. I spoke with—"

"You're hired," he cut in. "Plain and simple. You're fuckin' hired."

CHAPTER 21
May 1998
Portsmouth

Vanessa Dickey pulled into the "Guest" parking slot next to Dee's Mercedes, hoping she hadn't caught him off-guard by visiting without first calling. She figured if she had come at the wrong time, she'd just turn around and leave. No sweat, she thought. But leaving, she thought further, would be heartbreaking. The 25-year-old X-ray technician was crazy about Dee, practically swooning each time the two met. She first saw him in a local mall, recognizing his face from television interviews he participated in while promoting his most recent book, The Psychological Implications of Promoting a Non-Existent God. She boldly walked up to Dee, introduced herself, and would not depart until the two traded cell phone numbers and e-mail addresses. She eventually talked to him by phone before manipulating him into giving up his home address. This was her first visit, unannounced, unplanned—classic Vanessa Dickey.

The six-foot-two-inch former high school basketball center who graduated from a Roswell, Georgia—postsecondary school six years ago, confidently strode from her used teal green Acura Legend, passing a cute stray dog feasting on a turkey drumstick as she went, and knocked on Dee's locked storm door. No answer. She knocked again. Still no answer. She knocked one last time. Her knock went unanswered. Turning to leave, she realized the Mercedes was Dee's car. She considered whether he'd probably looked out of a window, saw it was her and decided not to answer. No way, she deduced. Then she heard a click. It was the dead bolt to the front door. Her heart began to race as she spun back into the direction of the townhouse's front entrance. Dee's face appeared; he wore a smile. The storm door swung open.

"Hi there," Dee greeted. "What a surprise."

"Hello, Dr. Powell," she began, her voice a bit shaky. "I'm—I'm sorry I didn't call first. You were—were kinda on my mind, so I just figured I'd—you know, pop in."

"No problem," Dee said, his smile still in place. "C'mon in. You're just in time for lunch."

***

On Father's Day, Dee received a call from Vanessa who wanted to go out on a date. He declined, citing other plans. That was a lie, of course. Dee didn't have any other plans; he seldom did. He simply did not want to get too close to Vanessa, a true beauty. She was tall, light-complexioned, with smooth skin and elegant legs. However, Dee's ideal mate was not one who forced herself on a man during her very first visit to his home, attempting to give him a blow-job at the dining room table during lunch and without being asked to. That turned him off. Since then, she'd called about five or six times, each time asking Dee out on a date. When would the bitch get the message, he wondered. So, instead of running from the issue, Dee decided to face it.

"Vanessa, I have to tell you something," Dee said as if it were the most important thing he would ever say in his life. "I am truly not interested in dating you. Please don't call again." Without waiting for a response, he hung up.

An hour later, Dee heard a knock at the front door. His first thought was that Vanessa Dickey had come to give him a piece of her mind, causing him to consider not answering the knock. But almost immediately he dismissed the thought, reasoning aloud, "This is my damn house." He darted down the stairwell, cut left and left again before reaching for the knob and dead bolt simultaneously. The visitor was not Vanessa but just as confrontational, causing Dee to freeze in disbelief. It was none other than Dee's father, Rev. Tyler Powell. The Window Wizard storm door was unlocked so Tyler Powell was basically already inside the door.

"Well," his father sighed, "you gonna let me thru or what?" Dee countered with a straight face, "I don't make a habit of letting strangers into my home." Rev. Powell offered a dry smile. "I'm sure you don't," he responded, walking into the residence as Dee moved back a few steps to let him proceed, before adding, "and if I thought you had a sense of humor, son, I'd take that as a joke." The preacher went straight into the living room. Dee closed the front door and walked into the living room as well. Rev. Powell had not spoken to—nor seen—Dee in over two-and-a-half years. He sat on the couch, looking around at the furnishings as if to remind himself of what they looked like since the last time he visited. Dee sat next to him in silence.

"Well, you can say something," Rev. Powell urged with a smile, this one not so dry as the first.

"I—I don't know—know what to say," stuttered Dee.

"Well, you can start with 'Happy Father's Day, Dad'," he matter-of-factly stated.

CHAPTER 22
Summer 1998
Portsmouth

The TSE office was bustling with the usual faces—Andy, Shardae and Rhonda—as the three bodies zipped back and forth. It was 2:15 in the afternoon the Monday after the Independence Day weekend. Andy was usually off on Monday and Office Services Technicians Latoria and Ronica were not due in until 3:30. Today, however, was the first Monday of the month, marking TSE's regular Family Day where all the Teleworkers converge to share monthly recruiting numbers and to simply meet each other. Being that everyone worked from home, it—Family Day, that is—became a TSE tradition. So as Andy, Shardae the finance chief, and administrative assistant Rhonda readied up the office for the five o'clock affair, it was clear that corporate love was in the air.

Andy went into the bathroom to take a quick piss when he noticed the morning paper's front-page headline: ATLANTA PROSECUTOR DIES IN SHOOT-OUT. He reached for the Virginian-Pilot with his right hand, reading and pissing simultaneously. According to the article, Chief Deputy District Attorney LaPrecious Rhodes, who was being investigated in Atlanta for a series of killings, got into a shoot-out in Maryland with a detective, wounding him before turning the gun on herself. The picture of the fallen prosecutor reminded Andy of actress Victoria Dillard. "Pretty girl," he said aloud, shaking his penis to rid it of any remaining urine in its shaft before replacing it back inside his slacks. He dropped the newspaper back on the floor, flushed the toilet, and then exited without washing his hands.

***

Family Day ended at eight o'clock that evening and the affair was a grand success. All of TSE's Home Teleworkers showed up, fun was had by all and, Andy was happy. Indeed, he had reason to be. TSE by now was in the entire Hampton Roads and Peninsula areas, covering not only Norfolk, Portsmouth, Virginia Beach, Chesapeake and Suffolk but Hampton and Newport News as well. Additionally, TSE just opened up in the Metro-Richmond market, covering the city of Richmond and the surrounding counties of Henrico, Hanover and Chesterfield. Andy, just a week before, laid out plans to enter the Petersburg Tri-Cities market, giving TSE coverage in the cities of Petersburg, Hopewell and Colonial Heights. For the first time in his life, Andy was legally earning good money-- $78,000 to be exact—and he loved every minute of it. It made him happy to see the successful faces of his 66 Home Teleworkers because he knew were it not for their untiring recruiting efforts; he would not be earning what he is. Following Family Day, therefore, Andy told the office staffers they could all go on home. The two hours left to work would be on him.

As the five left the office building and spilled into the parking lot to each of their respective vehicles, Andy said good-bye to Shardae, Rhonda and Latoria without looking at them. But when he said good-bye to Ronica, he looked square into her eyes, produced an ever-so-slight smirk, and then climbed into his black BMW. She got into her 1990 Honda Accord, also black, and was the last car out of the parking lot. Each of the five hit the Route 44 expressway but the last two cars got off two exits later, pulling into a LaQuinta Inn motel next to a 7-11 on Witchduck Road. They said nothing as they exited their vehicles; rather they went straight to Room 240, rented by Ronica before she arrived to work. It was a normal ritual on Family Day—at least for her and Andy. The two had been having an affair since they met three months before, beginning just days after he hired her to replace Krista Wynn, the former office worker who had gone off to India on a religious mission. So, the good-bye Andy offered in TSE's parking lot was not really a good-bye at all. That was probably where the smirk came from.

An hour later as Ronica lay naked across the queen-sized bed, she gazed at Andy as he stood in the small motel bathroom drying himself from a hot shower. He never used soap; just real hot water. It was his way of not going home smelling like a fresh shower as well as rinsing away the scent of recent sex. Ronica decided to break the silence.

"Andy, what do you think that lady would do if she knew you were banging an 18-year-old girl?" Ronica had a habit of dehumanizing Andy's wife by calling her not by name but simply "that lady". It was the teen's way of clearing her mountain of guilt for sleeping with a 31-year-old married father of six.

Andy's response was simple. "She'd probably want to know why." He kept drying himself.

"That's it, you think?" Ronica queried.

"Yep," Andy's replied. Then he added, "She'd also probably want to work it out."

"Work it out?! Ronica seemed shocked. "You're fucking a girl who's only two years older than the triplets! What can be worked out from that?"

"You don't know Vicky," he seriously said.

***

"Your birthday is in two weeks, honey." Vicky said. "Do you have an idea what you want?"

Andy was sitting in the condo's living room, his head buried in stat sheets from the office.

"Honey?" Vicky called out from the kitchen. "Did you hear me?"

"Yep," he stated. "Gimme some booty; that'll hold me." He kept working.

Vicky seemed insulted as she left the kitchen and marched into the living room, looking sternly at Andy. "You need to watch your mouth."

"I was kidding," he said.

"Don't kid that way," she scolded. "One of the children may hear you."

"And?!" Andy exclaimed, becoming angry. "What— you don't think they know we screw at night?!" His voice was serious. "C'mon Vicky, we're both grown and the kids ain't crazy. Not by a long shot."

"Well," she began, trying to calm the situation, "maybe I'm a bit old-fashioned. It's just that—"

"Maybe? Maybe?" Andy repeated incredulously. "No, Vicky, you are very old-fashioned. You still think oral sex is sinful, you're scared to talk dirty and you've got this weird belief that any positions other than missionary is gonna banish us both to the fiery pits of Hell. There's no maybe in it. You are very old-fashioned."

"I can't help that," she contended.

"Yes you can," he countered. "You simply don't want to try."

"Andy," she began, attempting to change the subject, "I just wanted to know what you'd like for your birthday."

"A new address!" He said, rising and storming out the front door.

***

Andy pulled into the parking lot of a small convenience store adjacent to a public housing project called Grandy Village. His pager had just sounded but the battery in his cell phone was dead. He spotted the double phone booth as he drove, noticing one was available while the other was in use. As he got out the 740i, the person—a female—using the other phone stopped long enough in her conversation to eye him head to toe. She looked impressed. Andy grabbed the other phone, dropped in the quarter and dime, and began dialing the number displayed on his pager. 7-5-7 he began, peering at the rest of the numbers, 4-4-1, he continued, 2-1-2-1. The other party picked up on the second ring, answering with a simple "hello".

"This is Andrew Smith. I received a page from this—"

"Yes, Mr. Smith," the voice cut him off. "My name is Lorenzo Craig. I own a home in Sherwood Heights in Norfolk. I have a huge basement flat for rent, if you're interested."

Andy was floored. "How do you know—who told you I was—who are you again?" His confusion was apparent.

Lorenzo let out a casual laugh. "Lorenzo's my name, Lorenzo Craig. And to answer your questions, I'll say this: The walls have ears."

"What the hell are you talking about?" Andy asked, visibly amazed as he looked around, again noticing the female using the other phone. She was tall—at least six feet—and quite thick body-wise. She was close to 200 pounds but very proportionately built. Andy saw no visibly offensive fat tissue. His thought was interrupted by the strange caller's response.

"To be honest, sir, my friend is your neighbor in Holly Hill Condominiums. He overhead you on at least two occasions arguing with your wife and saying that you would be moving out, so he relayed that to me.

"My neighbor? Andy asked. "The nosy guy, Aubrey?"

"That's him," Lorenzo acknowledged. "His life-partner, Jake, did some business with your company once and kept your card. That's how I paged you. So, sir, about the basement flat?"

Andy grinned. "What type of work do you do, Lorenzo?"

"Sales."

"It figures," Andy followed up. "Gimme your address." The exchange of information continued for the next minute with Andy promising to visit in an hour or so. After hanging up, he decided not to leave the phone booth. He stood there, gazing at the tall female who looked to be in her mid-thirties. While she talked on the phone, she looked at him like she was irritated by his gaze but

Andy knew better. He knew the look was superficial so he never wavered. Finally she finished her conversation, hung up, then snickered before asking Andy, "What are you looking at?" She tried to seem stern, tough. Andy wasn't moved.

"You," he said simply.

"Why?" She asked, now attempting to sound proper.

"Cause you're tall, for one," he answered with the obvious look of lust in his eyes. "What are you, six feet even?"

"Noooo," she said affectionately. "I'm six-one."

"Mmm," Andy said the lust still visible. "I like that."

She tried to look taken aback. "I bet you do, but I don't know you."

"Now you do," he shot back. "I'm Andy, Andy Smith. What's your name?"

"Jessica."

"Jessica what?"

"Why?"

"Just asking."

"Jessica is all you need to know right now." She snickered again.

"So tell me where you live, Jessica." The two began to walk towards his BMW.

"Right there," she said, pointing to Grandy Village.

"Oh, so you live in those government-subsidized homes?" He had stopped walking as he asked his question.

"The what?!" She exclaimed. "'Government-subsidized homes'? Naw, man, I live in the projects. That's the projects. Where do you live?"

"The suburbs over in Portsmouth."

"Oh," Jessica replied, impressed. "Can I get a lift home? It's only two blocks from here."

"Sure."

***

It was Monday, August 24, two days before Andy's birthday. He would be 32. The past week-and-a-half was a total blur for him. He'd taken off from the office, leaving Shardae in charge. Over the past ten days, he'd managed to move out of the house—the second time he'd left Vicky since they first met in 1986—and move into an $85.00-a-week basement flat, meet a 36-year-old single mother of four from a Norfolk housing project and have sex with her that same day and every single day since and still manage to find time every other day to hook up with Ronica. A total blur indeed.

His new residence was quite cozy. It was situated to the rear of the spacious Sherwood Heights home owned by Lorenzo Craig and his wife Lynette Drew-Craig. Andy's entrance was followed by a long pathway along the side of the home, expertly decorated with colorful concrete slabs and stones along the way. A sliding door was his front door of sorts. Once inside, a sink and counter-top was to the left right next to a full bath. To the right was a sitting area equipped with a couple of wicker chairs and a small table. A short hall began just past the bathroom, with two doors in sight. The door to the left led to the Craig's kitchen. It was locked. The door to the right led to Andy's bedroom, a simple set-up complete with a twin bed, desk and chair, chest of drawers topped with a 14-inch television, and a shorter stand with a mini-fridge atop it. The closet, though not a walk-in, was still quite spacious. Free basic cable, a local phone line, the TV, fridge, and furniture all came with the flat. To Andy, it was an exceptionally good deal for only $85 a week even though cost did not concern him. Hell, he earned nearly $80,000 a year! Yet with Andy, especially considering the nature of the work he did, good deals always made an impact.

He was lying across the twin bed in his room when he heard a rap on the sliding door's glass. He went to investigate. It was Ronica, laid out in an expensive silk Collette Dinningan dress, courtesy of Barney's New York. Ronica picked it up earlier in the month during a weekend trip to the Bronx. Andy led her inside the flat. It was her fifth visit since he'd moved in. They'd have two-hour lovemaking sessions before she climbed back into her Honda Accord and head back to her home in Portsmouth's Charlestown Townhouses. She enjoyed sex with her boss; he helped make her feel like a woman instead of a teenager. His touch often sent shrills down her spine even before the lovemaking began. Once inside of her, Andy made Ronica convulse in orgasmic ecstasy in ways she never fathomed possible. She could do nothing afterwards except curl into an infant knot, stick her thumb in her mouth, and then silently swoon in the sensual feelings pulsating through her young tender body. Two hours with him seemed like two days on a remote island with every possible amenity. It was amazing. So, as Andy took her by the hand to lead her from the sitting area to his bedroom, she knew full well what was in store for her. No need to tarry so she immediately began peeling off the yellow $255-dress she wore, stripping down to a matching white bra-and-panty set with tiny red cardinals. Andy too began undressing, ridding himself of his purple Guess shirt and Mecca slacks. He wore no underwear. Naked, he removed Ronica's under things with carefulness, causing her to become aroused by his delicateness. Following fifteen minutes of intense foreplay, Andy plunged inside the youngster for the first of several times over the next hour-and-a-half.

***

"Happy Birthday, Andy," sang Jessica's youngest daughter, Keetra. "I hope you have a nice birthday." The child's voice was not Billboard material but she meant well and Andy was moved.

"Thank you, Keetra."

Jessica and two of her other three daughters stood nearby. Cookie and T.G. were already digging into the cake. The group of five was in the small kitchen of Jessica's Grandy Village apartment gleefully celebrating Andy's 32nd birthday. The girls instantly took to the successful businessman. Their mother typically dated another type of guy and he was a far cry from Andy. For a change, the girls could be around someone with an expensive outfit because he worked hard in an office as opposed to hustling crack cocaine on a street corner. The BMW Andy drove was in his name and not some unsuspecting relative's name to help him hide his assets. Ironically, Cookie, who actively pursued younger drug dealers in order to woo them with her adult body, still supported her mother's choices for sleeping partners regardless of whether they carried laptops or illegal handguns. As the oldest child still living at home, Cookie knew what it took for a female in the projects to survive: a very pretty face or some good damn pussy. It was just that simple.

As Andy cut a piece of birthday cake for himself, his pager sounded off. It was Ronica's number followed by her code, "18", then "911", signifying an emergency. She never sent a "911" page, Andy realized, so this must be important. He pulled out his cell phone and began dialing. With Jessica, Andy didn't have to go into other rooms to answer pages or make calls. She didn't care who he was sleeping with. All she ever asked of him was for some of his time, an hour or a whole day, or somewhere in between, whichever worked for him. It does not take much to satisfy the girl from the projects, Andy said within as he pressed the Send button on his phone. Ronica answered immediately.

"Hello," she began, her voice slightly quivering. Please say this is Andy."

"Yes, it is, Ronica," he confirmed. "You sound funny. What's going on?" Concern was in his voice.

"I need to see you, Andy. It's really, really important. I need to see you today. Like I said, it's really—"

"I get the picture," he cut her off. "I'm at a small gathering in Norfolk right now. Meet me in an hour back across the water at Portside. We'll talk then."

"Okay, Andy," she concluded before adding, "it's really important."

"I got you, Ronica. One hour. Portside."

***

"You hit the what?!" Andy marveled, his eyes wide in utter shock.

"The lottery," replied Ronica. "The Cash-5 Game. It's worth a hundred grand." Strangely, she was calm.

"Un-fucking-believable!" Andy spewed.

"Now to the meat of the matter," Ronica went on, taking Andy by the arm and leading him down the boardwalk of Portside in downtown Portsmouth as she continued talking, "which is why I called you."

"Okay," said Andy. This sounds kinda deep."

"It is," she acknowledged. "You see, my dad killed himself when I was twelve. The insurance didn't pay off but some other stuff did—stuff he'd sat aside for me, his only child. Anyway, 'cause I was only a kid at the time, my momma became the guardian over the trust—that's the 'stuff' I was talking 'bout—and she has control over it 'til I'm twenty-one. With this lottery hit, she'll control that too.

"Understand me, Andy, when I say I love my momma and I trust her. No question about that. It's just that I know how over-protective she is and how she holds on to every penny. She gives me $900 a month to buy things; my other money comes from TSE. With this lottery hit, she'll simply parlay the $60,000-plus net payment over the rest of the trust's remaining three-year period and simply triple my monthly pay-out to $2,700. That's actually very comfortable. But, Andy, I want that money now. I want to buy a small house—maybe a HUD house worth forty or fifty G's and needing five or ten G's worth of work on it—so I can set out on my own right now. Even though I don't plan on being at TSE forever, the money from there is sufficient—along with the other $900—for my needs. So momma doesn't need to up my monthly; however, she would never let me buy a house before I'm twenty-one. Thus, I need a way to control my own money. You've got to help me, Andy."

Andy was speechless. He did some law work while in prison but never anything dealing with a case like Ronica's. He was without an answer.

"What can I do?" He asked her, baffled.

"Are you ready for this?" She asked, breaking into a smile. "Are you really ready?"

"I'm not sure," Andy asserted, looking at the weird smile she wore, "but bring it on anyway."

"We can get married," she said softly.

Andy felt faint.

CHAPTER 23
New Year's Day, 1999
Suwanee

Jimmie Lee had been back home for the past week and today he was packing his things to head back out tomorrow. He'd enjoyed himself during this return home more so than the several years before. He knew not why. He just knew this return was more pleasant.

When he first arrived two days before Christmas, William, the White Plantation's driver, held a postcard in hand as Jimmie Lee disembarked the Trailways and headed towards the car, this one a 1998 Cadillac Concours, gray like the 1994 Fleetwood it replaced six months earlier. Jimmie Lee accepted the postcard and William's usual cordial greeting at the same time. He read it just after climbing inside the plush automobile, its umber interior shiny from consistent cleaning and the sienna carpeting just as clean. The card was from a North Little Rock address and the note on it was just four lines:

> Dear Jimmy Lee: This is Van from Richmond, Virginia. I met you in 1996 in Kansas in the city of Lawrence and got your Georgia address. I moved to North Little Rock last year. When

you make it to Arkansas, drop by for a visit.
Sincerely, Van Morrison.

Jimmie Lee could hardly remember a Van Morrison other than the singer. He vaguely recalled his visit to Kansas within which he stayed only two months, a far cry from his usual stay times in other states. Nevertheless, he attempted to resift his memory cells in an honest effort to bring to life this Van person. Then it hit him: there was a rather tall guy enroute to California that Jimmie Lee had met in Kansas—possibly while in Lawrence—a couple of years ago. The guy's name may have been Van, though in Jimmie Lee's mind it seemed more along the lines of Vic or Vinnie. Hell, Jimmie Lee thought, it's got to be Van; the other guesses are simply too close, too close for it not to be Van. I'll keep this card with me, he silently agreed.

As he packed his things, he heard the faint sound of an Earth, Wind and Fire hit from 1977. The ballad, Love's Holiday, was smooth and relaxing in spite of its age. When it was made, Jimmie Lee realized, he was about seven or eight years old; now he's 29. Boy, he thought, that was a long time ago.

His mind trailed off to 1989, the year he began traveling. He envisioned the wonderful celebration here on the White Plantation where Emma Lou and many folks here in town came calling just to see him off. He'd received his high school equivalency diploma and was ready to start his national trek. He recalled how happy his adoptive mother was and how splendid all the kind townsfolk were. That was nearly ten years ago. "Wow", he said aloud but not too loud, "nearly ten whole years"!

Right then a voice startled him out of his thoughts. It was Alexandria, the family's cook, who said, "Ten whole years for what, Master James?" She had walked into Jimmie Lee's bedroom to let him know it was time to eat when she heard him talking to himself. He simply shrugged, saying nothing. She didn't give it more thought, stating simply that lunch was ready and turning to leave.

"Alexandria?" Jimmie Lee asked, their backs to each other, her facing the bedroom door and he the bed.

"Yes?" She answered, grabbing the brass door knob but still not turning around just yet.

"I heard you lost your virginity."

Alexandria was repulsed. She spun around with the quickness of a deer. Her eyes burned with rage, her mouth tight with furiousness. She nearly cursed but retreated.

"Master James, that is absolutely none of your business!"

He smiled and said nothing as she stormed from the bedroom, slamming the door with such force that it jarred a wall painting loose from one of its fastenings, leaving it rocking side-to-side precariously. He knew what he was doing—starting trouble, that is. He'd heard the rumor too so he figured he'd wait until it was time for him to hit the road again before bringing it up.

Apparently, Alexandria had been drinking real heavy on Christmas night. The professed virgin was not known to get liquored up so it was a shocker to the locals. Be that as it may, it was no shocker to four local guys who—like Alexandria—were also getting juiced up. They saw what they classed as an opportunity divine and decided to pay for all of the gal's drinks for the night. After the party of five ran up a $268 tab, the boys paid and then left—with Alexandria, of course—to head to the outskirts of town, ending up in a cow pasture where Alexandria had sex with all of them one by one all night long and well into the morning. Only one guy, Joseph Babcock, the only non-drinker, was sober. This gave him the task of tracking how many times everyone experienced an orgasm. All total, the boys came 26 times; Alexandria erupted in orgasm nine times. It was indeed a sex-laden, memorable affair. It was also the first—and last—time that Alexandria would consume any alcoholic beverages. And she still toyed with the thought in her head as to how she would one day explain to a prospective husband that she lost her virginity by having sex with four guys in a cow pasture. One thing was for sure: Babcock and his pals, Clifton, Zach and Maurice, probably wouldn't mind explaining.

Jimmie Lee allowed his thoughts to settle down long enough to continue packing. He was practically done. He surveyed the spacious bedroom in a mental note of things, then resolved in the fact that he hadn't forgotten anything. He was done. Down the spiral staircase he went, walking the entire length of the first floor's main corridor, then turning into the dining room where the walls had been recently painted from gold to gamboge. He enjoyed his lunch—eating alone as Emma Lou was in town shopping—in spite of the fact that Alexandria would not look at him and afterwards he returned to his bedroom for a short nap. The packing had worn him out.

Emma Lou's frail hand stroked the side of Jimmie Lee's cheek. It caused him to stir but not awake. She did it again. This time he awoke, a thin dry white line trailing from the corner of his mouth and extending two inches toward his chin. It was dried slob. Upon realizing Emma Lou was there, he smiled. Still woozy, he sat up, looked around briefly, and then smiled again.

"Hey Momma Lou-Lou," he said in a still sleep-filled voice. "How long I been asleep?"

"Heck, only the good Lord knows that 'cause I sure don't." She laughed. "Plus, you're heading out tomorrow; no need to sleep the night before away." She laughed again. "Listen, get yourself together and c'mon downstairs. I've got something to talk to you about."

Ten minutes later, Jimmie Lee was descending the spiral staircase, its smooth sepia wood banister feeling good to the touch, the matching bay carpet—trimmed with tan borders with flakes of sorrel lining the inside of each border—feeling just as good to his shoeless and sockless feet. As he hit the first floor, he found himself smack center of the main house, the spectacular great room to the left, the sensational family room to the far right, and to the immediate right was the engulfing corridor, leading to the study and library, sitting room, kitchen and dining room. He turned left, heading into the massive great room where a brilliant fire was flaming it up inside a large fireplace, one of three in the home. The great room's décor matched that of the staircase, with auburn Ethan Allen sofas— two of them—and a love seat, as well as a chestnut easy chair by La-Z-Boy accompanied by a matching ottoman. Bronze end tables flanked each sofa and to the right of the love seat was a refinished round lamp table with a copper top and three rust legs. The carpet was cinnamon, complimenting the russet walls and chocolate baseboards. Jimmie Lee often called this the brown room instead of the great room for the color brown and its shady relatives were the very nucleus of its existence.

Emma Lou sat quietly on one of the sofas, her large-print Bible in hand, reading silently to herself. She was in the Old Testament, her attention focused in the Book of

Psalms, Chapter 121. She did so each year on the night before Jimmie Lee was slated to depart Suwanee. She knew in her heart the good Lord would protect her son from the evils of the world. Her contribution to the helping hand of the Lord was an earnest prayer using the words of the 121st Psalm. Prayer changes things, she was known to brag. She looked up as Jimmie Lee entered, their eyes met and then a smile from both their faces appeared.

"Hey," she began, sitting the Bible down with her right hand and patting the seat next to her with her left, "c'mon over here and have a sit-down."

"Okay," he said simply. He sat down beside her on the soft leather of the sofa, feeling enveloped by the luxuriousness of this Ethan Allen piece.

"Comfy?" She asked.

"Yes, ma'am," was his answer.

"Listen," she went on, "you know this family has dealt with the same law firm for the past fifty years, don't you?" She didn't wait for an answer. "Edwards, Graham & Griffin has served in Gwinnett County for 55 years and my late husband hired Jonathan Edwards in 1949 to be our family attorney. His granddaughter, Sheila Edwards Mason, is the attorney assigned to the White account since Jon died back in 1996. She knows my wishes, my last wishes."

Jimmie Lee decided to cut in. "Momma Lou-Lou, what gives?" The look on his face was of obvious befuddlement.

"I'm seventy-eight years old; I suffer from osteoporosis and this old ticker of mine"—she pointed a finger to her chest—"ain't getting' any younger. My days are numbered, Jimmie Lee. I've made certain last wishes and you need to know what they are."

"You've got plenty of time to live, Momma Lou-Lou."

She laughed. "Always the optimist, ain't you, boy?" She laughed again, and then settled down to get serious again. "I know you don't like talking about death but it's something all of us will have to eventually face. When it comes, though, it is not well to weep. Why?" She didn't wait for him to answer. "Because death is no enemy to man, not at all. It's a friend, Jimmie Lee, a friend who, when all of life's works are done and over with, just cuts the cord that binds the human boat to earth that it may sail on smoother seas."

"But Momma Lou-Lou," Jimmie Lee interjected with raised eyebrows. "There's no language that can describe your worth and as far as I can remember, yours has always been tried and true."

"Exactly," she stated with a warm passion. "But the good Lord would not call me unless and until my tasks here on earth were all done."

"I say again: You've got plenty of time to live, Momma Lou-Lou."

"Let me continue," she reminded him. "I'm leaving my biological son and daughter twenty-five-point-five percent each of my total monetary estate. You will receive close to the same—twenty-four-point-five—and the help will split the remaining twenty-four-point-five percent. The café goes jointly to your older brother and sister who'll probably have you oversee it since they're so far away and all. Saving the best part for last: you get the plantation." Jimmie Lee's mouth fell open in pure shock. "Yes, yes, that's how I want it, Jimmie Lee. All total, my entire estate is worth $27.7 million."

"What?!" Jimmie Lee was dizzy from the information. "When I first set out back in 1989, you said you were worth less than $9 million!"

"I've made good choices, son; good, wise choices." She smiled and patted his thigh. "Ask the folks over at Primerica Financial Services and they'll tell you the same thing. Larry Richgood, Tony Reecer, Anita Sobet—they're all at the top of their game."

"Jesus H. Chr—," Jimmie Lee attempted to say.

Cutting him off abruptly, Emma Lou admonished, "You'd better not use His name like that."

"Sorry," was Jimmie Lee's quick response, instead saying, "Gee-whiz."

"That's better." Emma rose. "I'm going into town to check on the café. Summon the driver from the servants' quarters and have him bring the car around."

"Yes ma'am," Jimmie Lee said.

CHAPTER 24
Spring 1999
Norfolk

"Here at A&G Select Imports," bellowed the obese salesman, "we make excellence affordable."

Dee heard the salesman's words slide into one ear and out of the other, his eyes fixated on the luxurious black-on-black 1997 Mercedes-Benz S320 with smoked, mirrored windows. It had a ridiculous 75,000 miles on it—probably a constant road trip vehicle—and selling for an amazing $42,000. Dee was in love with it, high miles included. He was trading in his Mercedes and also putting $9,500 down. The bank gave him an 8.0% APR with a 5-year note. He'd pay $507 per month until 2004. To Dee, it was an excellent deal and he didn't need the salesman's input to prove it. Obviously the salesman, a former New Jersey prison guard, was trying to make a sale here at A&G's new Norfolk location, a massively overdone 280-vehicle lot situated at Mapole Avenue and East Princess Anne Road, formerly the Marshall Manor Apartments site torn down a year earlier.

"Bob," Dee said, speaking over the noise of cars passing along the busy Princes Anne Road, "shut the hell up." Dee then produced a smile. "I'll take it."

Dion Gooden-El with S. W. Greene

***

"Fuck!" Dee exclaimed, under his breath. "Where's a good movie when you need it?" He was sitting at his dining room table in his Yorkshire Square townhouse in Portsmouth bored to death. That's when he decided to take in a movie. He grabbed the Virginian-Pilot newspaper, turned to the arts and entertainment section and began perusing the movie theater listings in search of a good, decent motion picture. Initially, he was stumped. Then he saw something that grabbed at him. It was a catch line about movies: SICK OF SEEING THE SAME OLE TYPE OF MOVIES IN THEATERS? If so, VISIT THE NARO IN NORFOLK'S HISTORIC GHENT. Under the catch line was a short listing of movies. The first one was a French film made in Canada called "Britons". The second was "Conquest At Owhyer, 450 A.D". The listing ended with a third film called, "The Buena Vista Social Club". Dee liked the sound of the third film for some inexplicable reason. What he did not know was that that same film just might one day make him filthy rich.

On the drive to Norfolk, Dee relaxed to a local oldies station, 104.7 KISS FM, which poured out four beautiful love songs during the 19-minute drive, including "Betcha By Golly, WOW" by the Stylistics, a 1972 release; Earth, Wind and Fire's 1975 "That's The Way of the World"; The Temptations' "Hey Girl, I Like Your Style" from 1973; and a 1976 Norman Connors work of art called, "You Are My Starship". Dee was soulfully involved in the smooth oldies, feeling like new money in his newly-purchased Mercedes-Benz, dressed smartly in a Roberto Villini suit worth $600 and a pair of $195 Pierre Cardin dress shoes, and sporting a perfect haircut only a few hours old from Rachel's Cuts, a downtown Portsmouth barber shop owned by Richmond native Rachel Dickey, ironically the sister of Vanessa Dickey,

158

the girl who pursued Dee with an unrelenting passion before he finally convinced her she was wasting her time. Seeing the NARO up on the left, Dee spotted a space and parked.

The Buena Vista Social Club was a documentary and Dee absolutely loved it! It was emotional, historical, understandable, and so spectacularly real in its overall depiction of Cuba's mid-20th century singing legends.

The following day, Dee decided to do some research on the Buena Vista Social Club. He searched the Internet, visited the local public library, and even called Havana in an effort to talk with the executive producer of the film. The information was very helpful; however, Dee noticed one omission: no one had ever written a book on the Buena Vista Social Club. Articles—in both English and Spanish—were plentiful; a dissertation from a Texas college professor was available on the Net and, of course, the "docufilm". But no book. Dee's excitement moved into overdrive as he pondered the possibility of writing the book on this fascinating subject, a subject he never thought would even interest him, a subject he didn't study in college. This was the one, Dee felt. This was his first national bestseller.

***

By July, Dee had been in constant contact with a Ms. Mendolia from the Cuban Historical Society in Havana. Although she was not a native Cuban, she'd lived there for over 28 years and had been Chief Historian of the Society for the past four years. Dee was satisfied with her many e-mails, faxes, letters, and phone calls.

He also had a new presence at the townhouse four days a week. Nakia Mangood, an NSU Evening Program student, worked 20 hours Monday thru Thursday as

Dee's personal assistant. The 4-foot-11-inch, light-skinned tenderoni was pretty quiet and dressed well and only had to be told once what to do. Her job was to organize the voluminous amounts of web pages that had been copied, the literally hundreds upon hundreds of pages from various books from the local library, and all of the scores of data and information from Ms. Mendolia.   Indeed, Nakia worked hard and was well worth the $206 Dee paid her every week. He even promised her he'd mention her on the Acknowledgements page of the book he'd been hailing as his soon-to-be very first national bestseller.

CHAPTER 25
Fall 1999
Portsmouth

A week ago autumn began. Yet signs of it were already visible: leaves falling, the shift in daily temperatures, and the absence of children during the day. Yes, autumn was on the scene. It was all around Portsmouth and, in particular, on Choate Street, where Andy and Ronica now lived; where today marked 13 months of marriage—yes, marriage—following a circuit court civil ceremony a couple days after Andy's 32nd birthday. They were also celebrating a year in their new home, a small but cheerful blue one-story single-family dwelling, donned with ultramarine shutters and a cobalt front door. Its price tag was $55,000, which Andy and Ronica paid in cash from her 1998 lottery winnings, and required $11,000 in repairs which Andy hired a small but highly efficient construction team to handle, to which it agreed and finished everything in record time. Andy—who assumed the costs of the repairs—wrote the team's check the same day it finished the vast project. Now he and his new 19-year-old bride were all set, nice and comfy in their new home in a new neighborhood—Douglas Park—situated in the heart of the city.

The entire TSE staff went into shock when it was abruptly announced that Andy and Ronica had married. Latoria was affected the most. The delicious-looking, nubile 17-year-old was convinced that she and her boss's once-a-week secret sex sessions were enough to keep him from marrying someone else in the office. No one knew of her love affair with him—not even her best friend from the neighborhood—and she made damn sure it stayed that way, taking precaution after precaution to pick out-of-the-way motels and always keeping her schedule with her birth-control pills. But more stunning to her was that while she toiled so diligently to shield her own love affair, she, like everyone else in the office, was a victim to a totally different secret love affair. Two secret affairs going on at once. The questions then began flowing like water: Who else? Was Mr. Smith screwing the entire office? What about Ms. P? Or Rhonda even? How about that girl Krista who used to work here? What about her? Just how many of these girls is Mr. Smith fucking? The thoughts angered Latoria. And to think, she silently confessed, I even swallow his cum when I suck his dick. Anger continued setting in. I'll fix his ass, she decided. I'll fix him good. The morning following the nuptials announcement, Latoria tossed out her birth-control pills. She decided she'd put a baby on Andy Smith. "That'll teach him," she said into the bathroom mirror as she flushed the pills down the sink. "Yeah, Moeesha," she said, speaking to her still asleep and not-in-earshot daughter, "you're gonna have a sister or brother and that mothefuckin' Andrew Smith is goin' to take care of 'em." The look in Latoria's facial expression showed she meant every single word. A year later she still was not pregnant but only God Himself knew how hard she was trying.

Meanwhile, Andy had all but forgotten about Vicky whom he bought out just days after marrying Ronica and basically continued full-throttle with his own life. His ex-wife's fifty-five percent interest in TSE reverted to him and the two hadn't spoken since. He was elated to be sole owner of TSE and the superficial power it gave him made sure his daily, evening, nightly, and weekend schedules remained full and almost unbearable. He continued his daily progressive work ethic at TSE, now earning $104,000 a year; his super-secret sexual liaison with office teenager Tori, now 18, had still been taking place since January of last year on a once-weekly basis, usually following work in the late-evening; his nights were indescribably busy and sex-laden as he matched Ronica's untamed energy pound-for-pound; and he saw Jessica, the girl from the Norfolk housing project, twice each weekend. At times, he was simply too exhausted to do anything at all. Yet he pushed forward. He had to. He had an image to protect. His daily sermons in the office suggested as much: positive mental attitude, success, money. Indeed, his life was zooming full-throttle and he loved every hectic minute of it!

***

It was the week before time fell back an hour when Andy, lounging comfortably in his office—an absolute rarity—with the backdrop of an impending sunset visible through the window, was startled by his administrative assistant's scream. He leapt to his feet, darted out his office and into the short hall, going two doors down to Rhonda's tiny office. Ironically the door was closed when she screamed; it opened as Andy reached for the knob.

"What in the hell?!" Andy exclaimed as Rhonda snatched open the office door. "Tell me there's a mouse or something in there."

"No," she said. "A fax."

"A fax made you scream?" He asked, shaking his head in disbelief. Then he began reading the fax. It was from Mandy Lyle, Chairwoman, President and CEO of American Financial Services, a Duluth, Georgia-based financial services concern worth $700 million. A vast amount of its services centered on TSE's core business: credit information consulting. The fax, Andy soon realized, was a hostile takeover offer. He was floored as he read the powerful four-paragraph letter:

October 13, 1999

Dear Mr. Smith:

As Chief Executive Officer of one of the nation's largest financial services companies, I have authorized our Chief Financial Officer (CFO) to offer you what I believe is a fair and reasonable price for a one hundred percent (100%) stake in Townes-Smith Enterprises, Inc. (TSE). American Financial Services Co., Inc. (AFS) is prepared to take over the entire operations of TSE for $2.92 million, a portion of which will be in cash, another portion in short and long-term debt, and another in AFS common stock.

This is an unsolicited tender offer. It represents our firm commitment to acquire TSE, a very successful—and yet very small—company in the highly competitive credit information consulting field. We will stop at nothing in order to bring this takeover to fruition.

Our CFO will contact you within twenty-four (24) hours of transmission of this facsimile.

Thank you very much for your attention and cooperation in this matter.

Sincerely,

Mandy Lyle,

Chairwoman of the Board

President and Chief Executive Officer

Cc: Daniel Matiya, CFO

Andy read the letter again and then a third time. Rhonda said nothing. Andy's mind kept re-playing the sentence, "We will stop at nothing in order to bring this takeover to fruition." His look was serious and inquisitive and—however slight—excited. "We will stop at nothing…," he silently re-played for the umpteenth time.

***

The morning before Thanksgiving was a mixture of joy and pain. Andy was joyful he'd negotiated a slightly sweeter $2.93 million price for TSE. He would receive $293,000 in cash, short-term debt of $586,000 paid off, long-term debt of $879,000 also paid off, and AFS common stock worth $1,172,000. Andy, however, was in pain too. It was the end for him and his dream of a massive corporate operation. He employed 94 folks—including 90 Home Teleworkers—up until today where only four remained and it was their last day. His operation had begun in the Hampton Roads and Peninsula markets, expanded to the Metro-Richmond and later Petersburg Tri-Cities markets, then finally making it to Roanoke a few months before the takeover. Yes, to Andy, there was joy and pain.

He, Shardae, Rhonda and Ronica—Latoria had quit in disgust when the takeover offer was accepted by Andy three weeks ago—all packed the last of their personal effects in cute little boxes from a local gift shop that had ironically gone out of business last week. Each received a severance check of $2,930 or one percent of Andy's cash pay-out from the takeover. Latoria refused hers; Shardae expected more but said nothing; Rhonda and Ronica were satisfied.

Speaking of Latoria or Tori as she'd been called by Andy, she had much bigger plans in store for good ole Andy. Even though she'd refused the money, she still had money on her mind, having sex with Andy every chance she could, hoping for a pregnancy. What she did not know on the day TSE closed its doors was that she had accomplished half her goal: she was indeed pregnant after a year of intense trying. She was only five weeks along; the first missed period would come two weeks later. A store-bought EPT would confirm it all.

That evening, Andy pulled into the dead-end Choate Street where his and Ronica's home sat. Ronica remained with him in the car before the two went in.

"Well," he began, "we've got some extra time on our hands now, baby."

"Yeah," she answered, "all of us." She added a smile.

Andy, who had been looking straight ahead, turned to Ronica and, looking puzzled, asked, "What do you mean 'all of us'?" She was still smiling.

"I took a trip to the doctor during lunch today," she began. "He called the office to tell me to drop by. I went yesterday to get some tests done. His lab tech was off and didn't come back 'til today. The results of the tests were positive for—" she paused for several seconds, a tear eased from one eye. Continuing, she said, "—positive for a baby."

Andy couldn't believe his ears. He looked stunned, was speechless, frozen in space and time. Only Ronica brought him back.

"So what do you think, Andy?"

"I can't believe it," was his reply.

She frowned. "I wasn't expecting that type of reaction. Are you happy or what?" She frowned again.

I don't know, Ronica."

"You don't know?!" Ronica shouted. The joy in her tone was gone. "What the hell you mean you don't know?"

"I didn't expect a baby so soon."

His words caused all hell to break loose. For the first time in a couple years, Ronica Smith did something unladylike: She reached out and hit a man—her husband.

***

Andy's car glided down the interstate heading from Portsmouth to Norfolk. He was on his way to visit Jessica, his project chick, on the anniversary of the Japanese's bombing of Pearl Harbor. He had nothing else to do. TSE was closed, he and Vicky had completely severed all ties, and he hadn't seen Ronica since Thanksgiving morning when he moved his things out the house and into a local hotel next to a Hardee's near the Chesapeake city border in Brentwood. The BMW continued to glide down I-264, holding steady at 54 miles per hour thanks to the 740i's cruise-control setting. Only a mile remained before Andy would be at the mouth of the downtown tunnel.

His attire was different than usual. Typically dressed in a suit, Andy's look today was quite the opposite. He looked angelic for one, and ten years younger for another, laid out in a milky Polo shirt and pants, a thick snow-colored jacket by Phat Farm, an ivory Sean John hat and oyster Nautica boots. In the front passenger seat sat a walnut-colored gift box with a mahogany ribbon and bow. Inside was a Donna Karan outfit: A scarlet leather mini-dress complete with cinnabar stiletto pumps. The outfit was a gift for Jessica and well worth the $299-price tag. He smiled internally at the idea of giving his project chick expensive gifts. She never asked for anything from him. She only wanted some quality time. She screwed his brains out during those times. But with gifts lying about, her screw-factor doubled, sometimes tripled, causing Andy to nearly lose consciousness or so it seemed. The ecstasy was just that intense. His internal smile moved outward, appearing on his face. The car pone broke the smile though.

"Andy!" He answered aloud, causing the phone to pick up automatically while he drove.

"Yo," greeted the female voice. "What's up, Andy?" It was Tori. Andy hadn't heard from her since the takeover announcement.

"Tori?" Andy asked.

"Yep," she replied. "It's me." She sighed.

"Listen, Tori, I know you didn't agree with the takeover, but—"

She cut in. "I'm pregnant, Andy, and it's yours. I just found out last night. EPT from Wal-Mart. I'm gonna need $300 a week to take care of pre-natal appointments and all the other shit associated with preparing for a new baby. Come over this afternoon—my mom's out of town—so we can work out the details."

By the time she finished talking, Andy had pulled the black BMW to the road's shoulder, bringing it to a complete stop, putting it in Park and cutting off the engine. For the second time in two weeks, he'd been stunned to speechlessness with news of an unexpected pregnancy. He felt numb. Finally, words flowed from his lips.

"But Tori, you said you were on the Pill."

She seemed as if she just couldn't wait for him to say that, instantly becoming incensed. "That's right, motherfucker! I was on the Pill until you started fuckin' that bitch, Ronica! Then last year you married that bitch! So I said, 'Fuck it! I'll put a baby on his ass!' Now what, you motherfucker?! You wanna deny it's your baby?!"

He reached out, saying nothing, and pressed one button on the car phone's dashboard console: "End." The call disconnected. He turned the phone off so she couldn't call back. He reached for his cell phone and turned it off too. He could see the tunnel ahead. He restarted the luxury import's engine, shifted it into Drive, and headed into the Portsmouth-Norfolk tunnel. He would find solace in the one person who never asked him for anything and who could make him forget everything: Jessica Courtier.

***

Andy spent two days delivering all 302 of the Christmas gifts he'd purchased. He visited Vicky and her six children, his first visit in over a year, and dropped off nearly a third of the gifts there. The rest were divided among his other family, Ronica and her family, his former employees, some friends and, of course, Jessica, Cookie, T. G and Keetra. His visit to Ronica was not pleasant so it ended as quickly as it began.

It was Christmas morning and he was sitting in his new townhouse in Portsmouth's Yorkshire Square, having moved in three days earlier. All of the furniture was brand new, thanks to Haverty's of Virginia Beach, and ran close to $22,000, excluding electronics, appliances and household accessories which cost a separate $14,400. His monthly payment on the townhouse was quite reasonable though—$600—and he was satisfied that he was getting his money's worth. Why it even mattered to him was beyond him. He had a quarter-million dollars in the bank and a stock portfolio worth over a million. Why did he care about a $7,200-a-year leased townhouse? The only reason he didn't buy a house was because he wasn't sure if he'd end up back with Vicky—a long shot for sure—or Ronica, both of whom had bought-and-paid-for homes, or whether he'd eventually—albeit doubtfully—pull Jessica and her three girls still at home out of the projects and into a nice big house in the suburbs. That money-hungry bitch, Latoria Taylor, wasn't even in the picture. She'd been worrying Andy for the past three weeks. He finally agreed to pre-natal care checks of $304 bi-weekly. She angrily accepted. So here he sat, chilling out on Christmas, sipping on a bottle of gin and waiting for Jessica to call him to let him know she and the girls were ready. They would spend all day together, sorta like one big happy family.

***

Jessica Courtier was almost ordinary. She had a GED—normal for project residents—as opposed to a high school diploma. She did, however, manage to attend Norfolk State University for a brief period in 1993 and 1994 but was forced to drop out. College was not-so-ordinary for her surroundings. Her 195-pound frame was outside the ordinary but the fact that she was "phat" instead of "fat" brought back the normalcy, the normalcy of project life. She knew one day she would get out of the projects. She perfected dance moves, which in turn made her better in bed, to aid and assist her in gaining the ticket out she so badly deserved. Every man she met she treated nicely. She never begged, never dug for gold. She just offered herself in hopes that one day some handsome man would make her happy by saying eight magical words: "I am taking you out of the projects." She was an offspring of ghetto life and underachievers. Project life and bad shit happening in the family was all she knew. Her three brothers were not impressive: Jasper, the 2-time imprisoned rapist was gone for life; Quentin died from bad pussy, having contracted HIV, the virus that causes AIDS; and Roy as no where to be found, last heard of living in Southeast D. C.'s rough Langston Lane area and strung out on the drug, Love Boat. Her sisters were equally unimpressive: Mary Lou stuck in a dead-end job in Williamsburg and Joan not working at all, relying on her live-in boyfriend, an ex-con whose street hustles barely took care of all the bills. Lillie Mae, Jessica's mom, was a 70-year-old alcoholic who was known in the area as the Candy Lady, hustling neighborhood kids out of quarters for frozen Kool-Aid in Dixie cups. Indeed, Jessica was, for the most part, almost ordinary. Even still, she really wanted to one day leave the stink of project life, even though she never voiced it aloud. Tonight, however, on New Year's Eve, that would change. She would ask Andrew Smith to take her and her three teenagers out of Grandy Village and into a new house—his—where they'd all live until the lease expires before buying a much larger house, one with four bedrooms, somewhere in Norfolk or Portsmouth.

Meanwhile, a freshly cleaned black BMW 740i exited the Norfolk side of the downtown tunnel and continued eastbound onto I-264. Inside the expensive vehicle, the factory-installed stereo system belted out the 1973 soul classic, "I Wanna Know Your Name" by the Intruders. The driver of the vehicle hummed the smooth beat. He was in a fantastic mood, awaiting the turn of the century, ready to take Jessica out to a New Year's Eve bash at a private party being hosted in a downtown Norfolk hotel by Norfolk-Southern outgoing Chief Morale Officer, a Yorkshire Square resident Andy Smith met the day he moved in a week earlier. Andy was dressed as sharp as a nail, donning Gucci's newest cocoa suit and a pair of coffee Gucci dress shoes. The BMW made its way to the Ballentine Blvd. exit of the interstate where Andy reduced his speed. Just then a new song came on the stereo, "Don't Say Goodnight" by the Isley Brothers, soon to celebrate twenty years of pleasure to listeners. Minutes later, just as the Isley Brothers tune ended, Andy pulled in front of Jessica's Grandy Village apartment. She was already out front, waiting patiently for her beau, dressed superbly in the scarlet Donna Karan strapless leather mini-dress and near-matching pumps Andy had bought for her for Christmas. Her height was extended to 6-feet-7-inches by the six-inch stilettos. Andy got out, smiled graciously as he opened the passenger-side door for her, kissing her on a cheek as she got inside the vehicle. She wore no coat—she liked showing her body—and moved quickly to get out of the evening's cool air. Back inside, Andy complimented her on her look and the two headed to the Marriott downtown. Her naturally long black hair was silky smooth and landed just past her shoulders. Her simple brown eyes were brought out by the black mascara she wore. She looked as beautiful as she did the day he met her sixteen months earlier.

"You are so very beautiful this evening," he said. "I am so fascinated that we'll be bringing in Y-2-K together. You are indeed a diva."

Jessica looked over at Andy with a smile. "Actually, a diva doesn't necessarily look good."

"Says who?" He inquired.

"That's a fact," she explained. "You see, a diva is a stately, grand woman, a 'trophy', who may or may not be a beauty.

"Okay," he said, absorbing her words, before asking, "What are you?"

She grinned broadly. "To people who don't know me, a 'fox' which is simply a good-looking female. To people close to me, a 'brick' or 'brick house'."

Andy couldn't resist. "A 'brick house' is a well-developed woman, right?"

"Basically," she answered. "More specific, it's a woman with a sexy, attractive shape, especially if she has round and large buttocks in proportion to her body." But deep in her seat of emotions, she knew she was more than that. She was a freak and a hoochie. Her sexual practices had no limitation; she'd do anything sexually. Her sexual promiscuity was obvious. It worked for her though. Here she sat in an expensive automobile with a man who was worth over a million bucks and the two were heading to a party with people who probably couldn't describe a project apartment, much less having lived in one. So whether Andy saw her as a diva or brick house or her true nature as a freak or hoochie, she was progressing at a steady pace to attaining her ticket out of the projects, out of the ghetto. Tonight she would make her plea for that ticket, for the ticket holder was the driver of the cushiony vehicle within which she sat.

"A brick house, huh?" Andy repeated. "Works for me."

Five minutes later, they entered the Marriott's spacious parking lot. The valet, a tall African-American boy about 21 with a name tag that read "Bernard Tatum" waited as Andy and Jessica got out of the 740i before jumping in to park it for them. Andy retrieved the invitations from his inside pocket and they headed inside. Less than a minute later, the two were seated in the massive Presidential

Ballroom, half consumed by 313 chairs and tables and the other half made into a dance floor. It was nine o'clock sharp.

Three hours and several shots of liquor later Andy was nearly toasted as the MC counted down the last ten seconds of 1999. Balloons and confetti fell from make-shift buckets extended from the ceiling. Lights flashed, DJ sirens blared, hand-held horns sounded and hats flew off heads. People hugged those they knew and those they didn't. Andy held Jessica close and whispered "Happy New Year" into her ear. She returned the same whisper to his but added "I love you." Andy's intoxication subsided briefly at hearing the latter words. He looked into her face. She was crying.

"What's wrong?" He inquired.

"Nothing," she stated. "Everything's right."

"Then why are you crying?"

"Because I'm happy."

"I am too, Jessica. I am too." He held her close again while his mind drifted to his marriage to Jeanette who cried tears of joy on their wedding day. Ole womanizing Andy had done it again.

"Andy?"

"Yeah, baby."

"I have something to ask you."

He looked her directly into the eyes, realizing this was very serious, hoping the 37-year-old wasn't pregnant, and then nodded to denote he was ready to listen.

"Here it goes," she began. The next three minutes of talking would be crucial. She took a breath before continuing. "Andy, from the very depths of my soul, my very being, I really love you. Really I do. From the day I first met you at the telephone booth in front of the Junior Market on Westminister when we instantly hit it off to you celebrating your own birthday with practical strangers—the girls and me—soon after to the days, weeks and months that followed where you showed me love, was always truthful, displayed such a peaceful demeanor, exercised so much freedom in expressing yourself sexually and being so just to my girls. I've love you from the very beginning.

"My life has meaning, relevance. It is only because you're in it. Life was a crazy haze before you, where men of questionable character toting guns and possessing illegal drugs seemed to draw to me like flies. Instead of not being able to see the forest for the trees, I could see neither the forest nor the damn trees. With you, Andy, I see both now. Clear. Crystal clear. You gave my life meaning with your constant motivational speeches on success and prosperity. You made my life relevant with the free-flow of positivism and optimism. I love you so very much." Her tears flowed freely now.

"There is nothing, absolutely nothing, and I mean nothing at all, that I want more than to be in your presence for the duration of your life. I want what's good for my girls, at least the three still at home with me, because they need a better life in their teenage years. I want what's good for me because I have never told you 'no' to anything you've ever asked of me. I want what's good for us as a couple because we're perfect as a couple: we look so good together, our bodies are in sync at every turn, we never fight, we appreciate one another and we love and respect each other. I'm sick without you. I'm literally sick when I'm not with you. My stomach churns like a Maytag washing machine in operation, my throat has this permanent lump in it until I see you or hear your voice again, my hands shake nervously and I can't seem to get it together. The sickness subsides only when you're present—whether actually or telephonically—and stays out of sight during that period. This sickness must be love; nothing else could explain it." She composed herself somewhat, wiping her eyes with her index fingers.

"Andy," she summed up, "I'm worth the risk. My girls are worth the risk. I'm not a dumb woman—far from it—so I'm smart enough to know one day I'm due to get out of the projects. I'm a good woman and I deserve a ticket out now. Please take me out of the projects. Please give me and my girls a better life. Give us our own house and each of them their own room. You and I don't have to get married. You can even have a second piece of pussy on the side, although I doubt that you'll need it. I just want us to share a home, a warm residence filled with love and happiness and a taste of the good life. I'm worth it, Andy. Will you take me out of the projects and out of ghetto life?"

Andy's inebriated state had receded somewhat more during Jessica's emotionally charged speech. He began poring over her words, re-drinking some of the most heart-moving ones, before realizing she was still awaiting an answer from him. He already knew his answer—it would be cut and dry—and thought back to two famous folks known for such type of curt responses: Ronald Reagan and Malik El-Hajj Shabazz, the latter of whom was more popularly known by his former name, Malcolm X. Ronald Reagan would be in a press conference and a reporter would ask him a question consisting of ten run-on sentences. Classic Reagan would answer with a flat and simple "yes" then immediately look about for the next reporter's question, never once flinching. So too with Malcolm X whose most famed episode of such curtness came when a Caucasian female college student stopped him on the grounds of a university, spent several minutes explaining how she wasn't a racist, wasn't raised a racist, liked everyone regardless of their race or nationality, spent time learning and understanding the so-called Black cause and wanted to know what she could do to help. Malcolm X looked at her and smiled ever-so-slightly before saying, "Nothing." She was crushed. Now Andy would have to offer a response to someone who had dug deep, very deep, for all the right words in order to get her a ticket out of the projects. He produced a faint smile, glanced at his watch to see it was just turning 12:04, and then wiped the smile from his face. His hand touched one of hers; their eyes were locked on each other. She was no longer crying; just smiling, waiting. Then his answer came.

"No."

CHAPTER 26

January 2, 2000
Memphis, Tennessee

The Trailways bus terminal in Memphis had been recently painted. Its walls were a fresh neutral, baseboards a brilliant silver and chairs all painted dun. Everything else had been painted alabaster. The mix was delightful. Plain but delightful.

Jimmie Lee disembarked the 55-seat coach on the cold Sunday morning. It was 32 degrees with a wind chill factor of one degree. He was dressed for the weather with his wool plaid shirt and corduroy pants covered by a heavy wool coat and steel-toe insulated boots. He topped that off with gloves and a cap. Where he'd just left was no where near as cold but he knew where he was going would be, so he dressed appropriately before leaving the White Plantation en route to the county bus terminal. For sure, Memphis proved him right meteorologically.

Jimmie Lee saw some pay phones. He thought of calling home but realized his stomach was calling him instead. He dipped inside taking note of the smell of fresh paint as he headed to the café. The warmth of the terminal enveloped him seemingly instantaneously and he was pulling off his wool coat by the time he'd made it to the café's marble and steel counter. He ordered fried eggs, bacon, hash browns and grits. Then he ordered cold milk and chilled apple juice, two glasses of the latter. Moments later his meal was ready and he wasted no time eating the couple of eggs, four slices of swine and both hash browns. The grits were so hot that he saved them for last. Intermittently he drank the 12 ounces of milk and 16 ounces of apple juice, the latter of which was his favorite breakfast beverage. Leaving $10.00 on the counter-top, Jimmie Lee grabbed his coat and left the café to head back to the pay phones. The $3.00 tip would be for the café's counter waitress.

Jimmie Lee grabbed the receiver of the first available phone, keyed in his calling card number and PIN, then after pausing for the special tone he dialed his home number: 7-7-0, 3-2-3. Before he could finish the last four digits, a strong hand landed on his shoulder. He turned to look into the face of an obese man around fifty years old, donning a smile like Jesus.

"Howdy, son!" The man began, the smile never leaving. "If you're calling for a ride, no need." His hand left Jimmie Lee's shoulder just long enough for him to extend it for a shake. Jimmie Lee obliged him.

"The name's Marvin, son. Wherever you wanna go, I'll take you. No charge, of course."

"What's the catch?" Jimmie Lee inquired as he returned the receiver to the cradle of the pay phone.

"No catch," said Marvin.

"There's always a catch," insisted Jimmie Lee. "Nothing's ever free."

Marvin let out a hearty laugh. "Yeah, yeah, son, you're sorta right. To be honest wit cha, I only ask that you take my bizness card wit you. That's all."

"What are you selling?"

"Selling?" He asked, somewhat incredulously. "Heck, I ain't selling nothing, son. I'm giving. Yeah, yeah, giving."

"Go on," Jimmie Lee stated, waiting.

"I give jobs. I run a day-labor firm here in the city. You're dressed for work, it looks to me, so I figured I'd get the ups on ya and give ya my card, that's all. No harm there, is it?"

Jimmie Lee paused a moment before admitting to Marvin, "Guess not."

"So, about that ride?" Marvin asked.

"Yeah, thanks," Jimmie Lee responded. "Nearest motel. Not too cheap, but not too expensive either."

"Gotcha, son," Marvin replied as he reached for Jimmie Lee's aging backpack. But Jimmie Lee stopped Marvin and toted it himself.

A half-hour later Jimmie Lee was settling in in Room 326 of Memphis' R&D Motel, owned by a brother and sister named Russell and Danielle who'd inherited it from their favorite aunt some years before. His room was a simple one, consisting of a queen-size bed flanked by sugar maple night stands and a 25-inch elevated RCA color-TV secured in place by a not-so-discreet chain and steel wall mount. There was also a mirrored dresser made of red maple and a tiny bathroom. He packed his things in some of the dresser's six drawers and the rest he hung in the closet next to the john. Then he decided to attempt to call home again.

Emma Lou was lounging on one of the auburn Ethan Allen sofas in the vast great room of the main house when the phone rang. She leaned leftward on the soft leather sofa to take a hold of the GE cordless telephone that had been resting on one of the four bronze end tables that flanked the great room's two sofas. She answered on the second ring.

"White Plantation, Emma speaking," she greeted.

"Hey there," saluted Jimmie Lee.

"Well, hello, Jimmie Lee," she ecstatically greeted. "You in Memphis already?"

"Yes, ma'am," he answered. "Got here nearly an hour ago. Got a motel room and a job offer."

"What?!" Emma Lou exclaimed. "A job offer? Already?"

"Yes, ma'am. A man named Marvin offered me a job as a General Laborer. I accepted it. I start tomorrow."

"Good, good, son. You're on a roll already. You had breakfast yet?"

"Yes, ma'am."

"Good, good. Listen, I was doing my morning Bible reading when you called. I'm already dressed for church. I'll be leaving in ten minutes or so, but I want to finish my morning reading before I leave the Plantation. So do this for me: Get all the way situated, get you a nap, and then once you're up and about, call me back then. You okay with that, son?"

"Yes, ma'am," he answered honestly. "I'll call in four hours. How 'bout that?"

"That would be high noon, then."

"No, ma'am, eleven o'clock," he corrected.

"Different time zone, remember?" She warmly admonished.

"Oh yeah, high noon there, eleven here. Gotcha covered, Ma."

"Talk to you later, son."

"Okay, Ma." He always ended each phone call with "Mom", "Momma", or "Ma".

Jimmie Lee hung the phone up; Emma Lou attempted to do the same. Instead her finger missed the Power button, her hand dropped the cordless phone, her other hand clutched her chest, the hand formerly holding the phone joined the other hand at her chest, her face contorted, sickly gasps spewed from her mouth, her knees buckled, she fell to the cinnamon-carpeted floor and began a slow, painful process of dying. Emma Lou was suffering a heart attack. She could see her Bible still resting on the sofa as her life inched away. She wanted to reach for it but couldn't. So instead, as she lay dying, she silently recited a familiar portion of Chapter 11 in the Gospel according to Saint John, the latter part of Verse 28: "The Master is come, and calleth for thee." Thirty-three seconds later, Emma Lou White died from sudden heart failure. She was 80.

Jimmie Lee, oblivious to what had just taken place roughly 370 miles away, decided to get a nap. He stripped down to his undershirt, boxers and socks, climbed under the cotton sheets of the bed and closed his eyes to rest. As he did so, little did he know Emma Lou was doing the same, only her rest was—unlike his—endless. For the second time in his life, Jimmie Lee had lost his mother.

Three-and-a-half hours later, Jimmie Lee awoke from his slumber. He brushed his teeth, washed his face, and then clothed himself. He headed out to the front desk to find the nearest fast food joint or other satisfactory eatery. The desk clerk, a juicy looking gal named "Natalie", directed him to Arnita's Diner a few blocks away. He braved the now 33-degree temperature by walking all three blocks, arriving in less than ten minutes.

The diner was packed. Jimmie Lee found a seat way in the back. The table was small, had a salt-and-pepper aluminum stand in its center and a laminated menu sat under the stand. An ashtray was near the table's round edge. Jimmie Lee looked over the menu before deciding he'd have the lean beef steak, asparagus, mashed potatoes and a couple brown & serve rolls. The soup-of-the-day was beef & vegetable stew, so he desired that as well. Just as he was deciding on a beverage and possibly a dessert for later, his server approached. She was a fair-skinned teenager with too much make-up, four gold teeth in the front of her mouth and a jaw-full of Juicy Fruit chewing gum. Her name tag read "TaMisha". Jimmie Lee was amazed at what today's teens represented to the rest of society, but quickly brushed off his judgmental thoughts. He placed his order, adding a Pepsi and two pieces of chocolate fudge cake for dessert once he was done with his early lunch. The diner was pre-pay only so Jimmie Lee settled the $13.32 tab before TaMisha left the table. He gave her twenty bucks and waved off any notion he wanted change.

As Jimmie Lee awaited his order, he admired the diner. He noticed the various grades and types of wood. The tables were made of cherry, the chairs of cedar. The counter looked like walnut, while the counter stools bore a striking resemblance to hickory. The floors were definitely butternut and the walls were trimmed mid-way and at the baseboards with hemlock. "Instead of Arnita's Diner", he said to himself, "it should be Wood Diner or Tree Diner."

He laughed internally. He also took note of the patrons, a mixture of young and old alike, male and female, mostly white. Some smoked, some didn't. Some drank beer, others were satisfied with soda. Everyone, however, was eating and they all seemed at peace. Peace, Jimmie Lee thought, is the absence of war, confusion, chaos. He liked that. That's what his travels were all about; enjoying himself without having to experience a host of craziness.

TaMisha brought over Jimmie Lee's lunch several minutes later. The plate's food was piping hot, the Pepsi was ice cold and the chocolate fudge cake was topped with chocolate ice cream. Jimmie Lee looked a bit puzzled and stared up at the waitress to inquire but she flashed a gleaming smile and winked at him, signaling that the ice cream was on the house, probably without owner Arnita's approval. He did not protest but instead dug into his meal as if he had not eaten breakfast nearly five hours earlier.

***

Jimmie Lee toured downtown Memphis after lunch, forgetting that he was supposed to call back to Georgia. When he realized his memory lapse, it was nearing five o'clock. He instead continued his tour, extending it to Graceland, home of Elvis Presley, before making his way back to the R&D Motel. It was 7 p.m. It was also dinner time. He was beat, so instead of leaving the comfort of the motel room, he ordered out, calling a local pizzeria for a large pizza. It arrived nearly 35 minutes later, topped with extra cheese, ground beef, mushrooms, onions, olives and pickles. Only two slices were left as Jimmie Lee dozed off to sleep, an old episode of the original Star Trek series on the television. Once again, he had forgotten to call home. He had no clue what lay before him in the days to come. No clue whatsoever.

CHAPTER 27
January 3, 2000
Portsmouth

Andy had only recently left the warmth of his townhouse when he saw them. He was two blocks from home, heading to the 7-11 convenience store to buy a few items when two women flagged him down on Airline Boulevard near a Pizza Hut. He pulled over.

"Hi," returned Andy. "What's wrong?"

"Our car broke down. Can we get a lift?"

"Sure," Andy welcomed. "Hop in."

The first woman, the prettier of the two, climbed in front while the quiet, less-than-personable one got in back.

"I'm Tiffany," began the one in front. "She's my best friend. Her name's Shalita."

"Andy, Andy Smith," he greeted. "I have to go to the 7-11 up here. Once I pick up my items I can take you to wherever you need to go. I ain't doing shit right now anyway. That cool?"

"Sure Andy," Tiffany responded.

"Where ya'll heading anyway?" Andy asked, looking

into the rearview mirror and making eye contact with Shalita, hoping she'd join in on the conversation, as her silence made him somewhat uneasy.

"Churchland," replied Tiffany.

"Whew!" Andy exclaimed. "That's a ways, a good ways."

Tiffany smiled and rubbed Andy's shoulder.

"I thought you said you won't doing nothing right now."

"Yeah," he remembered. "I did say that, didn't I?" He sighed. Glancing at his watch, he noticed it was eleven o'clock.

Then Tiffany perked up. "How about this: Let's go to your house, I'll call Triple-A from there and we'll chill until the tow truck comes. I'll just give them your address, they'll come get me and Shalita, take us to the car, tow it, and then take us home. How about that?"

Andy liked the idea. "Cool," was his response. He and Jessica had broken up two days earlier and he'd been chilling at home ever since. It was pretty late at night and he left the house with the intention of coming right back. Having a couple girls over might lighten up his stress somewhat. After all, he really did like Jessica. And, of course, he missed her. But commitment was not on his mind. Past commitments proved unsuccessful. Hence, all Andy wanted to do in his post-Jessica era is enjoy himself. He found his way to freedom by working day-in and day-out to get out of prison and then became a successful businessman. He was rich now, at least in his eyes he was, and he would let nothing get in his way again. Tonight he'd enjoy some social entertainment from one good-looking and one not-so-good-looking female. Nothing could go wrong, he thought as he pulled into the 7-11 parking lot.

Absolutely nothing could go wrong, he thought again. The feeling made him smile inside.

"Ya'll want something from outta here?" He asked.

"Just beer," said Tiffany. "A 12-pack of Bull."

"Red Bull?" He wanted to know.

"Naw, Schlitz Malt Liquor Bull. That cheap shit that'll fuck your stomach up. That's the best shit to buy."

He shook his head in comical disbelief, then headed into the convenience store. He would have left his key in the ignition but the quiet, ugly girl in the back still had him a wee bit edgy. He bought what he'd left the house for—cheddar cheese, salted butter and some clams—and a 12-pack of beer. He threw in a box of condoms just in case the tow truck took too long. He let out a barely audible snicker. Five minutes later he was back in the black 740i with Tiffany and the strange bitch in the back seat, Sha-something.

"Say your name for me," he requested of her, looking into her face through the rearview mirror as he started the BMW's engine.

"Shalita," Tiffany answered.

Andy, never removing his eyes from Shalita's face, said, "What? You can't talk for yourself?"

Finally, she let out a slight smile and then repeated Tiffany's answer, "Shalita." She said nothing else.

Tiffany rubbed Andy's shoulder again.

"She don't talk much, Andy."

"I see," he said, pulling out of the convenience store's parking lot and back onto Airline Boulevard en route to Lancer Drive.

***

By 4 a.m., the tow truck had never arrived, all of the beer was gone, and Andy and Tiffany were engaged in deep conversation. Shalita was in her own world. Andy and Tiffany were lounging on the end of the couch in the living room having just discussed Andy's entire life story, from his upbringing with his mom, Kayla, to his 10-year prison stay to his current status of success and prosperity. Somewhere in between, he discussed his three wives and numerous girlfriends. Meanwhile, Shalita sat at the other end of the couch purportedly listening to a Sony walkman she'd pulled from her purse. The walkman was actually without batteries. Shalita had been listening to Andy talk for quite some time. She was listening, plotting all the while, waiting for the right moment to make her move. After hearing a sigh from Andy, as if to indicate he'd run out of words, Shalita felt it was time.

"I think I saw one more beer in the 12-pack's box," she said suddenly, rising to go to the kitchen.

"It talks," Andy joked. Tiffany let out a short laugh. Shalita ignored the joke and continued on into the kitchen. Once there, she opened the refrigerator and made a superficial search for one last beer. She knew there were no more left. With the Amana fridge door still open she eyed the entire kitchen in search of a weapon. She found one—several actually—atop the counter: A set of Cutco knives. She pulled the two largest ones using both hands and then used her elbow to close the door of the refrigerator. With that, she placed both hands behind her back and headed into the living room, stopping at the entry way separating the short hall from the living and dining rooms. Andy and Tiffany's backs were to her when she spoke.

"There's no more beer," Shalita stated.

"I said that an hour ago," Andy reminded her. "And even with Virginia's new law of buying beer until two in the morning, we're still a couple hours too late to go get more."

"Any money in this place?" Shalita asked bluntly. The question caused Andy to turn around. He looked at her standing there, hands behind her back, face laced with utter seriousness. He realized something wasn't right. Just then, Tiffany stood and walked over to where Shalita waited. Shalita repeated her question word-for-word.

"What's behind her back?" Andy asked himself. He too stood, asking curtly, "What's going on here?" He moved toward the women in an attempt to exercise his masculine authority, his home-court advantage, but was abruptly halted in his tracks when Shalita's hands both became visible. His knives, he recognized.

"Listen," he began. "I don't have time for this bullshit. This is my home, for God's sake."

"We just want all the money that's in the house, Andy," Tiffany politely stated.

"I don't have time for this bullshit," Andy repeated, shaking his head with hostility. "I've got credit cards and checks; I don't keep cash on hand."

"Tie him up, Tiff," commanded Shalita. "We'll tear this place apart until we're satisfied."

Andy allowed his mind to focus on his prison stay briefly enough to remember what an old cellmate of his told him once: Never quit, always survive. With that he lunged towards Shalita and punched her in the face as hard as he could. The blow stunned her, bloodying her nose in the process. She stumbled backwards and fell to the floor. One knife fell from a hand; the other she still gripped. He made an attempt to step across her in order to head to the kitchen. He'd call 9-1-1, he hoped. As he stepped over her, she grabbed one of his ankles with her free hand. At that same instant, Tiffany jumped onto his back. Her weight caused Andy to lose his balance. Both tumbled to the floor. Shalita still had Andy's ankle. She sat up, let go of his ankle and moved her hand to his neck. She pressed the blade of the knife in her other hand to the side of his face.

"I swear to God I'll kill you if you make one more false move," screamed Shalita.

Tiffany scrambled to her feet while Shalita slowly brought her and Andy to theirs, holding his throat and the knife to his face the entire time. She again demanded to know where money was in the house.

"Other than a few bucks in my pocket, I don't keep cash in the house," Andy said through a strained voice. It's kind of difficult to talk normal when your throat is being gripped by a crazy bitch holding a knife to your face.

"Bullshit!" Shalita screamed. She was becoming frustrated and spat as she spoke. "I want all the fucking money in the house or somebody's gonna die!"

Never quit, always survive—Andy couldn't help but rehear those critical words. He speedily sent his knee into Shalita's crouch area with all the force he could muster. He knew she did not have testicles—at least not anatomically—but a fierce whack to the vulva might have some stopping power. And stopping power it did indeed have. Shalita squealed in utter pain, dropping the other knife and again falling to the floor, this time balling into an infant-like knot from unspeakable pain. Andy shot into the kitchen and reached for the telephone. A hand grabbed the back of his shirt collar and jerked him backwards. It was Tiffany. She had retrieved the first knife from the floor and was now holding it to Andy's throat from behind.

"Try that with me, motherfucker!' She challenged, guiding him backwards out of the kitchen and back into the tiny hall. "Get up, bitch!" Tiffany shouted to Shalita. He ain't did nothing but stun ya! Get yo ass up!" As Shalita got up, still smarting from Andy's knee strike, Tiffany continued guiding him backwards until they were back in the living room. Shalita arrived a few seconds later, still limping and obviously not quite pain-free, knife in hand.

"Now, Andy," began Tiffany, her voice patient but serious, "we can do this two ways: the right way and the wrong way. The right way is you let us tie you up while we go through the house to get what we came here for. The wrong way is you continue to resist and fight to the point that we kill you and then go through the house to get what we came here for. Either way, we get what we came here for. Pick your way, Andy. Pick your way."

Silence fell over the room, save for the trio's heavy breathing. Andy contemplated his answer. While he did so, he also reflected on his old cellmate and those profound words, "Never quit, always survive." But right now, his life was in danger and the wrong choice could cost him it. So he surrendered.

"I choose the …right way," he stated slowly.

"Good choice, Andy," Tiffany said. "Now, very slowly, let's go over to the couch. Have a seat and be cool."

"Gotcha," Andy said, complying. "I'm cool."

"Go find something to tie him up with, Kat," Tiffany told Shalita. Andy took note of the fact that Tiffany called her by a different name. He said nothing. As Shalita or

Kat or whatever the gangster bitch's name was left the living room in search of rope or its fair equivalent, Andy came to realize that along with all the things he could call himself, one of them was "ex-lawyer", albeit jailhouse lawyer. The lawyer label made him one thing for sure: a great liar. And even though his lawyering days were over, his days of telling lies were not, at least not right now. He heard the girl called Shalita head to the second floor of the townhouse. Tiffany was still behind him as he sat on the couch, the knife at his throat still, but the pressure from the blade eased somewhat. He thought back to those survival words again. A lie began to form in his mind.

"Tiffany," he calmly started out. "Like I told you earlier, there's no money in here like talking about it, but I have something fairly close to money, close enough to make you happy."

Tiffany was interested. "Like what?" She asked, the knife's pressure easing a bit more.

"Jewelry," Andy said softly, alluringly. He had to hurry, this he knew, so he repeated it but with some descriptiveness.

"Jewelry, some gold, some platinum, all high quality, straight from the finest of the finest jewelry stores across the state." His voice seemed sensual, almost sexual.

"Where?" She wanted to know. Again, the knife's pressure eased even more, this time to the point the actual blade was only barely touching Andy's throat. Only when he exhaled could he feel it; his inhalations allowed him to escape, however brief, the coolness—and, of course, sharpness—of the blade's edge.

"In a false compartment behind the reel-to-reel's face over there," he responded, slightly nodding forward toward the home entertainment system. "Just pull the face straight off; the reel-to-reel's not real."

Tiffany's greed arrested her. The knife came away from Andy's throat; Tiffany came around the side and in front of the couch, facing Andy. She waved the knife, telling him not to move. Turning, she focused her attention on the reel-to-reel. Needing both hands to pull the face off required her to place the knife in her mouth, her teeth clinching the length of the serrated blade's edge horizontally. Andy could wait no longer. He believed Shalita, a.k.a. Kat, would return at any moment so he dashed into action.

Andy lunged forward at Tiffany, passing over the coffee table as he went, and in a half-second had taken hold of the back of her shirt and waist. He violently jerked her rearward, causing the back of the female villain's knees to slam into the coffee table, effectively throwing her off balance. She and Andy fell against the table's edge. The knife fell from her mouth. Andy began pounding her with blows; lefts and rights came in consecutive patterns, swift and unrelenting. Most were to the face, some to the side of the head, a few to the upper body. Within twenty seconds, she was incapacitated enough to afford Andy an easy escape so he took it, scrambling with the speed of an antelope. He leapt to his feet, barreled across the sofa, sprinting toward the hallway again, this time with the intent to reach the townhouse's front entrance. Although only seconds passed, it seemed like hours as Andy's heart pounded while he attempted to save his own life. He could feel the thudding in his throat; it scared him. Nevertheless, Tiffany's partner in crime, having heard the commotion, was already en route to the first floor and, with the speed of a cheetah, beat Andy to the front door. Just as he reached out for the knob, her left hand—balled into a fist—heavily struck his wrist and lower forearm; then her right hand, still grasping the other knife, came down at Andy from an upward swing. He ducked just in time. She swung again, this time with Andy pinned in the corner by the door's hinges and a side wall. He knew he was going to get stabbed on this one—he knew it—so he raised both hands, palms facing outward, shielding his face. She came down again, grunting from the forcefulness of her swing, sounding somewhat like a Venus or Serena Williams grunt as they slam a return serve against a worthy opponent in a championship match. Andy heard—and felt—the sickening tear of his flesh, then saw blood spurt across the front door, his palm now laying open, gushing with blood. The girl raised her hand again but this time Andy was ready, in spite of his injury, to fight for his very life. And fight he did. With his free, uninjured hand and, ironically, with his bloodied one, Andy reached for the knife with all the skill he could muster. He was successful! His cut hand gripped the girl's wrist; his good hand locked around her palm and the end of the knife's handle. He tightened, as best he could, his hold and then butted her with all his might, almost knocking himself dizzy as he made her weak-kneed. Her state of confusion was enough that Andy got a hold of the knife, but instead of holding it on her while police were summoned, Andy inexplicably turned it upward in his good hand, raising it high, then plunged it into the girl's face. He raised it again, plunging it into the side of her head. It took somewhat of an effort to remove the knife. As it exited, Andy heard footsteps behind him. He spun around to meet Tiffany who was knifeless and—again for no understandable reason—chose not to hold her at bay in order to call police. Rather, he buried the large knife into her chest, pulled it out, and then drove it in yet again as she slid to the floor. Blood was everywhere. He was bleeding, both girls were also. Blood now covered the walls, floor and most of the door. The sick smell of serum filled the brief hallway. The three of them were silent. Both girls were on the floor, Tiffany gasping her last breaths, the other not moving at all. Andy looked from one to the other then slid to the floor himself, the loss of blood somewhat weakening him. I've gotta live, he told himself. With that thought in place, he struggled to his feet, tore his shirt off and used it as a wrap for his blood-soaked hand, then fumbled for his car keys with the other hand. He retrieved them from his pocket but dropped them as he pulled them out. He bent to pick them up. The knife was still lodged in Tiffany's chest. She was no longer gasping. The only breathing Andy heard was his own. Call the police, a voice inside him said. "No," he said aloud. "I've gotta live. They won't get here in time. This is a good neighborhood. They're downtown in the projects, in the ghetto hoods in the bad neighborhoods. It'll take too long for them to get here. I've gotta live. "Never quit, always survive'." He had the keys again. With them tightly in his hand, he managed to turn the front door's dead bolt to the unlocked position and thereafter twist the knob so as to allow the door to open. It stopped after about four inches, as Tiffany's partner's corpse was in the way. Andy pulled the door harder, gaining about four more inches. He forced himself through the opening, stumbling to his car. He started the engine seconds after climbing inside and began his life-preserving trip to the nearest hospital, Maryview Medical Center, where he collapsed just inside the Emergency Department's entry doors. Unbeknownst to Andy, he would soon be on an operating table for a three-and-a-half-hour procedure in order to save his hand and his life.

CHAPER 28
January 3, 2000
Memphis, Tennessee

The telephone on the other end rang six times before Jimmie Lee decided to disconnect. It was unusual for Momma Lou-Lou to not answer, he thought, but he was also aware it was still early—six in Memphis, seven in Suwanee—so he'd pretty much made up his mind to call back later during his lunch break or, at the very latest, after work. Momma Lou-Lou, he thought, must have had a long day yesterday and is sleeping a bit late this morning. Typically, she was up at the crack of dawn.

After hanging up, Jimmie Lee made a second call, this one to the local taxi service, and requested a taxi at his motel room. While he waited outside his room door, he reflected on his life. He was a law-abiding drifter from Georgia who'd spent a decade traveling the country, working odd jobs as he went, attempting to cover all fifty states. He had nearly half the states still to go. He was single, had no children and no other responsibilities. These factors proved advantageous as he trekked across the nation. Today he would continue with his simple life by working yet another odd job—as a day-laborer here in Memphis—in hopes of meeting a new face, learning something new, whatever the case may be. Meeting new faces, he thought, was pretty cool. One that stuck in his mind more than any other recently was Van Morrison, originally from Richmond, Virginia, now living in North Little Rock, Arkansas. Jimmie Lee and Van met in Kansas nearly four years ago. When Van wrote to Jimmie Lee a year ago, the latter almost could not recall the former. Several minutes after studying the postcard, Jimmie Lee remembered. Not too much more thought went into the postcard after that. Yet, in recent days, Jimmie Lee has consistently thought of Van and even entertained going to Arkansas next. It neighbored Tennessee and he could look Van up. Who knows what the future may hold for him in Arkansas, he wondered. That thought was interrupted by the arrival of the taxi which had pulled up curbside where Jimmie Lee stood waiting. He hopped in, the cabbie turned on the meter, and they were on their way.

***

The job for the day—for the week actually—was up in Jackson, about forty miles Northeast of Memphis. A vanload of workers was sent. Jimmie Lee sat right behind the driver. The ride was comfortable and lasted less than 45 minutes. Jimmie Lee and the crew would help clear the annex of the Casey Jones Home and Museum to prepare it for its first refurbishment in over 36 years.

***

An hour later, Jimmie Lee was busy at work. He and a guy named Jason were moving a solid steel file cabinet equipped with a built-in combination lock. The cabinet was huge and heavy. Just as the two workers negotiated a turn with the bulky item, a young woman with a refulgent smile happened by, meeting Jason's eyes. He lost his thought momentarily, as well as his grip on the cabinet. Jimmie

197

Lee had no warning. The steel cabinet came down hard, knocking him off balance. He was able to clear all but one part of his body—his right hand—from the tumbling mass. His screams could be heard for miles, it seemed.

CHAPTER 29
January 4, 2000
Portsmouth

Andy's eyes opened slowly, his stupor stimulated by a warm, soft hand. The anesthetic given him during surgery made sure he enjoyed a total loss of the sense of pain and touch. He had been on the operating table for almost four hours. His hand's injuries were profound: two tendons in his little finger and one tendon in his middle had been severed and he lost hundreds of cubic centimeters of blood prior to—and following—his arrival in the Emergency Department. No guarantee he would again have feeling in his hand existed. Doubt existed as to whether he'd even be able to extend all of his fingers normally. None of this information was known to Andy right now. In spite of his medicated slumber he knew only that someone was touching him caressing him, calling his name. As he neared a satisfactory state of consciousness, a face appeared in his sight. A familiar face it was. A woman's face. Long hair. Sweet perfume. It was Jessica. She was back. She smiled.

"Hey Andy," she opened with. "Don't try to talk yet. Take a minute to compose yourself. You haven't been out of surgery but a few hours. Relax."

He defied her. "Jess—Jessica," he began. He coughed.

"Shhh," she interjected. "Relax, baby." Her voice was lustrous, pacific. And relax he did, no longer wanting to talk. He said nothing for a couple minutes. Yet his peace was interrupted by a suit-and-tie guy who walked into the private hospital room. The guy looked vaguely familiar. Jessica moved a little off to the side; he took her place directly in front of Andy.

"Mr. Smith, can you talk?" The stranger asked. He was very well-built, towered between six-feet-five and six-seven, and bore a look of intense seriousness that could crack glass.

"Barely," answered Andy. He coughed again. "Let me try my hand."

"My name, sir, is Detective Sergeant Theodore Iverson. I'm with the Portsmouth Police. I need to ask you some questions, Mr. Smith."

"Fire away," Andy told him, finally remembering where he'd seen the cop before. It was during his early-1987 arrest for bank robbery, ironically in a hospital room but at Portsmouth General. Back then, Det. Iverson escorted two FBI agents and a robbery investigator from the Norfolk Police Department into Portsmouth for purposes of jurisdiction only. This was the first time Andy had seen the detective in nearly thirteen years. Andy was anxious to hear the cop's questions.

"You came in here cut up pretty bad early this morning," he began. "Initially, hospital authorities thought it was a gunshot wound at first, notifying us, but later discovered it was a stab wound. I hung around anyway. I've been waiting six hours. Tell me something good." He smiled. "Who did this to you?"

"A couple girls," Andy confessed.

"Girls?" Det. Iverson inquired. He didn't look at Andy as if he was amazed that females jumped a man. Instead, he looked at Andy as if a light inside of his cop-thinking mind had just illuminated. His eyebrows raised, he moved a bit closer, reaching inside his suit jacket for a small pad and pen. "Tell me about these girls, Mr. Smith. Tell me something good." The serious look left him long enough for him to smile again.

"They flagged me down on Airline, near the Pizza Hut, telling me they had car trouble." He paused briefly, coughed, then continued. "I gave them a ride to my house in Yorkshire, they called Triple-A, we got to drinking, Triple-A never came, and then all hell broke loose all of a sudden."

"Mr. Smith, were these two girls Black, early-30's, one cute, the other a bit rough-looking?"

"Yeah," Andy replied. "How did you—"

"Aunya King and Katherine Young, also known as the Black 'Thelma and Louise' outlaws," the detective stated. "We've been looking for them for several weeks. You're their fourth victim. We're in luck though, Mr. Smith, because you're alive. Your three predecessors were not so lucky."

"My predecessors?" Andy asked.

"Just a play on words," the detective admitted. "I was talking about the other three victims."

Andy was somewhat taken aback. "They're all dead?"

"Yes sir, Mr. Smith, I'm afraid so. Now what I need you to do is tell me if you heard them say anything about where they were heading? Anything at all?"

Andy looked troubled, confused even. "Where they were heading? You mean they still got away?"

Now Det. Iverson seemed confused. "Of course, sir. I didn't know anything until I got the chance to speak with you. Once you said 'girls' and the car trouble line, along with your stab wound or wounds, I knew it was King and Young. You passed out when you came in, so no one knew anything. In short, yes, they got away, sir. At least for now."

"Man," Andy said amazingly. "They actually got away."

"Seems that way," the detective stated. "Now, Mr. Smith, if you could sign this release form, I can get your house keys from Hospital Property. Then I'll head over to collect trace evidence from your residence. It'll help build my case once I catch them."

Like a flash of lightning, everything came together for Andy. Now he understood. "So, so you haven't been to my townhouse?"

"To or in; no sir." The detective had no clue what was to come. The sentence that did come both shocked and floored the nineteen-and-a-half-year police veteran."

"I think they're dead, both of them, inside my house," said Andy. Jessica, who was still standing near the bed, gasped and then nearly fainted.

***

The swarm of detectives, uniform patrol officers and police technicians asked questions, canvassed neighboring townhouses, took photographs and collected physical evidence. Their case began from a stabbing; it was now a double-homicide. Two female victims lay dead in Andrew Smith's posh townhouse. One had two stab wounds—one through the nose and the other through the temple—and the second female had been stabbed three times, all in the chest, with a knife still lodged in her left breast. It was almost dusk; the throng of police personnel had been there close to seven hours. Their leader, Det. Iverson, gave all of the orders, directed the entire investigation. It was obvious he was in charge. His work here was now done; his crowd's work was as well. They would all leave. He, however, would have to see Andrew Smith again. The seasoned police detective had lots of questions.

***

The next day, Andy was slated to be discharged from Maryview Medical Center. His stitches were to come out in ten days, physical therapy to start soon after, and a long recovery to follow. A nurse wheeled him out of Room 372, rolled him down the long hall and into the elevator enroute to the first floor lobby. Once there, he thought he would see Jessica. He did not. He saw his doctor, flanked by two uniform patrol officers, standing in the lobby. None of them were smiling.

"Mr. Smith, Andrew Smith," said an officer. "We will be taking you to police headquarters to the detective bureau for investigative interrogation. Please stand up."

***

"Andrew Smith," started Det. Iverson, "you have the right to remain silent. If you give up that right, anything you say can and will be used against you. You have the right to an attorney before and during any questioning. If you cannot afford an attorney, one will be appointed to you by a court of competent jurisdiction. Do you understand these rights as I have read them to you?"

Andy was taken without cuffs to the detective bureau and placed in a room alone. He had not been photographed or fingerprinted. He was there for nearly an hour before Iverson showed up. He held in his hand a Miranda rights form, a small tape recorder and a legal pad with pre-written questions scrawled on it. He sat across from Andy in the small room. Without greeting Andy, the detective started reading from the rights form. He was now finished and awaited Andy's response.

"I understand my rights, Detective."

"Having stated you understand your rights, Mr. Smith, I now would like to take your statement with regard to the homicides of Aunya Tiffany King and Katherine Shalita Young, a.k.a. Kat Young. Do you desire to make a statement, sir?"

Andy's jailhouse lawyering days kicked in. He had advised thousands of prisoners never to talk to authorities once they have read off the Miranda rights. The authorities were attempting to solve a case. That's all they were there for. They weren't there to help, to clear up anything. They were there solely to solve a case. Andy knew this all-too-well. He would not let Det. Iverson convince him otherwise.

"I plead the Sixth Amendment, Detective," Andy said.

"You mean the Fifth, don't you?"

"No, Detective, I mean the Sixth Amendment. I'm not pleading the Fifth because I have not done anything that would incriminate me. I am pleading the Sixth because I simply want a lawyer present when you question me."

"Who's your lawyer?" Iverson asked, becoming impatient.

"You'll have to give me one," Andy advised. "Since I haven't done anything that would incriminate me, there's no need for me to hire a lawyer. You'll have to give me one."

"You know we don't do that," the cop stated.

"Then I'll be leaving, sir," said Andy. "Where's my coat?" Andy was smart, brilliant in the law. He knew that by pleading the Fifth Amendment right not to incriminate himself, the police could hold him for several hours, photograph him, print his fingers, etc., while they hurriedly develop their case. But in pleading the Sixth Amendment right to counsel, the police could not hold him for any period at all. They'd have to develop their case on their own time. "My coat, Detective?" Andy repeated. To this, Det. Iverson sighed, rose and left, then returned about forty seconds later with Andy's coat. Andy put his left arm in a sleeve, draped the right side of the coat over his right shoulder, and then left. Outside he hailed a Safeway Cab Company taxi and gave the driver his Lancer Drive address. During the ride, Andy knew he'd have to move and do so very quickly. He knew he had fucked up. Now he'd have to save his life again, this time from losing its freedom. He had just one solution: run.

***

The Trailways bus station had its usual Saturday morning traffic. It was January 8th and many Norfolk-based Moorish-Americans were loading onto buses enroute to North Carolina to celebrate the birth of their Prophet, Noble Drew Ali who graced the Moors with his 1886 parturition. Among the crowd of ordinary people and the distinguished Moors—with their crowns, turbans and fezzes consuming the masses of other heads—was one fellow who looked not-so-ordinary. He appeared nervous, uneasy, bothered. He was around 5'8", African-American and in his mid-30s. Working his way onto the Southern states-bound bus, the fellow carried a small suitcase in one hand and a one-way bus ticket to North Little Rock, Arkansas, in the other. The name on the ticket did not match the man's name, but the man's face matched a name: Andrew Smith.

CHAPTER 30
January 9. 2000
North Little Rock, Arkansas

When Jimmie Lee disembarked the Trailways bus, he took care not to hit his right arm which had been expertly wrapped prior to his leaving the hospital in Memphis. Although he could have afforded to use his debit cards, Marvin Aaron—Jimmie Lee finally learned the man's last name—insisted on having his day-labor firm foot the bill. No protest came from Jimmie Lee who left home each January with two debit cards with $1,000 each in credit and $500 in cash. Instead, he thanked Marvin and asked to be driven to the local bus terminal. There he bought a Memphis-to-North Little Rock one-way ticket and climbed aboard. He was near the end of the bus's long ride, with only two stops left, i.e. West Memphis, Arkansas and then a straight shot to the small city next to Arkansas's capital. The other riders remaining had not been so lucky. Their bus's second stop was in Raleigh, North Carolina, its third was Charlotte, on into Tennessee to Nashville, then hitting Memphis. The bus originated in Norfolk, Virginia. Here, Jimmie Lee stepped off a bus into a new phase in his life: recovery. The beginning of that recovery started with his cautiousness not to hit his arm on anything, including the rails of the bus he'd just disembarked.

Jimmie Lee sat his bag down on the sidewalk to reach into his pocket just as a man brushed past, prompting Jimmie Lee to look at the man, expecting some manners but getting none. The man was a few years older than Jimmie Lee and looked to be in a haze. Jimmie Lee pulled out a postcard. It bore Van Morrison's address here in North Little Rock. A map of the city—Jimmie Lee looked around briefly—would tell how far Van was from the terminal. But first, he realized, he really, really needed to call home. He hadn't been in touch in a week. Momma Lou-Lou, he thought to himself, is probably worried. If only he knew.

Instead of using a pay phone inside the bus station, Jimmie Lee opted for one on the outside. He found one just around the corner right in the midst of a cab pick-up point. Two cabs were waiting. He dialed the number in Suwanee. Emma's only daughter, Eboni Jintao, answered on the first ring.

"White Plantation; good morning," she greeted.

"Eb?" Jimmie Lee inquired. "This you?"

"James! She said excitedly. "Jesus, James, why haven't you called?"

"It's a long story, Eb," he said, then going on with, "but I'm sure you'll understand."

"James," said Eboni, her voice going from excitement to abrupt normalcy, almost solemnest. "I have something to tell you."

"Yeah," he replied. "I'm sure you do: You stayed past New Year. What else is new?" He laughed.

"James, this is serious." This voice was sad, very sad.

"What happened?"

"Momma passed away last Sunday." Eboni's voice was still sad, very soft.

Jimmie Lee felt dizzy.

"No way," he said, his voice sad too and low.

For the next three minutes, Eboni explained how William, the family driver, was slated to take Emma Lou to church. When he arrived at the front of the main house and blew the horn, she didn't respond. He decided to go inside where he found her lying in the great room. She was already dead. He summoned the Sheriff who called one of Suwanee's two doctors, both arriving about the same time. The doctor's finding: acute heart failure. Arrangements were made and the funeral was initially delayed. Ultimately, she was buried this past Friday. The family, that is Eboni and her brother Ivan, waited as long as they could, hoping to hear from Jimmie Lee. The undertaker could hold the body no longer so the funeral took place two days ago. The reading of Emma White's Last Will and Testament is scheduled for tomorrow, Monday. Her estate by now—thanks to aggressive investments and mounting interest—is worth $38.4 million, nearly an $11-million surge from a year before. Jimmie Lee's cut: just under $9.41 million. That includes the massive plantation, Eboni concluded. She waited for Jimmie Lee to respond.

"I gotta go," he said with a sadness that seemed deeper than the Pacific Ocean's average depth of 13,000 feet. "I just gotta go," he repeated, his voice cracking, as he hung up the pay telephone. Eboni was left with a dead line.

Jimmie Lee walked over to the waiting cab—the other one had a fare and had departed—and got in. He told the driver to just drive until he said stop. It seemed like hours before Jimmie Lee finally came back around. Actually it was less than forty minutes. He asked to be taken to any nearby store in order to buy a map. The driver complied, pulling into a convenience store parking lot. Jimmie Lee went in, got the map, came out, sat it on the hood of the taxi, opened it up, and then reached into his pocket for Van's postcard, matching the street name on it to the list of streets on the map. He found the street, asked the driver how far away was Magnolia, and was told it was only a block down, just over some railroad tracks. Jimmie Lee paid the meter fare, thanked the patient cabbie and started walking.

Magnolia Street ran parallel to the railroad tracks. It went left and right. He turned right. The first address was a brand new duplex homeless shelter with the left door reading 384 and the right being 388. Stunningly, Van's address was 386. Confused, Jimmie Lee went inside the right door.

"No men!" The clerk yelled. Jimmie Lee was just inside the door.

"What?" He asked.

"No men in here, ever," she repeated, a Marlboro cigarette hanging from her lips. She shot a thumb over her shoulder. "See the sign?" There it was, in big letters, "No Men Allowed." Jimmie Lee backed out slowly as she told him to go in the other door. He did.

"Yes sir?" The other clerk inquired. This one a man.

"I just went next door and she—"

"That's the women's shelter," he cut in. "This here's the men's. I need some I.D. from ya and your bag has to be searched. Then sign this."

"No, I'm not here for a room."

"You sho' ain't," the man replied. "You done said a room. Boy, ain't nothing here but one big dorm. What you need, sir?"

Jimmie Lee handed him the postcard, then pointed to the address.

"Oh hell, sir, that house is long gone, 'bout a year ago. They built these shelters here six months ago. The faggot who owned the house that used to be here got high on weed, drank some home-made wine, and then snorted some dope before he passed out holding a cigarette. Burned the house to the ground. He died in the fire. Everyone said it was karma. He'd treated a lover of his like shit following a nasty break-up. Told all sorts of lies on the poor guy. The dick eater's dead now. Karma's a motherfucker, ain't it?"

Jimmie Lee cringed at the awful language.

"Can I stay here tonight?" He asked feeling too drained to go out and find a motel room.

"You sho' can, sir," the clerk answered. "Just sign here in the book and let me go through your bag. Oh yeah, I need to see some identification, too."

Instead of signing the book, handing over his bag, or showing I.D., Jimmie Lee pulled a twenty from his pocket and stuffed it in the clerk's hand.

"Give me a bed."

***

A week later, Jimmie Lee was still living in the homeless shelter. He had no sense of time or motion and spent hours at a time walking the streets of North Little Rock

211

among its 61,000 residents. He never called back to Georgia. He really did not know what to do.

Today, a Sunday, was no different than any other day except that Jimmie Lee, during one of his aimless walks, trailed into the neighboring city, Arkansas' capital. It was much larger than North Little Rock with population of 180,050. His stroll landed him in an area near the city's airport. He stopped at the corner of Sixth Street in order to re-tie his boots and, using just his left hand, did a good job. That's when he noticed it.

Right in front of Jimmie Lee was a small church, Sixth Street Church of Christ that looked like a tiny two-bedroom cottage that had been converted into a church. He peered inside the dusty front window pane and saw just four people sitting on one of the only three pews within. He looked closer and saw the lone preacher delivering his sermon from the pulpit. Emma Lou loved church, Jimmie Lee recalled. He decided to step inside.

"…not conformed to this world, but be ye transformed by the renewing of your minds." The tall, dark, lanky preacher eyed Jimmie Lee without smiling then nodded slightly as if to say come on in. "In other words, folks, you cannot conform to this world in its ungodly state. You have to gear your mind to be renewed, a transformation, if you will." Jimmie Lee sat down in the second row by himself. One churchgoer turned around and smiled and mouthed, "Welcome."

A short while later, the service concluded. The other four attendees shook the preacher's hand and promptly departed. Jimmie Lee stayed behind.

"That was pretty good," Jimmie Lee said, standing up. The two did not shake hands because of Jimmie Lee's cast.

"Thanks, son," the preacher stated and showing yellowed teeth as he spoke. "I'm Brother James, the acting minister here. Our regular minister, Brother Christopher, is in Africa. He's expected back in a few weeks. I'm just filling in for him while he's gone. You oughta hear him preach. Now he's a good one!"

"My name's Jimmie Lee, Jimmie Lee White. Sorry I can't shake your hand."

"Yeah, I was noticing that," Brother James admitted. "What happened?"

"You got time?" Jimmie Lee asked.

"As much as God's willing to give me," he said, pointing over to the pews where the two seated themselves.

***

Eight days after Jimmie Lee met Brother James, much had changed. By now, Jimmie Lee called him James and had dropped the Brother portion. His character outside church did not warrant such an honorary title. He was a bitter and racist man who complained all the time and seemingly had nothing but negative things to say. He belittled Sixth Street Church of Christ's preacher for leaving the country to find a wife instead of focusing a search within the United States. He blamed every aspect of his personal failures on the nation's majority race. Nothing seemed to satisfy him. Jimmie Lee did not see any of it coming. The day they met, James convinced the Georgia-born transient to move out of the homeless shelter and in with him in his tiny, one-bedroom apartment near Fifty-Third Avenue and Geyer Springs Road. Jimmie Lee got the couch. Now he regretted the move.

Also during the past week, Jimmie Lee had his stitches removed from his right hand; the cast was replaced with a soft but quite hefty wrap of gauze and an ace bandage. He would start physical therapy tomorrow—Tuesday—at a local hospital. He had also been out looking for work, applying for all sorts of jobs, not even taking into account how long it would be before his hand fully healed. He filled out applications at restaurants, grocery stores, gas stations—you name it. James, however, had no faith in Jimmie Lee's efforts.

"Boy, ain't nobody gonna hire you with that hand messed up like that. Nobody! You just wasting your time." Jimmie Lee heard this over and over. Today he'd had enough.

"You know what, James," Jimmie Lee began, his mouth tight with frustration. "If a man listens to you, he'll never go anywhere. You're the most negative person I've met in 30 years of living! I'm going to get this hand back in proper working order and I'm going to find a job too."

"Yeah?" James asked. "You think so, huh?"

"Know so," Jimmie Lee corrected.

"I don't think I like your tone, boy! James shouted, becoming upset almost instantly. "I'm old enough to be your daddy, boy!"

"But you ain't!" He fired back.

Jimmie Lee grabbed his belongings and stormed out the apartment. He heard James call after him but kept walking. He exited the apartment complex and walked onto Geyer Springs Road heading towards College Avenue. Up ahead, on the far left, was a small building; on the immediate right, a huge church. Jimmie Lee glanced up to see the church's name, Geyer Springs Church of Christ, strolled a few more yards, passed the Church, then looked over at the small building. It was the church's office. He crossed the street and went inside.

"Praise the Lord; good afternoon!" A jubilant front-desk clerk greeted. "I'm Sister Billie Jean. May I help you, young man?"

"Yeah, I need to know where's the nearest motel."

"One's close by," she answered. "Go up yonder to College Avenue, turn left, go down about twelve blocks, and then you'll see the College Motel on the corner of Sixty-Fifth and College Avenue. You can't miss it."

"Twelve blocks, huh?" Jimmie Lee asked, a bit taken aback.

"You walking or driving?"

"Walking."

"Wait a sec." She turned in her chair and was about to call out to someone. Before she could, a man popped out from a back office.

"I was just about to summon you, Brother Dale," she admitted. You still going to the Sonic Drive-In for lunch?"

"Yes, ma'am," said the man who looked around forty with a receding hairline.

"Could you drop this man off at the local motel on your way?"

Brother Dale paused a few seconds, glancing at Jimmie Lee.

"I'll pay you," Jimmie Lee offered.

"Oh no," the man stated. "That won't be necessary. Just come to church next Sunday. How 'bout that?" He smiled.

"Deal," said Jimmie Lee.

***

By the start of February, although Jimmie Lee had had no contact with his family back in Suwanee, his life had forged on. He got a day job as a full-time cashier at the Target on the corner of College and Casher Avenues and today he was starting his night job. He'd been hired part-time at a nearby Sonic Drive-In. He was going to therapy twice a week and his hand was steadily improving. By now he could use his thumb, index and middle fingers; the ring was still bent slightly forward and the little was completely unusable, bent completely forward into a curl. Yesterday he moved out of the motel and into a private home on Little Rock's notorious Southeast side of the city. The assistant manager at the Sonic Drive-In offered it to him the day he was interviewed and hired for the night job. The assistant manager needed a roommate and—upon hearing that Jimmie Lee was staying at the run-down College Motel for $99 a week—proposed that Jimmie Lee could rent a room at his place for $65 weekly. Yes indeed, life was moving on for Jimmie Lee. Life was moving on.

***

Sandira May Williamson was one of the assistant managers of the Target where Jimmie Lee worked four days a week. His 10-hour days were Monday, Wednesday, Friday and Saturday from 7 a.m. to 5 p.m. He went to therapy on Tuesday and Thursday, and church on Sunday. Sandira, known as "San" by those close to her, was due to graduate in May from the University of Arkansas at Little Rock. The school's acronym, UALR, was phonetically pronounced, "Yuler". San saw Jimmie Lee on each Monday, Wednesday and Friday; her work days were Monday thru Friday from 6:30 a.m. to 2:30 p.m. She attended evening classes from 5 to 9 p. m. The two conversed often and she'd grown to like Jimmie Lee, really like him. She pondered how to approach Jimmie Lee beyond their working relationship without looking desperate, chasing a man. With Valentine's Day only 72 hours away and no date, San had to do something, and soon.

"4-0-1 to the Customer Service Center," San announced over the store's P. A. system, calling Jimmie Lee's employee number. San, at 23-going-on-24, oversaw the Target's customer service operations at the front of the store, handling refunds, exchanges, rain checks and general customer complaints. She was good at everything but the customer complaints, for her own temper was one to remember. Even still, she got the position a year before she was to earn her MBA with a minor in retail. It was Target's way of investing in its future.

Jimmie Lee, who was not at his usual Register 12 post when San paged him, came from the back of the store and walked over to San at the Customer Service Center.

"You called?"

"Yes, Jimmie Lee," she said. "Where's your money bag?"

Jimmie Lee looked baffled. "My money bag? It's only high noon. I don't get off work for another five hours, San."

"Oh yeah," she said, laughing. "What was I thinking?"

Jimmie Lee said nothing.

"Whatcha doing right now, Jimmie Lee?"

"Eating my lunch—at least I was 'til you paged me."

"Your girlfriend fixed it for you?"

"No," he answered ever-so-plain.

"Where ya'll going for Valentine's Day?"

"Who?" He asked.

"You and your girlfriend?"

"Nowhere," he said, then decided to stop playing head games with the five-foot-six single mother of one. "Actually I don't have a girlfriend, San."

"Oh really?" She asked with a tinge of excitement in her tone. "You wanna take me out on Valentine's Day come Monday?"

"Sure," he said, turning to leave. "I'll get your phone number before you go home today."

Jimmie Lee himself could not believe what he'd just done: set his first date with a girl. Up until now, he had neither dated nor had sex with a female and he was 30 years old! No one was particularly fond of San, male or female, so he had no competition to worry about. He'd considered asking someone out eventually; however, he never worked up enough nerve to do so. He had a couple prospects in mind: Lonita, another Target employee, and "Cocoa", his barber from Roberta's Hair Palace across from his night job, where he worked Tuesday thru Saturday from 6 to 10 p.m. Now it was a done deal. He and San, with her store-brought long black hair and big brown eyes, would enjoy Saint Valentine's Day somewhere in the city. He'd let her choose the location of the date.

***

San's Prussian blue Dodge Neon pulled onto Victoria Avenue just after six Monday evening. Jimmie Lee lived at 9311 with his roommate, Cedrick, whose nickname was Latasha. Cedrick also had a night job—at a club called

"Sheryl's Den"—where he set up stage shows for all the real happy guys. San parked and strolled up to the front door. She wanted to know how Jimmie Lee lived. She knew very little about him except that he was from Georgia and seldom talked about his family. Each time she would bring up questions about family, Jimmie Lee would quickly change the subject. After several attempts, she stopped prodding. She was not sure what would come of this date, her first one in several months. School, work, raising her small son and a general lack of interest from men who knew her all made dating regularly almost impossible. She took a deep breath as she rang the doorbell. It did not take long before the door opened. It was Cedrick.

"Yes, Miss Thang?" Cedrick inquired, showing more of his Latasha side.

"I'm San," she said, not smiling. "I'm lookin' for Jimmie Lee."

"Jimmie Lee?" He repeated with surprise. "For what?"

"We're going on a date," she said proudly, this time producing a slight smile.

"Jimmie Lee don't date, Miss Thang," Cedrick said matter-of-factly. "Who you think you foolin'?" He stepped back a few feet. "But come on in anyway and have a seat. I'll go get him."

Once Cedrick was gone from the room, San surveyed the living room where she was seated and the attached, open dining room. The house was exceptionally neat. The living room's walls were pearl, baseboards cream, and its carpeted floor was alabaster. The three-piece Leggett & Platt furniture set was a loud but stylish chrome yellow. The all-glass cocktail table by Steelcase was a tasteful addition to the room. The dining room's walls were also pearl. In it was a simple spruce 4-chair dining set. The carpet stopped at the start of the dining room. San was impressed. She leaned forward a bit, trying to get a distant peep into the kitchen. All she could see without getting up was that the walls were painted banana. Just then, Cedrick reappeared.

"You lookin' for something, Miss Thang?" He asked her, looking towards the kitchen as if to mock her.

"No," she curtly stated.

"I can't tell," Cedrick impudently replied. "Jimmie Lee is coming." He turned and marched off, smacking his mouth in a girlified manner as he left.

Jimmie Lee came out less than five minutes later. He was smartly dressed in new clothes: an indigo Ralph Lauren Polo shirt, navy blue Levi Strauss jeans, and white and lapis lazuli Reebok Classics. His hair was cut in a bald fade and he was freshly shaven. He no longer wore the ace bandage on his right hand, and in it were two dozen long-steamed American Beauties.

"Hi," he greeted. "These are for you." He handed her the red roses.

"Hey Jimmie Lee," she saluted, almost breathless. "Happy Valentine's Day." They embraced.

"Hi," he repeated, a bit nervous, then added, "same to you." Somehow it was too hard for him to say "Happy Valentine's Day" back to San. First-date jitters probably.

They left the house at 6:10 and drove clear across the other side of town to a pizza joint called "Chi Chi's" on Rodney Parham Road. Jimmie Lee had told San to pick a place. She asked what types of foods did he like and the two settled on pizza. That's how they ended up at Chi Chi's. Along with ordering the sliced pizza buffet, Jimmie Lee drank Pepsi while San opted for Coca-Cola, the nation's Number One soft drink. The couple made small-talk during the date and by 7:30 they were leaving. The ride back to Southeast was quiet and San dropped Jimmie Lee off at his front door.

"Had a nice time, Jimmie Lee," she told him. See you at work tomorrow."

"Wednesday, you mean," he corrected before getting out of the car.

"Oh shit," she cursed. "You're off on Tuesdays."

"Yeah,"

"Okay then," she said. "Wednesday it is." Before he could get the door open, she abruptly leaned over and kissed his cheek. It surprised him.

"Thanks," he said.

"Jimmie Lee," San said, "I can't figure you out."

"What's to figure?"

"I don't know…yet."

***

On the first day of each new month, Cecil Douglas, Target's General Manager, announced the Employee of the Month for the previous month. A minimum of ninety days' employment was necessary to be eligible. Jimmie Lee was hired on January 27 and started the next day. His 34 days of employment was a far cry from three months, so he sat there in the Employee Break Room trying to figure who would win.

Two people walked into the break room, one man and one woman, both dressed with a corporate America flare. The man was decked out in a gray Jones New York two-piece suit and slate Oleg Cassini shoes. The woman wore a sapphire skirt by Rosae Nichols at Traffic, L.A., a turquoise Roland Movret top and delft Anne Klein shoes. The man spoke up first.

"Hello, people," he greeted to the 41 full-time and two part-time staffers. "I'm Paul Wyatt. Some of you already know me. I'm the Regional Vice President of Arkansas-based Target locations. This woman here is not known to any of you—except maybe management—so I'll introduce her: This is Rebecca Ross, Regional Senior Vice President of Target stores here in Arkansas, as well as in Texas, Missouri, Tennessee, Mississippi, Louisiana, and Oklahoma. She's my boss."

"Hi," she took over. "Like Paul says, I oversee stores in seven different states. I usually only make it out once a year due to my busy schedule and large location-load, but today is a special day.

"You see, Target prides itself in recognizing excellence. We believe that strong, skilled employees make for great business, convincing customers to return again and again and again. Some of our employees take years to win an Employee of the Month award. Some take only months. Even still, there are some whose efforts are priceless, selfless and unending regardless of how long they have been with us.

"I was contacted by Paul a week ago with a request from Cecil to waive the 90-day minimum eligibility requirement in order to award the February 2000 Employee of the Month to an individual who's been on board for a mere five weeks. After reviewing his daily cash balances, weekly progress reports and his first monthly evaluation, along with the more than forty customer satisfaction cards bearing his name, I have decided to grant Cecil's request.

"Today, I present the Employee of the Month award to an employee who has been aboard just over a month: James Lee White. Give him a warm round of applause."

***

Jimmie Lee and San went out on their sixth date to the Saint Patrick's Day Parade in downtown Little Rock. He had opened up a bit more in recent weeks, talking about his childhood in Georgia, his birth mother and his decision to travel. He would not, however, go further, refusing to discuss the current state of his family, nor that he was now worth close to $10 million. In spite of his dates with San, his mind constantly trailed off to another young lady, his barber.

Cocoa's real name was Vonda Ford. She was 25, born and raised in Little Rock, graduated from high school in 1993 and the Arkansas School of Beauty and cosmetology in 1997 after completing a two-year program. She was hired as a stylist at Roberta's Hair Palace in 1997 and in 1999 became its Senior Stylist. She and one other stylist, a chocolate honey named "Deidre", were the only ones trained to cut men's hair.

Although single, she was engaged—albeit without a ring on her finger—to a so-called bad boy named "Black". She had two sons, one of whom lived with her and Black and the other with her sister in Phoenix. She, Black and the little boy all lived in Baseline Trailer Court, a block from Jimmie Lee and Cedrick's place. The trio had lived there for five years. Right now, though, Black was locked up.

In the oddest reality, Jimmie Lee was in love with Cocoa. She was blue-black, so dark her hue seemed to have been imported straight from Africa for her 1975 birth. Her skin was eloquently smooth; her light brown eyes were like gemstones from the purest region of the world and her long, shoulder-length, and natural sloe-black hair gave her a queen-like aura. Her beauty was more than magnificent; rather it was magniloquent, a step above the former. Yes, Jimmie Lee was in love with the five-foot-three model-material Cocoa and he needed to tell her about it.

"San," he began, turning to look her in the eye. "I need you to drop me off at Roberta's Hair Palace when we leave the parade."

"I thought you got hair trims every Saturday. Today's Friday, Jimmie Lee."

"I know," he acknowledged. "I'm going a day early."

"Okay," she said. "I'll wait for you and then take you home."

"No, no," he responded. "Just drop me off there. I'm going to leave from there to go to work at Sonic."

"I thought you got the day off."

"No, just from Target."

"What about your uniform?"

"I got an extra one at work, at Sonic."

***

A couple hours later the parade had ended, San and Jimmie Lee shared lunch and then they made their way back to her car. Once inside, she started the engine and turned on the radio. Her all-time favorite oldies song was playing—The OJays' 1975 classic, "Let Me Make Love To

You"—and she nearly melted upon hearing the lyrics, as if it were her first time ever listening to the quarter-century-old slow jam. She looked at Jimmie Lee with a twinkle in her eyes.

"I have my own place, Jimmie Lee," she stated. "I am surprised you've never asked to come over."

"You have a son, too."

"Yeah, but he lives with my mother. I get him each weekend. This weekend, though, he's in Chicago with my uncle. They left last night and won't be back until Sunday morning. Won't you come over tonight?"

Jimmie Lee paused. His mind drifted to Cocoa. His mind always drifted to Cocoa.

"Maybe another time," he answered.

San put the 1997 vehicle in Drive and headed to Roberta's Hair Palace. The 21-minute drive was silent all the way. When they arrived, Jimmie Lee turned to her, thanked her and—stunning her—leaned over and planted a kiss on her lips.

"Good-bye, San."

Unfortunately for her, the farewell held a much deeper implication than she could ever, ever imagine.

CHAPTER 31

April Fool's Day, 2000
Portsmouth

"April Fool, Nakia!" Dee blurted as his personal assistant opened the second envelope and removed the check.

"Dr. Powell!" She shouted. "It's a thousand bucks!"

"Yep, sweetheart," he said, leaning over to kiss the young, desirable girl on a cheek. "You're worth every bit of it. Sorry to let you go."

Dee's primary research on his third book, The Buena Vista Social Club: A Documentary, was complete. His secondary research would be done in South Florida where he was traveling to in a couple more weeks. This past Thursday was Nakia's last day and he instructed her to come by Saturday—today—to pick up her final paycheck of $206 plus a $100 bonus check. He put them in separate envelopes and told her to open them before she departed. She and her best friend, a lampblack cutie named "Kita" who stood a few inches taller than Nakia but was a few years younger, arrived to find Dee relaxing out front a few feet from the townhouse's front entrance. They parked their 2000 Nissan Altima—a gift Kita received from her father—next to Dee's 1997 all-black Mercedes and followed him inside the home. Little did Nakia know her bonus check would be ten times greater than promised. For a change, she got a good April Fool's Day joke.

Dee's research in South Florida would be sponsored by the University of Miami's Cuban-American Studies Department. They would cover up to sixty days of research with a maximum of $4,230 in expenditures. Dee would foot the rest of the bill. His first book, released in 1992, has sold close to 180,000 copies. His second book was approaching 160,000 copies sold since it hit in 1997. He thus had no problem with money. Whatever he spent over the University of Miami's allowance would be taken care of.

His Publisher was pressing hard for an October release. Dee was not so sure. He would not complete all of his secondary research until June. That left only four months. He would have to write as he researched. That was a lot to ask of him, he felt. But the driving force that kept him from saying no was the fact that he was finally leaning towards his first national bestseller. He deserved it. He was polished and a bit uppity; hated but envied by most average working-class African-Americans. He was highly educated and smart enough not to have thrown his money away on foolish buys such as unnecessarily large homes, brand new vehicles, or a wife. So everything he got, he deserved. Included in this would be a national bestseller. Hence, if the Publisher wanted October, then damnit, Dee would have to work his ass off to make it happen. No longer was he unsure about meeting the publishing deadline. He would.

After Nakia, Kita and Dee talked inside the house a few minutes, the girls announced they would be leaving. Dee saw them out. As they got out front again, Kita turned to Dee with an odd look on her face.

"What's up, sweetheart?" He asked.

"Is it true they had a murder out here not too long ago?"

"Yes," Dee acknowledged. "It was a double-homicide. The guy said it was self-defense but he went on the run before the police could confirm it. They're looking for him as we speak."

"Yikes!" She said.

***

Two weeks later, Dee covered all his furniture with sheets, cleaned out the Sears refrigerator, put light timers on the first and second floors, forwarded his home phone number to his cell phone and packed ten outfits into two suitcases before driving his Mercedes-Benz to a storage company to lock it away for the next two months. From the storage company, he took a taxi to the Norfolk International Airport, boarded a Delta Air Lines flight to Charlotte and on to Atlanta, changed planes and flew to Fort Lauderdale for re-fueling before flying straight to the Miami International Airport. It was Saturday, April 15.

CHAPTER 32
Friday, April 14, 2000
Little Rock, Arkansas

Target's General Manager Cecil Douglas summoned Jimmie Lee to the management offices the moment the latter arrived to the store. Cecil was beaming from ear-to-ear when Jimmie Lee stepped in.

"Have a seat, Jimmie Lee," he said without speaking. "I've been waiting to see you. I got an e-mail when I came in thirty minutes ago. It was from Ms. Ross, the regional Senior V. P. She asked me to see if you'd like to go into a fast-track program. Would you?"

"You mean management training?" Jimmie Lee asked in disbelief.

"Yes sir," Cecil answered. "You're the best freakin' employee I've had in years! You're here on time every single day, you're neat and clean, you're mannerable, polite, understanding—hell, I can't name it all—and all the customers like—no, love—you!

"Man, I'm tired of employees thinking they can steal the store's money and get away with it. I'm sick of the constant pricing errors because these folks are too lazy to do a price check. I'm really tired of customers complaining they can't find anything and then when they ask for help, some employees make it seem like the customer is bothering them or something.

"If I had ten more employees like you, Jimmie Lee, I could turn this entire Target around. So, I was thinking, the only way to get ten more like you is to have you in a position to lead and train. Then you can clone as many more 'Jimmie Lees' as we need to turn this operation around. I'm dying here, man, with loss of inventory, cash shorts, and poor customer service. I need more like you.

"I called Paul Wyatt, the state regional V.P., and asked him to recommend you to Ms. Ross. He did. And like I said when you walked in, she asked me to see if you're willing to give a fast-track program a try. What do you say, Jimmie Lee?"

Honestly, Jimmie Lee did not know what to say. He was trying to deal with the fairy tale love affair he had with Cocoa, with whom he had not yet had sex. Although he had never been in love before, he knew this was real, this was true. He and Cocoa had gone on dates every single night for the past month. Some nights he would be exhausted from his job at Sonic, especially after having worked all day at Target, but love kept him from complaining, love gave him a burst of energy to go with Cocoa to wherever she wanted, love made him forget he was tired, love made him forget what the very word "tired" even meant. The day San dropped him off at Cocoa's job seemed like only yesterday, with him walking into Roberta's, spotting Cocoa in her usual work area, casually strolling over to her and— with a single tear rolling down his cheek that only he could get away with—told her that he loved her and the two of them needed to talk about it. No greeting, no warning, no nothing. Just a single sentence accompanied by a single tear. Cocoa was speechless, gripped in a state of awe, paralyzed by the evidence of true love in the eyes of the man who stood before her. She had a customer enroute; she rescheduled when the lady arrived. Then Cocoa and Jimmie Lee left, drove downtown to the riverfront and talked for hours. She learned absolutely everything about the man whose hair she trimmed each week, a man she'd known for less than three months. He left nothing out—nothing at all—and made sure Cocoa was never in the dark. About anything. Not even the death of Momma Lou-Lou. Not even the millions of dollars waiting on him. The millions he wasn't even sure he wanted. All he wanted was Cocoa, all he wanted was happiness. So now, faced with an opportunity to advance in the discount retail industry, he felt haunted. He simply did not know what to say to Cecil; however, he knew he had to say something and he had to say it now.

"Fast-track management training program it is, Mr. Douglas," he stated without blinking. He was astonished at how he could lie to Cecil so easily.

***

"I'm quitting, Dionne."

The Sonic Drive-In store manager was counting out a cash drawer when Jimmie Lee abruptly announced he was leaving the night job he had held for the preceding two-and-a-half months. She was awestruck by the information.

"What on Earth are you gonna quit for, Jimmie Lee?" She inquired. "You're one of my best people, if not the best."

"Gotta go," he said.

"And?" She asked, surprised by his curtness.

231

"Just gotta go," he said. Then without warning, he walked to the time clock and punched out. It was eight o'clock.

Confused, Dionne said, "You haven't finished your shift, Jimmie Lee, and it's Friday, our busiest night."

"Gotta go," he said for the third time, walking out of the restaurant and into the night air.

***

"Come go with me, Cocoa."

"Jimmie Lee, I can't just get up and leave like that. I have a son, he's in school; I have a job; my boyfriend gets out of jail in July. I can't just up and leave."

Jimmie Lee had left the Sonic and walked to Cocoa's trailer court, arriving around 8:20. She was surprised by his knock at her door. He'd never come to her place. He knew better. Neighbors might see him and later leak it to her thug of a boyfriend upon his release from the Fort Smith jail where he was serving a 434-day sentence for various petty crimes. She let him in anyway, peering about as he entered, making sure she did not see anyone close by her trailer who might pose a threat as a leak.

He began by telling Cocoa he really did not want the nine-plus million dollars waiting on him unless he could take her back with him. He agreed to take her son too, and later send for the other son living in Phoenix. If he could not get her to go with him, he told her, he would return to drifting instead of going back to Suwanee. Too much sadness back there, he explained. His only lure back to Georgia was her and he wanted her to go with him but she did not seem open to the idea. In fact, she seemed scared by it.

"Tomorrow," Jimmie Lee began, "I'm going to call in sick to Target—I just quit the Sonic job—and go to the bus station in North Little Rock where I'm going to buy three one-way tickets to Georgia. Then I'm coming back to Cedrick's place, pack all my things and head over here. I'm going to knock on your door, wait for you to answer, then ask you if you and the boy are ready to go. If you say 'yes', then we're leaving Little Rock for good. If you say 'no', I'm going back to the bus station, cash in the tickets and buy a single one-way ticket someplace else. I don't have any idea where."

Cocoa knew Jimmie Lee was serious. She knew he loved her. Most troubling for her was that she loved him as well. She was scared though. Her boyfriend, with whom she'd been engaged for over a year, was quite violent. He would find her, she believed, and kill her for leaving him. She thought she loved Black but Jimmie Lee's love for her trumped her own for Black, shaking her to the reality that she did not love Black at all. She feared him and confused her fear with love. They had a son together, for God's sake. She couldn't leave, even though she knew she should. Black was no good for her. She did not realize it at first. That was six years ago. As his nasty side unfolded, she knew she'd made a huge mistake hooking up with him. By then she was pregnant with their son, her second child. Her sister in Arizona, fearful that the older son was being exposed to too much violence in the home, came one day and took the boy from Cocoa and carried him back to Phoenix with her. That was three years ago. Now she was being asked to leave Arkansas—for good—with her remaining child. He who asked her loved her, this she knew, but fear, pure, gripping fear, would not let her leave. In spite of Jimmie Lee's seriousness, Cocoa had to think of something, anything, to somehow slow his pace. There was only one answer.

"Jimmie Lee," she started out, her voice lowering to a whisper, "I need to put my son to bed." From the time Jimmie Lee arrived until now—it was 8:35—he had been standing. So too was Cocoa. Her son was engrossed in a cartoon on a cable network that catered to young children. He looked up only briefly, saw it was the nice man who'd been with him and his mom on several occasions recently then went back to the cartoon.

"Have a seat," Cocoa told Jimmie Lee, taking his hand and guiding him to the sofa. "I'll be back in a few." She lightly kissed him on the forehead, then on his nose, then his lips.

"Come on, Mister Man," she said to her son, her voice returning to a normal pitch. "Your bed time was five minutes ago. Thought you got away, didn't ya?" He giggled, then got up off the floor and followed his mom into the rear of the trailer.

She was gone for at least ten minutes. When she returned, she told Jimmie Lee her son liked to hear a couple of songs before he went to bed. She always accommodated him. She enjoyed singing.

Cocoa dipped into the tiny kitchen and returned moments later with two glasses of German Gewurztraminer wine. She handed one to Jimmie Lee who actually did not drink. He asked what it was, she told him, and then he attempted to give it back to her.

"It's okay," she cooed, "at least this one time. It'll relax you." She sat down next to him.

"I'm not a drinker, Cocoa."

"Shh," she told him. "Don't worry, baby, it's light. I won't give you anything that would hurt you." She scooted a little closer to him, held up her glass to offer a toast, he acknowledged the offer, tapped his glass lightly against hers and they both said the same thing at the same time.

"To us," they toasted in unison. The commonality of their thoughts made them laugh.

Cocoa picked up a remote control from a nearby end table and turned off the television. A second remote was on the sofa which she picked up after replacing the first one. She pressed one of its buttons causing the stereo system to come to life. She pressed another button and a homemade oldies CD began playing. It began with the Commodores and their 1976 bombshell, "Just to Be Close to You." She sat the second remote on the table with the first one and scooted even closer to Jimmie Lee, their fully-clothed bodies touching. With her free hand, she rubbed Jimmie Lee's head and kissed him on the cheek, then ear. Her hand left his head long enough to click the light switch on the wall behind the sofa. The room fell dark, illuminated only by the white light from the kitchen and the blue stereo console. She rubbed his head again.

"How's the wine?" She asked in a purr-like tone.

"It's okay," he said, not really having anything else to compare it to.

"Go ahead and kill it," she instructed.

"What do you mean?"

"Just drink it straight down. It won't hurt you. It's light."

The taste of the wine was light, true, but this German-made joy juice was a sneaker, a creeper of sorts, and knocked you to your knees if you aren't careful. Normally one glass would not do it; however, Jimmie Lee was not a drinker. Couple that with Cocoa filling the twelve-ounce glass more than half-way and Jimmie Lee was in for something. Cocoa knew this and intended to capitalize on it.

"There you go, baby," she stated as Jimmie Lee gulped down the rest of the smooth wine. She took his empty glass and sat it on the end table with the two remotes. There was no cocktail table in the room. She sipped on her own glass a few more times and handed it to Jimmie Lee, asking him to finish it off. He almost said no, but then realized he couldn't say no to her, not to Cocoa, the love of his life.

The next song on the CD, a 26-year-old groovy ballad by Blue Magic, began. The song came out a year before Cocoa was born. Her mother listened to it all the time. It eventually grew on Cocoa as well. It was called "Stop to Start" and was beautiful.

Cocoa, dressed in an azure Adidas sweat suit, unzipped the top and removed it. Underneath she donned a sky blue halter top. She kicked off her suede Adidas tennis shoes and sat them aside. With the matching azure sweat pants still on, sock less feet and cute little halter top, Cocoa stretched out on the sofa, placing her head in Jimmie Lee's lap. She felt the hard bulge in his pants as she did so and was elated her efforts were effective thus far. While laying there waiting for the wine to kick in on Jimmie Lee, she began discussing her childhood, detailing her younger years with her mom and dad and sister. She recounted life in Little Rock and her recollections showed she enjoyed the memories. When she was conscious of the fact that Jimmie Lee's bulge had subsided, she scooted up to a sitting position and casually climbed into his lap. Once there, she started a long string of light, playful kisses all over his face, neck, and ears. The bulge quickly returned. She began focusing on his lips with her kisses, probing the inside of his mouth with her warm tongue, tasting the flavor of wine as she did so. In the background, the Spinners replaced Blue Magic with their own 1974 hit, "Love Don't Love Nobody". The wine slowly took its effect on Jimmie Lee. Cocoa knew it eventually would. She moved into the next phase.

She climbed off Jimmie Lee's lap long enough to remove her sweat pants. Under them was a pair of booty shorts, their color matching the halter top. She tossed the pants to the other end of the sofa where they landed atop the sweat shirt. Saying nothing, she unbuckled his belt, undid the button on his jeans, unzipped his pants and reached inside his Hanes boxer shorts, expertly pulling out his concrete-hard penis. Damn, she said to herself, he is definitely from the country. Slithering down on her stomach, her head again in his lap, she began a slow series of soft—very soft—kisses to his phallus, beginning at the base near his hairy testicles and painstakingly moving North to the head of his throbbing love muscle. Once at the head, her kisses turned into light licks, then not so light, then slurps. Sounds came from Jimmie Lee's throat he'd never heard. A warmth inside of him began rising by the second. Cocoa advanced, taking his penis' entire head and about an inch of his shaft into her mouth, moving up and down with perfect timing. Her hands moved to the remaining portion of his shaft and she gripped the 8-inch pole with them both. Slowly she took more of him into her lovely warm mouth, consuming just over half with each downward motion. A surge was moving from within Jimmie Lee's loins, one he had never before experienced and before he could figure out what it was, he lost his breath, a gasp came from his mouth and his penis began spitting hot, molten semen inside of Cocoa's jaws. She slurped and slurped as he ejaculated, swallowing down every drop of the steaming liquid. She thought he would never stop spewing semen. Secretly she wished he wouldn't. After all, Black had to serve three-fourths of his jail sentence of more than 14 months. He had been gone for seven months and she had not cheated on him during this particular jail stay—at least not up until now. Removing Jimmie Lee's still-hard penis from her mouth, she looked up at him to find him out of breath, his head resting in a backwards position on the sofa's top portion. She giggled at the sight.

Getting up, she took him by the hands, helped him up, giggled again as he staggered a bit—either from the wine or blow-job or a combination of both—and led him towards the back of the trailer to the room next to her son's. As they departed, Jimmie Lee recognized "Lady" by the Whispers as the 1980 song played out of two 50-watt speakers in the tiny living room. Less than a minute later, he could barely hear the song because by now he was in Cocoa's darkened bedroom and she'd closed the door once they'd entered.

"Sit on the bed," she told him.

The only light in the room came from the moon as it shined through the only window in the 11 x 14 bedroom. Cocoa found a Zippo lighter and began lighting several candles along the dresser's length, atop a bureau across from the dresser and one each on flanking bedside stands. She reached over, kissed Jimmie Lee on his forehead, and then unbuttoned his shirt, helping him out of it. She had him lay back on the bed, thereafter sliding off his pants. Next she took off his shoes—amazingly his pants were not hindered by them—and his socks. Moving up, she removed his undershirt. He was clad in only his boxers. Looking directly into his eyes, Cocoa slid off her halter top, bringing it down around her waist and on down her legs to her ankles and off one foot at a time. Her breasts were a perfect 34B. She peeled off her booty shorts, revealing silky, smooth black vaginal hair. Jimmie Lee was still lying on the bed, only his legs and feet hanging off the side, gazing unceasingly at Cocoa's wondrous body. His penis was erect again, stretching against the material of his cotton boxers. Cocoa leaned over, removed the boxers, then climbed onto the bed atop Jimmie Lee. She began probing the inside of his mouth again with her luscious, wet tongue, rubbing her naked body against his. Her kisses moved to his chin, neck, chest and stomach. She kissed his pubic region, each upper thigh, sliding off the bed and onto her knees as she worked. Then she took hold of his hardened shaft—using only one hand this time—and kissed his balls over and over before proceeding directly to the tip of his penis. There she greedily began sucking it again, pumping his shaft vigorously as she went. He moaned and groaned. Letting her hand fall away from the shaft, her mouth consumed half and then all of Jimmie Lee's penis with her lips stopping at the base. Her jaws tightened, her mouth became a chicken-choker, and she sucked Jimmie Lee until he again blasted off inside her mouth, filling it with even more semen than before.

Cocoa climbed to her feet as Jimmie Lee lay spent on the bed. He could hardly move. She reached up, pulled back the cover and top sheet and told him to climb in. He did; she followed.

"Stay here tonight," she told him, "and get up early to go handle your business at the bus station. We'll wait here for you, packing our things while you're gone." Then she added, "I'll give you all of me tonight, Jimmie Lee, so you'll know for sure that I love you."

***

The next morning around six, Jimmie Lee called Target—San answered—and told her he was sick and couldn't work. San was taken aback by his call-in, but agreed to relay the message to Cecil. He took a shower, dressed, and headed out without making too much noise. Cocoa never heard him. She was fast asleep; her body fatigued from hours of sex the night before. She took him to places he never knew existed, having vaginal sex with him four times. Each time he ejaculated; twice she experienced orgasm. On the last encounter, though, an inaudible explosion inside of her took place but she didn't know it yet. The explosion occurred when one of Jimmie Lee's millions of sperm collided with one of her eggs. This collision happened in spite of her being on The Pill. It is well-settled; however, that The Pill is not 100%. The explosion—conception—just proved it.

***

Ninety minutes after Jimmie Lee left Cocoa's place, he arrived via taxi to the North Little Rock bus terminal. He walked from Cocoa's trailer to his rented room on Victoria, packed all personal possessions he had—except his two Target smocks and three Sonic Drive-In uniforms—and sat them in two small suitcases at the front door. He woke Cedrick up, paid him a month's rent in case he had trouble finding a new boarder and then left without explaining why. On his way out the door, he yelled back to Cedrick to call the city cab company and have them send a taxi to the Wal-Mart two blocks up. Cedrick agreed. Jimmie Lee walked to the discount store, bought a small box of "Thank You" cards, and then went outside to wait on his

240

taxi. He filled out the cards—5 in all—to Brother Dale at Geyer Springs Church of Christ, Cecil at Target, Dionne at Sonic, Cedrick and Cocoa. The first four had the same end-note, penciled in by Jimmie Lee before he signed his name, saying "Sorry I'm leaving so abruptly." The one to Cocoa was different: "You made the right choice." He would mail the other ones once he got back to Suwanee; Cocoa would get hers today. Minutes later, the taxi arrived to take him to North Little Rock.

***

Jimmie Lee's taxi pulled up to the door of Cocoa's trailer. He instructed the cabbie to leave the fare meter running. Jimmie Lee dashed out, skipped the first step, then the third, onto the trailer's small porch. He knocked, failing to notice Cocoa's car was gone. He knocked again, a bit excited. No answer. First he wondered if she was still asleep, then he looked through the tiny window of the front door, noticing the living room's light was turned on. It wasn't when he left. He knocked once more. Still no answer. He looked around briefly, really eyeing for a nosy neighbor, when he realized Cocoa's Ford Probe was not in its parking space. He became baffled by this discovery, then slowly began to come to grips with the reality of what was going on: Cocoa got cold feet. Knowing it was useless, believing no one was inside, he continued knocking.

Someone, however, was inside. Two people actually. Cocoa's son was still fast asleep, his door closed, shut out from the knocking. Cocoa was sitting on the floor, Indian-style, just feet from the boy's bedroom. She was crying, crying as she reflected on the last three months, the happiest months of her entire life. Her cries turned into sobs as she reflected on her decision the night before to use sex to deceive Jimmie Lee, to make him think she'd

241

leave with him, to ease his mind. She had to slow his pace—his so very serious pace—and sex was the only answer she knew. Her sobbing turned into wailing as she realized how hurt Jimmie Lee would be, seeing her car gone, thinking she was gone, unaware that she'd gotten up an hour ago and hid the car a block away, walking back in bedroom slippers and a sweat suit. She thought about Black, that he'd find her, kill her. Cocoa's tears poured like rain in Hong Kong, slob ran from her mouth as she whimpered uncontrollably, unable to stop. She went from her sitting position into a tiny ball on the floor. There was no way for her to escape the excruciating pain she now felt. No escape whatsoever.

Outside, Jimmie Lee stopped knocking. He could not hear the crying, the sobbing, and the wailing. He knew nothing of the pain that ripped through the insides of the love of his life. His unanswered knocks were all he knew. He turned to leave. Before descending the four wooden steps, he reached into his back pocket, pulled out the "Thank You" cards, found Cocoa's , opened it and stared at it, then turned back around, stepped up to the front door and stuck the card—without an envelope—inside the door's mail slot, hearing it fall to the uncarpeted living room floor. He paused a moment, released the mail slot from his fingers, turned and walked off the porch. Before getting into the taxi, he looked at the trailer apartment once more before whispering a sentence that only he could hear.

"I was talking about the other choice, not this one, but thanks anyway."

Jimmie Lee climbed into the rear seat of the awaiting taxi. He looked lost, saddened by the absence of Cocoa and her son in the cab with him.

"Back to the bus station," were the only words he had for the driver. The tears that rolled down his face were without words.

CHAPTER 33

Sunday, April 16, 2000
Downtown Miami, Florida

The Royalton Hotel, with its 46-year history, was an imposing piece of architecture. It took up half of a downtown city block beginning on the corner of Second Avenue and stretching to the center of the avenue going towards Third. The lobby was spectacular with its high ceiling, gigantic chandelier and plush couches and lounging chairs, all made of hand-stitched white leather. The marble floor was brilliant, the Oriental rugs that covered it in various places appeared new, and the walls were expertly painted Paris green. The guest services counter, also marble, ran the length of the western portion of the lobby. Everything inside was so clean and neat that it all actually seemed brand spanking new. This sensational hotel was well worth its $155-per-night price tag.

Dee checked in yesterday evening. He paid for just five days, hoping to locate a flat or a room for rent within a private residence. His reception was warm and friendly.

"Bien venido!" The Cuban guest services clerk welcomed. "Habla usted espaniol?"

"Si, un poquito," responded Dee to the clerk's inquiry as to whether he could speak Spanish, letting the clerk know he could but not very well.

Exercising another option the clerk inquired, "Habla usted ingles?"

"Yes," Dee replied, relieved. "I speak English very well."

The clerk too seemed a bit relieved, and then began a fairly good job of communicating in Dee's native language. He confirmed the Virginia doctor's reservation, collected $787.50 for five nights' stay plus tax, and then handed him his card-key. A bellhop assisted Dee with his suitcases and the two took one of the elevators to the fourth floor. Dee's room—Suite 462—was a long walk from the elevators. The long hallway, its shag carpeting, its oil paintings on the walls between suites—all of this seemed to lessen the long ness of the stroll. Inside the hotel suite, Dee tipped the bellhop with five bucks and waved him out.

"Muchas gracias, Senor," thanked the bellhop.

"No hay de que," Dee answered, telling the young man not to mention it,

Dee unpacked, skipped supper and went to bed.

***

Today he toured downtown Miami on foot, trailed off into a rough area called Overtown adjacent to downtown, befriended a couple of prostitutes near a convenience store, thereafter making his way to a nearby Metro rail station. From there he went back downtown, grabbed a bite to eat from a street vendor and looked for a public telephone. He called his agent, Kristle Gray Hill, telling her he arrived safely and then promptly ended the call. He made a second call—to the home of Juan Ruiz at the

University of Miami—to set up an appointment in his hotel that night. Mr. Ruiz preferred weekend meetings.

***

Thursday morning, April 20, Dee checked out of the Royalton and moved into a private house in Opa Locka, a city with rich Arabian historical ties. He rented a room from a Panamanian-born woman named Yvette Quinn who'd placed an ad in the Miami Herald. The room, a 15-by-20 with a walk-in closet and private bath, cost $100 a week. It was perfect for Dee, although he could not immediately get used to all the shades of purple. The walls were amethyst—an odd color for walls, he felt—and the carpet was lilac. Even the headboard to the bed was heliotrope; prompting Dee to wonder how such a color could be acquired on the open market. Everything else was white. A bit girlified even still, he felt. All in all, though, Dee was satisfied, comfortable. That is all that really mattered.

That afternoon, following a short nap, Dee set up his laptop, pulled out some documents he got from Juan Ruiz, got comfy and began typing. He had twenty-nine chapters done so far. The book would have a total of thirty-six. The book would make him rich. Or, bring him down.

CHAPTER 34
Early-May, 2000
Dade County, Florida

Jimmie Lee had been gone from Little Rock for a wee bit over two weeks. Every day that passed brought thoughts of Cocoa. She was inside his head every waking moment. He did not want to leave her behind; however, in the end, the choice was no longer his. It was hers and she made it. He had to live with that choice, irrespective of how hard it was to live with. He loved her, this much he was sure of, but he questioned her love for him, for if she truly loved him like he thought, she would have left with him. Deep down, he wanted to talk to her one last time, to tell her everything was okay, that there were no hard feelings. He wanted to hear her voice one last time.

***

"Welcome back, Miss Ford," greeted Roberta Marina, owner of Roberta's Hair Palace in Little Rock. "It's been almost two-and-a-half weeks. You okay, gal?"

"Yes ma'am," stated Cocoa. "I was bad off sick and could barely move. I even went to the hospital." Her lies were convincing.

"So I hear," stated Roberta. "But you're okay now, right? I mean, you're ready to return to work?"

"Yes ma'am." Cocoa was not sure if she was ready but she had to make money somehow and sitting at home going through daily crying spells was not going to do it. She had a son to tend to, a boyfriend to send money to each month. She averaged a weekly net of $476. She needed to get back to work to catch up.

This morning, Cocoa had an appointment with a teen named "Shaunta". The 17-year-old wanted a perm-and-style and a light tint. Cocoa would receive half of the $46.80 cost. Later, the stylist had a "Thad" who needed a hair cut, and a "Stephanie" who wanted to increase the length of her hair by six inches. No others were scheduled; the work day would be light.

"Miss Ford, line two; Miss Ford, line two, please," said a male voice over the hair salon's intercom system. It sounded like the new guy—Cocoa could not recall his name—who worked in the back office catering to Ms. Marina's every command.

Picking up a nearby telephone, Cocoa saluted the unknown caller in her usual style, simply stating her name with a smile in her voice.

"Hello, Cocoa, how are you?" It was Jimmie Lee. He sounded distant, not just in voice but in mileage too.

"Jimmie Lee!" Cocoa shouted ecstatically. "Where in God's name in the world are you?!"

"In a small place between Carol City and Liberty City," he answered. "Opa Locka, Florida, specifically."

"Florida?" She repeated, calming down somewhat. "So you really didn't go back to Georgia?"

"Nope," he said in a flat tone. "Told ya that."

"I know, Jimmie Lee. Listen, I'm really sorry—"

"No, no, Cocoa," he interrupted. "Don't say that. You made a choice. I accept your choice. Don't feel like you have to apologize 'cause you don't. You don't owe me an explanation for anything you choose to—"

"But I do, Jimmie Lee," she insisted.

"Naw you don't, baby," he said mildly. "I love you for being you, for being honest with yourself and honest with me. I'll always love you for that."

Cocoa began to cry.

"No, no, baby," he soothed her. "Don't cry. It's okay. Everything's okay."

Through tears, she tried to speak; however, they were flowing so freely now that it was too difficult to form her words. She wanted to stop crying—at least long enough to say something comforting to Jimmie Lee, something apologetic enough to make sure her conscious would be clear—but her cries were nowhere near an end. Apparently Jimmie Lee felt so too.

"After you get this cry out," he said, "don't cry anymore. Everything is okay. I'll always love you. You were being honest. You don't owe me anything. So, don't cry for me again."

"Jim—, Jimmie Lee," she forced out. "I love you."

"I love you too, baby," his voice cracking, "but right now I gotta go."

"No, please, don't—"

"I gotta go, baby. Enjoy your life, Cocoa. Enjoy your life." With that, he hung up.

"Nooooo!" Cocoa cried, clutching the phone ever-so-tight and becoming so weak in the knees that she slithered to the floor. "Nooooo!" She repeated over and over. But Jimmie Lee was gone, gone forever, and could hear her no more.

CHAPTER 35

Mother's Day, 2000
Opa Locka, Florida

The chime of the cellular phone pulled Dee from his sleep. He rolled, grabbed it off the night stand and hit the Power button.

"Dr. Powell," he answered with sleep I his voice.

"Good morning, Doctor," greeted a warm Panamanian woman. The voice was that of Ms. Quinn, his landlady. "The early bird catches the worm."

"What time is it?" Dee asked.

"Almost 7:30."

"What can I do for you, Ms. Quinn?"

"Step outside, if you don't mind."

"Step outside?" He asked. "Now?"

"If you don't mind, Doctor," she replied. "I'm in the white minivan in front of the house."

Dee, with phone still in hand, climbed out of the comfort of his bed and walked to the window. He saw the van.

"I'm coming out," he said into the phone before pressing the off button. He tossed it on the bed, retrieved a pajama shirt from the dresser drawer—he already had pajama pants on—and headed to the front door.

"Good morning again, Dr. Powell," greeted Ms. Quinn as Dee reached the passenger-side door. Her mother was sitting up front. Dee recognized her from a brief introduction a week earlier.

"You already know my momma," she began, "and this young lady in the back is Nicky."

Dee looked in the back of the vehicle. His discovery took his breath away. There was a beautiful young lady around twenty years old holding a small child. She was clad in a cadmium Enyce halter top with matching short-shorts, a pair of wooden slides with an apricot strap across the top bearing the Fubu logo, and a tangerine hat with a very wide brim that tilted on the right corner, a red-orange feather extending from its fire-orange band. The hat was also an Enyce original. Her eyes formed a Chinese-look, although she was far from Asian. Big, bold brown eyes dazzled in the morning heat, a perfect nose followed, then a set of luscious lips topped with gloss. Dimples were implanted in each cheek. Four silvery earrings—each with a unique design—graced each ear. Looking her up and down again, he saw the navel ring—also silvery—that complimented her seemingly perfectly round belly button.

"So, Doctor, you gonna say something or just stare?" Ms. Quinn inquired, chuckling.

"Sorry," apologized Dee. "My name is Deloren Powell. Call me Dee." He reached inside the van, extending his arm in the space between the passenger-side door and passenger seat, so he could shake Nicky's hand. It was warm and smooth. He was swooning.

"Nice to meet you, Dee." She smiled. Her teeth were straight and even, perfect and white, an accent accompanying her words. She sounded Jamaican or African.

Ms. Quinn cleared her throat. "Listen, Doctor, today is Mother's Day. We have to go to the market. We should be back in an hour. Why don't you freshen up and get yourself together. When we come back, we're going to drop Nicky off here so you can treat her to a Mother's Day brunch or something. She's a nice girl, a mature young lady. What do you say, Doctor?"

How could Dee resist? He couldn't, actually. He knew so, and so did Ms. Quinn. Nicky, on a scale of 1-to-10, was an 11.

"I'd love to fix her a nice Mother's Day brunch," he replied. "I only ask that you give me two hours. I have to run to the grocer."

"It's a deal," Ms. Quinn happily said as she started up the engine. "We'll see you around 9:30, 9:45 at the latest." The she added, "You can let go of her hand now."

***

Her name was Nicky Phoenix. She was 23 years old and originally from Christ Church, Barbados. A former University of the West Indies student, she dropped out in 1997 after two years to come to the United States where she joined her sister, Brina, who was already living in South Florida. Nicky met a guy named Earl who swept her off her feet, got her pregnant, and then dumped her eight months into her pregnancy. She gave birth to her son, Carl, who would turn two in less than a month. Her mother, Audrey Phoenix-Banyo, and father, Calvin Banyo, remain in Barbados with Nicky's two brothers and a half-sister. The 130-pound beauty with her five-foot-seven-inch body is an illegal alien and has been working as an exotic dancer for more than a year. She and her son, along with their small dog, Jane, live in an efficiency apartment on Opa Locka's Dunad Avenue.

Dee sat across from her in the Sharar Avenue house's spacious Florida room off from the kitchen, listening as she gave him the run-down of her life, admiring her beauty all the while, including the long hair that ran down her back, the tattoo of a bottle of Barbadian rum on her left arm and the tongue ring he missed when he met her earlier that morning. Her accent added to her flawless looks—making her appear even more beautiful—enough that Dee decided she was a "12" instead of an "11".

The two of them—Carl stayed with Ms. Quinn—enjoyed a tasty brunch that included lean beef steak, puffed rice and green peas. Nicky even ate like a "12", using table etiquette that appeared to come from Ms. Manners herself.

Dee was impressed with everything about her with two exceptions: her illegal alien status and current occupation. He decided to pry.

"Why haven't you attempted to get a Green Card?"

"Too much hassle, too many questions."

"But you've got a son; you don't want to get arrested and risk being separated from him."

"That won't happen," she said as she stood to clear the table, "because I have mechanisms in place to insure his safe-keeping."

"I see," Dee stated, rising to give her a hand with the dishes. "When do you plan on trying to make your status here legal?"

"When I find a husband," she said, smiling at Dee as they stood in front of the kitchen sink, filling it with soapy water. "I want to get married."

"You've been here almost three years. Surely you could have married by now. Look at you: You're the perfect specimen of a woman."

"Thanks," she said, smiling even more, then added, "but I'm looking for love too. My future husband has to love me, has to be in love with me."

Who couldn't fall in love with you? He asked himself. She read his look and was curious about his thoughts.

"What?" She asked. "What just went through your mind, Deloren?"

"I prefer 'Dee'."

"Sorry, Dee." She began washing the dishes. He ran fresh, luke-warm water in the second sink to rinse the dishes as she finished washing them. "So what were you thinking just then?"

Honesty swept over him, so he told her.

"That was a very kind thought," she responded.

***

Finishing up Chapter 32 of his book, Dee immediately started on Chapter 33. Usually he waited for more research data to be compiled—aside from the voluminous amount he already possessed—but he was on a roll, he was feeling it, so he kept going. It was late—11:45 at night—and he had been working for more than four hours non-stop. Carl, Nicky's son, was asleep on the bed. Dee now kept him while Nicky worked. Her 3 days on-3 days off schedule did not conflict with his own since she worked late, going in at six each evening and getting off when the strip joint closed at four-thirty in the morning. Most of the time, like tonight, Carl was asleep by 7:30 p.m.—he was up around six-thirty each morning—and Dee used that quiet time to work on his third book.

Dee and Nicky had drawn exceptionally close in recent weeks. He kissed her for the first time a week after they met. When she was off, the trio spent a lot of time on 22ⁿᵈ Street, Miami's hottest shopping strip, eating lunch and/or dinner in the area following a day of spending. He was falling for her—and hard. Last week, after knowing her just two weeks, he told himself—but not her—that he was in love. Imagine that. Deloren Powell in love. He never thought it possible. His career meant so much to him; his desire to write a bestseller before choosing a mate meant just as much. Their closeness both scared and excited him at the same time. Yet something inside of him told him to plunge forward, follow his heart and make a decision as to what he should do. Before he could ask himself what should he do, the answer was upon him.

Dee shut down the laptop, packed away all his papers and notes, and climbed into bed, making sure he didn't awaken Carl. His efforts to fall asleep were futile at first, but sleep did eventually come. When he last looked at the clock, it read 2:15 a.m. It was Saturday, May 27.

***

Petruska's Jewelers sat on the corner of 22ⁿᵈ Street and 105ᵗʰ Avenue. The proprietor was the great-grandson of a pair of emigrants from Czechoslovakia who, during World War II, decided America was the place to be. They immigrated with their two children and the family's life savings, $320 in cash and 16 quarter-carat diamonds. Vaclav and his wife, Stanislavina, never looked back. Their one-location jewelry business recently entered its 58th year and 1999 revenues hit an all-time high of $48.5 million.

Dee caught a taxi from Opa Locka to Miami, arriving in less than twenty minutes. His mood was such that he tipped the driver with a twenty-dollar bill. He walked into Petruska's just as it opened.

"Good morning," Dee greeted. "My name is Dr. Deloren Powell. I'm from Virginia and am here doing the final touches on my next book."

"Welcome to Miami," the proprietor began. "I hope your stay has been pleasant thus far."

"Indeed it has."

"What can I help you with, Dr. Powell?"

"I would like to buy a ring, an engagement ring, possibly a trio set."

"And the price range, Doctor?"

"A thousand dollars, sir."

"Okay," stated the proprietor, somewhat expecting a higher range. "White gold, yellow gold, sterling silver, platinum—what's your flavor?"

"Well," Dee pondered. "I guess white gold would be fine."

"Step over here sir," the jeweler instructed, walking a few feet away to a case of wedding bands and engagement rings. "The bands here are priced up to $200 and the engagement rings run $900 to $1100 a piece. We'll make you the perfect trio set and deduct ten percent for the joint purchase."

While Dee examined the elegant gems through the glass case, he thought back to how he picked Nicky for her ring size. She had arrived at his place around 5:15 this morning, took a shower, then woke up Carl to get him bathed and clothed. The three of them had breakfast at the house, during which Dee jokingly told Nicky her fingers looked fat. She laughed it off and said she only wore a size 6. Dee got the info he needed. She and Carl went home around eight o'clock; Dee forthwith dressed and called a taxi. Now, here he stood, trying to find a simple but elegant ring for her. That's when he noticed it: A white gold, five-diamond engagement ring. A half-carat stone sat in the center flanked by two quarter-carat stones. The ring did not have to be matched up with bands. It had its own: two plain, smooth-edged white gold bands. The price tag was a comfortable $978.00.

"Right here!" Dee exclaimed. "I want this set right here!"

The jeweler was wiping a case's top surface when Dee yelled; however, the excitement seemed not to move the man who was used to customers doing that. He laid the cloth down, wiped his hands with some paper towels, and then reached into his vest pocket for a set of small keys, using one to unlock the case within which Dee peered.

"Right there," Dee said, calming down somewhat.

"Okay, Dr. Powell, let's put the set in your hands so you can feel the rings to make sure they are the ones you truly desire."

"Huh?" Dee questioned.

The proprietor laughed. "It's a jeweler's thing."

"I'll take them," Dee told him. "I don't need to feel them. I want them. Size six. MasterCard, Visa, Discover, American Express—take your pick."

"Okay, Doctor," the jeweler stated. "Let's go ahead and take care of everything for you."

***

Juan's, a tasteful American restaurant in South Miami Beach, was a popular spot for large gatherings. At a table capable of seating eight were Dee, Nicky, her sister here in Florida, Ms. Quinn and, of course, Carl. Dee summoned everyone to meet at Juan's for lunch, talking Nicky into calling her sister. Nicky questioned the request. Dee told her he simply wanted to meet her stateside family member. He'd already spoken with her mother and half-sister via telephone.

Just as lunch was arriving—consisting of a combination of dishes that included lamb chops, veal cutlets, uncooked burger, corn tortillas, sweet yellow corn, steamed eggplants and a whole lemon meringue pie—Dee took a fork and lightly tapped a glass, gaining everyone's attention except Carl who was already feasting on a bottle of whole milk in his high-chair.

"Brina, Ms. Quinn, I called you here as witnesses to a spectacular moment in my life. Nicky, I called you here because you're the subject that has made this moment spectacular. Ladies," he paused briefly to look at Carl, "and young man, I'd like to first read a poem by Virginia poet Robert Morgan Bennett. It's called "With All My Heart'." Dee stood for the reading; he slipped a small piece of notebook paper, folded in quarters, from inside his suit jacket. His romantic 20-second reading went as follows:

> With all my heart, on this day, I give to you my love. With all my heart, I kneel and pray, I give to you my love. With all my heart, I stand and say, I give to you my love. And with all

259

> my heart, forever and a day, I'll give to you my love."

He re-folded the paper, handed it to Nicky, then reached inside his suit jacket's other inside pocket. Out came a brown jewelry box with a "P" emblazoned in chartreuse on its top lid; thin electroplated gold trimming separated the top lid from the bottom. Dee moved his chair back a yard and got down on one knee, turning towards Nicky—Carl was at his rear—and thereupon opened the box that held all three rings.

Nicky gasped, her sister and Ms. Quinn were speechless and wide-eyed, Dee was smiling.

"With all my heart, Nicky Phoenix, I give to you my love. Will you return to Virginia with me and marry me?"

Nicky swallowed hard, looked at her sister, looked back at Dee, then broke into a tearful smile.

"Yes, Dee."

***

Memorial Day rolled around two days following Dee's proposal to Nicky. Ironically, the two still had not yet engaged in sexual intercourse. Nicky wanted to on the night of the proposal; however, Dee dissuaded her. He told her he wanted to wait until the two of them got married in Virginia. They would be returning in less than two weeks. Nicky was impressed with Dee's traditional values. So when he suggested they take in the vast Memorial Day parade held each year in Coral Gables, she was delighted to do so. After all, it was her first time since coming to the U. S. in 1997 attending any type of Memorial Day affair.

One of the parade's performing groups was the Coconut Grove Adult Basic Education Center. Featured was a team of dancers, all of whom recently received their GEDs from the ABE Center. They did a stellar performance. Dee commented on their skills.

"Talent runs from one end of the spectrum to the other. Whether you get a GED, high school diploma or nothing at all, talent can still find its way inside of you. When I got my GED, I knew I had other talents and I promised myself I would never let them go to waste."

Nicky was intently listening as he talked and something caused her to look baffled.

"Wait a sec, Dee," she said. "I thought you graduated from high school with honors."

"I did," he answered.

"But you just said you got a GED."

"No I didn't."

"Yes you did."

Dee looked strange. "Did I really say a GED?"

"Yeah," she replied.

"Oh, I'm sorry," he stated. "I meant my high school diploma."

***

"Dee," called Nicky from his bedroom, "where's your laptop? I've never seen it. You work here in this cooped up bedroom and no one ever gets a sneak preview of your next book."

Dee came out of the bathroom, wiping his face with a towel after shaving, and gave Nicky a weird gaze.

"I—I sent it out," he told her.

"What do you mean?"

"I mailed it home. I finished the book so I mailed the final manuscript and the laptop home to have my agent start on the publishing preparations."

"Why mail the laptop?"

Dee appeared intimidated by the line of questioning, responding, "Because I wanted to."

Nicky noticed the change in his intonation and decided—at first—to let it go. For some reason, though, she changed her mind.

"When did you mail it out?"

"Yesterday," he snapped. "Why?"

"Just asking," she said. "Dee?"

"What?! He nearly shouted.

"You don't have to get upset, Dee," she informed him. "I was just asking 'cause I've never seen a laptop close up before.

"Sorry, Nicky," he said as he walked out of the bedroom.

Nicky said nothing, sitting there, wondering, trying to piece this together. Something was amiss. She could not figure out what. What she did know was that Dee did not mail out his laptop yesterday. Yesterday was Memorial Day and the post office was closed. She made a mental note of the conversation and the issue about him earning a GED instead of a high school diploma.

***

Wednesday evening, Nicky prepared for work an hour earlier than her normal time. She was going to first head to an Internet café a few miles from her job. After doing a bit of research she would go on to the club. She was dressed in a khaki and lemon soft leather mini-dress by Guess and a pair of saffron lo-cut boots designed by Mecca. A drab handbag by Polo—its strap fawn—was draped over her shoulder. She drove the four blocks—two down and two over—to Dee's place and dropped Carl off.

The Internet café was tucked away between two other businesses—a wine seller and a job placement satellite office—near 4th Street and 99th Avenue. Nicky worked at the strip club at 7th Street and 105th Avenue about four-and-a-half miles away. She had plenty of time on her hands, gave the attendant ten bucks for the one-hour sitting and logged on.

She tapped into the website for the Library of Congress and clicked on U. S. Copyright Office. From there she keyed the title of a book, The Psychological Effects of Brown versus Board of Education, and waited for a response. Less than a minute later, the search request concluded. The result: Not Found. She then keyed the title of another book, The Psychological Implications of Promoting a Non-Existent God. Her wait for a response for this search request also took close to a minute. When it concluded, the result appeared on the screen: Not Found.

She grabbed her handbag without logging off and left the café. Her facial expression told it all: Who is Dr. Deloren Powell?

***

By Friday, June 2, Nicky had conducted more research on her fiancé. She went back to that Internet café to search alumni records, including year books, and failed to locate any student with Dee's name having attended the College of William & Mary. There were several dozen Powell's over the years but none named Deloren. The closest she came was Delano and he was Caucasian. She was not sure what was going on, yet she was in fact sure that Dee had a past, a dark one, one he wanted to hide and keep hidden. She was also sure she no longer trusted him with her son and decided to re-hire her former sitter. She justified the move to Dee by telling him the girl could not find any work. He went for it.

The next morning, instead of going to pick up Carl after work, she called the sitter and asked her to keep him a few hours longer than usual. The teen agreed. Nicky then drove back to the all-night Internet café and bought an hour's time. She sat down and started her mission. She searched residences in Virginia looking for any Deloren Powell in the state. There were none. She found a Delorna Powell in Portsmouth, Dee's home town, and wrote down the telephone number. The woman's address was listed as 1516 Darren Circle. Nicky chose not to write down the address. She paused her surfing mission long enough to find a public telephone. She pumped in four quarters for three minutes of talk-time and dialed the number.

"Hello," answered a groggy voice after several rings.

"Delorna? Delorna Powell?" Nicky inquired.

"Yes, this is she," the woman acknowledged.

"I apologize for calling you at five-thirty in the morning but I need to get in contact with your brother. It's an emergency."

"Which brother?"

"Deloren."

"Who?"

"Deloren Powell, your twin brother."

"You got the wrong person. I don't have any brothers; just one younger sister who'll be 50 in three more months."

"Ma'am," Nicky stated sincerely, "I'm very, very sorry to have awakened you." Nicky then hung up. She picked the receiver up one more. This time she dialed Dee's cell number. He answered on the third ring.

"Dr. Deloren Powell; good morning," he answered.

"Dr. Deloren Powell," she said, mocking him, "this is your fiancée. We need to talk. I'm on the way to your place now." She hung up before he could respond.

When she arrived to the Sharar Avenue house, Dee was standing in the front doorway waiting. He looked tired; not a sleepy-type tired but a weary one. They walked into his bedroom together.

"Dee," Nicky began. "I know you say you love me, but—" she paused "—you're a ghost."

"I'm a what?" He asked incredulously.

"A ghost," she repeated. "I can't find anything on you. I tried the university you attended, the Copyright Office in D. C., even searching your name. Nothing."

Dee became angry. "What the hell are you doing? You're checking up on me?!"

"We're getting married," she countered. "I have a right—"

"You have a right to nothing! You're an illegal alien, a stripper. You don't have any right to check on me!"

"But Dee, you have to understand—"

"Bullshit!" He shouted. "I don't want to talk to you anymore! Just leave! Now!"

"Dee, listen to me," she said as she softened her voice. "Whatever you're hiding, tell me. I can handle—"

"Get out, Nicky!" He screamed. "Get the hell out!"

Nicky left. Dee stood there in the middle of his bedroom looking a bit crazy. He was trembling, sweating and breathing quite hard. He began walking in small circles, mumbling inaudibly. He appeared confused, worried. Seeing Nicky from his window as she drove away hurt him, hurt him bad; nevertheless, he had to get it together. He had to or his entire world would come crumbling down.

Meanwhile, Nicky had other things on her agenda. She drove to 22nd Street to Petruska's Jewelers with the intention of waiting for it to open. She would try to find out if the man who bought her rings paid cash or whether he paid by check or charged it. When she got to the jewelry store, she checked the hours of operation. To her surprise, it was closed on Saturday and Sunday. She drove away, now heading to Ms. Quinn's place on Baghdad back in Opa Locka. Five minutes into her departure, something else hit her like stone: Dee said he bought the rings the same day he proposed. That was a week ago today. That, she realized, was a Saturday. Petruska's, however, was closed that day. Yet another lie.

It was around 8 o'clock when Nicky pulled up in front of Ms. Quinn's home. Maybe Ms. Quinn could give some input.

"Well, hello, my darling," the woman greeted upon opening the door. "Come in, please."

"Ms. Quinn, I need your help," stated Nicky the moment she stepped foot into the house.

"Sure," Ms. Quinn replied. "What do you need?"

"Do you remember seeing Dee's ID when he rented the room?"

"He paid cash, Nicky. Why do you ask?"

"Do you remember seeing his laptop?"

"No."

"Ms. Quinn, I don't think Dee is who he says he is."

"No men ever are, darling," answered Ms. Quinn, sitting down in the living room. "But what do you care? He loves you, he wants to marry you, and he's got money. Marry him, get your papers and come back to Florida in six months."

"But, Ms. Quinn, he's a ghost."

Ms. Quinn laughed. "Then call him 'Casper'."

"No, seriously, Ms. Quinn, I can't find out anything on him, anything at all."

"Maybe he works for the CIA. Who knows? Hell, who cares?"

"I do."

"Don't worry about it, Nicky. Go back to Virginia with him, marry him and then pick a big fight six months later and storm out the house with the boy. Call me and let me know you're coming. I'll pick you up from the airport."

Ms. Quinn stood up and headed to the front door. Nicky followed the cue.

"Ms. Quinn, aren't you concerned at all?"

"I am concerned about only one thing—you getting your papers to stay in America—and only that one thing. To hell with the rest! Marry him, cook him big meals, give him coochie every night and in six months come back to Florida."

As Nicky stepped out onto the porch, she turned one last time.

"Ms. Quinn, one more question: Other than Petruska's, what jeweler do you know with Saturday hours?"

"Lots of 'em."

"Any of them begin with a 'P'?"

"Just one," she answered. "Patterson's."

Nicky was surprised. "That's a grocery store."

"True," Ms. Quinn acknowledged. "But they have a jewelry store inside called 'Patterson's' as well. They sell real fine costume jewelry; nothing over two hundred bucks."

***

At 11 a.m. Dee walked the few blocks to the Opa Locka post office. He had a box there and was awaiting a package. He hoped it was there. If it wasn't, he would have to wait until Monday. He could not wait until then. He needed the package right fucking now! His future—and his life—depended on it.

CHAPTER 36
Saturday Afternoon
June 3, 2000
Dade County

Andy had lived in one other state—Arkansas—while on the run from the law. His stay in President Clinton's former stomping grounds was quiet and inconspicuous. No one even suspected Andy Smith was in the state. There he meticulously plotted his getaway. His goal was to leave the country and enter a non-extraditable nation. He chose Morocco. He learned the moment he arrived in Arkansas that all his accounts were frozen. The only monies he had when he left Virginia were $5,120 from a small checking account at Bank of America. He has since lived as frugal as he could. When his underworld connections from his years in prison gave him the go-ahead, he made his way to South Florida. Here he would pay $3,000 for a new identity, travel documents and tickets out of the country. He did just that. His run from the law would come to an end this coming Monday morning as he would board an airplane in Miami that would soon after end in New York City and ultimately end in Fez, Morocco. By now he was out of money—with only $51.30 to his name—and was more than ready to make his great escape.

Today, after having settled in a small city in Dade County several weeks ago, Andy would visit a nearby U. S. Post Office to check on whether his getaway items were there. He prayed they would be; if not, his plan would have to be re-drafted and he'd have to start from scratch. This was dangerous with so many authorities on the hunt for him, including Portsmouth Police, Virginia State Police and the FBI. But as long as his P. O. Box held the anticipated items, he was good to go or, better yet, as good as gone.

Arriving at the post office around ten minutes past eleven, Andy noticed the facility was practically empty, save for two men. Both, like Andy, were inside checking p. o. boxes. Both, like Andy, were in their 30's. One looked a few years younger; the other a couple years older. All three were African-American. And all three shared a common aura: they seemed troubled, anxious. Andy briefly put the other men out his mind and made his way to Box Number 514, pulling the long amber key from his pocket and inserting it into the box's lock. He paused, then took a breath, then turned the key to unlock the box. There was one package inside, a large ecru envelope measuring 9x12" in size and a half-inch in thickness which Andy hurriedly pulled out. No return address was on it, yet extra postage was, insuring it would make it to its intended destination and its intended recipient. He promptly exited the U. S. Post Office, taking notice that the other two men held packages as they left. One looked buff; the other, beige. At least that's what the colors looked like in the distance since Andy was seriously on the move.

Back at his Dade County hideaway, he tore open the envelope like a child tears open a Christmas gift. Inside were the following: a new Moroccan passport bearing his picture and the name Mohammed Jettou Bey; an international driver's license in his new name and issued from France, Morocco's closest ally; two additional forms of picture-identification, including a Casablanca library card and a Fez-based health insurance company benefits card; and, finally, a round-trip airline ticket to Morocco paper clipped to a travel itinerary. Andy, upon seeing the ticket, began crying tears of joy. He was free, finally.

Andy was slated to board a U. S. Airways flight from Miami International Airport Monday morning at 5:01, fly to Jacksonville for refueling, then on to Atlanta's Hartsfield International Airport. In Atlanta he would switch planes, have one stop-over in Charlotte, North Carolina, then on to JFK International Airport in New York City. Once in the Big Apple, he would de-board the U. S. Airways and board an Air France flight to Frankfurt at Rhein/Main Airport. After re-fueling in Germany, Andy would stay on that plane and fly to Paris. From Paris, Andy would board a Royal Air Moroc to Fez. The flights would consume fifteen hours of his time. He had no complaints. He was slated to arrive in Fez on Tuesday morning at 1:00, counting the five-hour time zone difference.

Andy, nevertheless, noticed one problem: gate fees. He did not have enough cash to cover them—seven in all—and would need an additional hundred bucks to do so. He had half that. He knew no one nearby. His only option: call in a favor.

He picked up the telephone receiver then put it back down. He picked it up again and again he returned the receiver to its cradle. Pausing at least a minute, Andy once more picked up the phone, this time dialing a number. It rang twice. She answered.

"Praise the Lord!" Greeted Shardae Pearson, Andy's former chief financial officer when he ran TSE.

"Praise the Lord?" Andy questioned. "I must have the wrong number. I was looking for Shardae Pear—"

"This is she," interrupted Shardae. "With whom am I speaking?"

"This is Andy, uh, Andrew Smith," he replied.

There was silence.

"Hello?" Andy said.

"Mr. Smith?" She inquired, her tone moving from religiously joyful to serious.

"Shardae, I know you've seen the news reports but I'm innocent. It wasn't like that. It was totally self-defense."

"Mr. Smith, I'm saved now. I gave my life to Christ almost three months ago. In your situation, you should be doing the same thing. He will make a way when there is no way. He will cleanse—"

"Wait," Andy cut in. "Just wait, Shardae. I believe you. I really do. Right now, though, I need a favor. I've never denied you anything, anything at all. I don't want you to deny me. Shardae, I need some money. I need one hundred dollars. You can send it via Western Union. I'll give you all the information you need."

"Mr. Smith, I can't get involved in—"

"Shardae," Andy said impatiently. "I've never denied you. I need you."

"I'm, I'm really, I can't," she said and hung up, infuriating Andy, causing him to nearly sling the entire phone up against the wall.

"What in the hell am I going to do?!" He shouted in utter despair.

CHAPTER 37
Saturday Evening
June 3, 2000
Opa Locka

"The wedding's off," Nicky stated as she walked into the living room of Ms. Quinn's home.

"Well, hello, my darling," warmly responded Ms. Quinn. "I see you're still questioning your nuptials with Casper." She chuckled. "Have a seat and tell me about it."

"The wedding is off," Nicky repeated. "Calling him Casper is on point 'cause he's definitely a ghost. I can find nothing on him. Now I discover this ring is fake. The 'P' on the box stood for 'Patterson's' not 'Petruska's'. He didn't pay a thousand dollars like he claimed. He paid a hundred. These stones are not diamonds. They're cubic zirconium. Patterson's had one more set left just like the one Casper bought. Instead of $978.00, the set was $97.80. This is not white gold; it's sterling silver. He's a fake, the ring's a fake, and the wedding is officially off." She was fuming.

"Listen to me, my darling," began Ms. Quinn, her voice soothing and motherly. "If you don't want to marry him, that's your choice and yours alone. But listen to me for a moment: The Saudi Arabian man across the street, the one who attends flight school, could be a spy or terrorist. Who knows? But that's not the issue. Just marry ole Casper in the name he gave you, then ask to be excused to go to the restroom but instead of going to pee, slip out of an exit, get to a pay phone and call me. I'll have you flown back here to Florida the same day. You need to get your papers. You need to be able to stay in the U. S. I say marry him anyway. You don't have to if you don't want to. It's your choice."

Nicky said nothing.

"Now, my darling," stated Ms. Quinn, standing. "Go home, take a long hot bath, spray on your most expensive perfume, dress up in your finest outfit, swallow down a hefty amount of sweet white rum, then call Casper over and give him your answer."

Nicky promptly departed the Baghdad Avenue residence and headed home. Her son, Carl, was with his aunt, Brina. Nicky's car drove past Dee's Sharar Avenue place. She looked at his window and saw the blinds were shut. She continued on home, arriving a couple minutes later.

She walked inside, noticing all the lights were off. I didn't realize I'd done that, she thought to herself. She sat down her keys and reached for a light switch. She never saw the ceramic vase as it was violently smashed into the back of her head.

***

When Nicky regained consciousness, she couldn't believe the horrendous pain she felt in her skull. It was almost toxic. A blindfold covered her eyes, duct tape sealed her mouth shut, her hands were tied tightly behind her back, and her legs were bound at the ankles. She was lying on her stomach on her bed. There were noises around her. Someone was rifling through her drawers, the closet, and all her belongings. A burglar, she deduced. After several long, agonizing minutes, the burglar climbed onto the bed and whispered something in her ear.

"I'm going to take the tape off of your mouth long enough for you to tell me where you keep your money. If you scream, I will kill you."

Nicky was shocked beyond her imagination. The shock stemmed not from the threatening words themselves; rather from the voice that uttered them. It was Dee!

He peeled off the duct tape slow and easy, letting it stop half-way across her luscious lips.

"Dee, why are you—"

A hard fist smashed into the side of her face.

"Where do you keep your cash?!" He shouted.

With blood filling her mouth, she began to cry. He punched her again, this time even harder.

"Where is the cash?!" He asked, shouting still.

"I don't—don't have any here," she said through tears and blood-soaked jaws.

Angry, Dee said nothing else. He moved to Nicky's waist area. He violently snatched down her vermilion Fendi slacks, allowing them to stop at mid-thigh. Next came her silk Chinese red thong, it too stopping at mid-thigh. Dee took his gloved hands and spread her butt cheeks two inches in width, then nastily spit a glob of spittle that landed a centimeter above her anal opening, oozing downward to cover the opening. He got up, unzipped his pants, pulled them down to his knees and climbed back onto the bed.

"For the last time, Nicky, where is the cash in this place?" He queried, his voice shaky but not loud.

"Please, Dee, don't—"

Before she could get her words out, Dee plunged his stiff penis into her rectum, causing her to shriek in indescribable agony. Her world was literally being rocked. Tears drowned her eyes inside her blindfold. She never thought she could face such savagery. Dee continued to plunge in and out, in and out, in and out. Finally, less than five minutes later, groans escaped from his throat as he ejaculated inside Nicky's virgin anus. He withdrew his penis. Fresh semen, Nicky's blood and bits of feces covered the more than half of his phallus that he'd managed to get inside her.

"Where is the cash?!" He asked, shouting again but obviously spent from his completed act of sexual violence.

"There isn't any in the house, Dee," she managed to say before her sobs replaced her words.

"Today is your lucky day, Nicky." Dee got up, went into the bathroom and washed up, returned and began to untie her. First came the ankles, then hands. Next he pulled the duct tape completely off and removed the blindfold. "Pull your thong and pants up. You can shower later."

Nicky did as she was told. Dee, standing there with a deranged look, watched her intently.

"Now," he said, standing her up. "I'm going to let you live. I'm not going to kill you. If you call the police, they'll find out you're illegal. Even though I may go to jail, guess what'll happen to you."

"Deportation," she said.

"Exactly," Dee agreed. "Do you want to get deported?"

"No," she stated, her tears beginning to flow again. "I want to stay here with my son."

"Then keep your mouth shut; understood?"

She understood very well indeed and nodded her head.

"Sorry we can't get married," Dee said as he appeared to prepare to leave. "For whatever it's worth, though, I actually did fall in love with you."

Thereafter, he left.

Nicky locked the door, turned off all of the lights, went back into the bedroom, laid face down on the carpeted floor and cried herself to sleep.

CHAPTER 38

Sunday Morning
June 4, 2000
Dade County

Andy was awakened by the ring of the telephone. He gathered himself, looked at the clock to see it was 7:23, then answered the phone.

"Yeah?" He greeted, wondering who was calling.

"Mr. Smith?" The voice greeted him. It was Shardae.

"Shardae?" Andy questioned. "How did you get—"

"Caller ID," she said, cutting him off. "I wrote down the number yesterday. I thought about what you said about never telling me no for anything. You were right. You've never denied me; I won't deny you now.

"This is what I did: After your call yesterday, I thought long and hard on your request of me. Then I decided to help. This is the extent of my involvement though. I don't want to have anything else to do with this, Mr. Smith. I saw the news, they talked about your penal history, your outlaw wife and her sister, everything. When I worked for you, I enjoyed it, but I never knew your history, Mr. Smith. I never knew. Notwithstanding that, I felt that since you never once mistreated me, never once, the least I could do was help you this one time.

"About twenty minutes ago I went to the Western Union and wired you $100. The area code on the number from my Caller ID was in Florida so I told the wire clerk Florida. The money should be there in half-an-hour, according to the clerk."

Andy, moved by Shardae's change of heart, nearly broke down. In spite of her recent conversion to Christianity that would typically require her to cooperate with the authorities, she saw the compassion in helping a man in need. Or did she? He thought suddenly. Could this be a set-up? He wondered before immediately dismissing the thought. No, he realized, this gal was his right-hand man, so to speak, during her entire TSE tenure. She wouldn't set him up; she'd just stay out of it. I was good to her, he recalled fondly.

"Mr. Smith, you still there?" She asked.

"Uh yeah, Shardae," he stammered. "I'm here."

"Again, Mr. Smith, this is the extent of my involvement, okay?"

"You gotta deal, Shardae," he said, relieved. "Thank you so very much."

After hanging up, Andy took a quick shower and dressed. The closest Western Union site was 5 ½ blocks away. He'd be there in no time. But, before he left the house, he needed to put something in his stomach; he was famished. It would take only a minute to grab a cinnamon-and-raisin bagel and take it with him. He walked into the spacious kitchen of the home in Dade County's Opa Locka where he'd spent the last couple months. For whatever reason, he did not see the glimpse of the body

through the living room window that had just took up a
position outside the house on its long porch. Maybe it was
because Andy was excited to have everything in place for
his departure from the country, maybe it was because he
wasn't wearing his contacts, and maybe it was because he
simply had his guard down.

Outside, twelve law enforcement personnel prepared
themselves.   One, an FBI special agent, possessed a
federal fugitive warrant and copies of murder warrants
from Virginia.   The special agent waited alongside six
scattered Opa Locka police officers who'd each covered
the perimeter of the residence. The remaining five were
members of the Metro-Dade County Tactical Response
Team.   Dressed in all black with goggles and helmets,
they donned bullet-proof vests and toted M-16 rifles. All
of them were positioned against the home from two
key vantage points, the front and back doors, negating
windows because they bore steel bars. The two at the
back door radioed to the three at the front that they were
in position.

Andy bit into his bagel and walked out of the kitchen,
passed the dining room and was then in the living room.
He opened the front door, spotting one of three Opa
Locka patrol cars. He had no time to respond or flee.

"Down on the floor! Down on the floor!" The three
voices shouted, seemingly simultaneously. Without waiting
for Andy to comply, one smacked the bagel from his hand
and roughly pushed him to the living room floor. He heard
footsteps coming from the kitchen, seeing two more all-
black figures from the corner of his eye. He heard one
radio to the police officers and federal agent that the
suspect was in custody and they were cleared to enter.
As a Tactical Response Team member cuffed Andy, he

thought back to Shardae, the one person he thought he trusted.

Shardae Pearson, following Andy's call last night, notified local police. They in turn contacted the FBI who coordinated with Dade County officials. While this was being done, the Feds tapped Shardae's telephone and instructed her to call Andy back the next morning. By then, the Tactical Response Team and Opa Locka police, as well as a Miami-based FBI agent, would be able to verify Andy was still in the Sharar Avenue home when they attempted to apprehend him. Shardae had set him up.

In came the city police officers led by the special agent, the latter of whom told the Dade County officers to stand Andy up.

"Andrew Smith," he began. "I am Special Agent Daniel Nicola with the Miami Field Office of the Federal Bureau of Investigation. You are under arrest for Unlawful Flight to Avoid Prosecution. I also have warrants charging you with Capital Murder in Virginia."

Andy looked into Agent Nicola's eyes and smiled.

"We just died guys. All of us."

"Pardon?" The federal agent inquired. "What the hell are you talking about? Who died?"

"All of us."

"And by 'us', you mean who?"

"Me, Jimmie Lee, and Dee; all three of us."

"Who is Jimmie Lee?" The agent asked, baffled. "And who is Dee?"

"Me," Andy confessed, still smiling. "They're me."

CHAPTER 39
June 9, 2000
Miami International Airport

Andy Smith waived extradition during a hearing on June 6th; Virginia received the paperwork the next day via Express Mail. Today he will board a plane that will take him back to the state he so desperately never wanted to see again. The two extradition officers from Virginia gave him a "gift" upon the trio's boarding of the DC-10. It was a Virginian-Pilot newspaper, dated June 5th, with a front-page article on Andy. The title told it all: FUGITIVE LED THREE LIVES. This story followed:

> A wanted Portsmouth man whom authorities sought for five months and then captured less than 24 hours before he could flee the country was apparently leading three different lives while on the lam.

> Andrew Smith, 33, has warrants on file in Portsmouth for capital murder surrounding a double-homicide in his home near the Hodges Ferry section of the city. Aunya Tiffany King and Katherine Shalita Young, already wanted by

police and dubbed the African-American version of "Thelma and Louise", an early-1990's motion picture about two outlaw women, were both found stabbed to death January 4. Smith was severely injured, according to police, when King and Young attempted to rob him in the residence. He was later questioned and released.

As the investigation developed, questions arose regarding Smith's failure to call police from the home at the time of the robbery attempt and the nature of the stab wounds received by the two women. When Smith could no longer be located, murder warrants were filed against him.

It took five months to locate Smith. By then he had lived in Arkansas under the name James Lee White and in Florida as Dr. Deloren Powell. Each alias came with an extensive history which Smith was able to perfect to the letter in order to avoid capture, authorities say.

"I think even in his mind, he believed he was James Lee White and Deloren Powell," opined Det. Sgt. Ted Iverson of the Portsmouth Police Department.

Andrew Smith will face an extradition hearing tomorrow in Miami. If he waives extradition, he will be returned to Virginia within a week to answer to the charges lodged against him here.

After reading the article, Andy handed the newspaper back to the officer without comment. After all, what could he say?

CHAPTER 40
July 16, 2000
Portsmouth

Ronica Little Smith, Andy's third wife, gave birth today to Diamond Tamika Smith. Ronica has decided to file for divorce and does not plan on visiting Andy or bringing his daughter to see him. Ronica continues to live in the Choate Street home she once shared with her estranged husband.

CHAPTER 41

July 22, 2000
Portsmouth

Latoria Taylor, who served as Andy's once-secret love interest while spearheading TSE, delivered her second child today. Audra Taylor however will be given up by Latoria and handed off to a family member who agreed to raise the child. Latoria has neither written to nor spoken with Andy since his capture in South Florida.

CHAPTER 42
July 24, 2000
Little Rock

Vonda "Cocoa" Ford ultimately discovered she was pregnant roughly two months after last seeing Andy, then posing as Jimmie Lee White, and was panic-stricken. After five weeks of considerable deliberation, Cocoa obtained an illegal second-trimester abortion. It was performed today, one week before her longtime boyfriend, Black, was to be released from jail. The sex of the child, who would have been due January 14, 2001, was never determined. Andy was never informed of the pregnancy or the termination.

CHAPTER 43

Labor Day, 2000
Opa Locka

In a miraculous method of conception, Nicky Phoenix became pregnant while she slept on the floor of her bedroom the day Andy, posing as Dr. Dee Powell, anally sodomized her. Apparently semen dribbled down from her anal area to her vaginal opening and worked its way inside her uterus. She stunningly discovered the pregnancy in late-July 2000 after experiencing morning sickness which she mistook for the flu. A due date was set for March 10, 2001. Right after discovering she was pregnant, Nicky and her son, Carl, dropped out of sight. The fate of her and Andy's unborn child is unknown.

CHAPTER 44
October 13, 2000
Portsmouth

"Madam Foreperson," the circuit court judge began. "Has the jury reached verdicts in this case?"

"We have, Your Honor," the 55-year-old grandmother replied.

"Mr. Smith, please stand and face the members of the jury," the judge instructed.

Andy stood, faced the nine men and three women, and took a deep breath. He faced two death sentences. He hoped the $54,800 he paid to his two attorneys would at least save his life. His 1987 suspended sentences were another matter, one he could not avoid. His fate with those sentences was already sealed. It was this case that worried him most.

The judge interrupted Andy's thought.

"Madam Foreperson, hand your verdict-forms to the Clerk."

After receiving same, the Clerk read them aloud to the hushed courtroom of less than 60 people"

"We, the Jury, in the case of the Commonwealth of Virginia versus Andrew Smith, as to Count cone, Capital Murder, as charged in the indictment, do hereby find the said Andrew Smith GUILTY of First-Degree Murder, a lesser-included offense, so say us all.

Signed, Agnes Breedlove, Foreperson."

The Clerk paused only momentarily before proceeding to the second verdict form. She read:

"We, the Jury, in the case of Commonwealth of Virginia versus Andrew Smith, as to Count Two, Capital Murder, as charged in the indictment, do hereby find the said Andrew Smith GUILTY of Second-Degree Murder, a lesser-included offense, so say us all.

Signed, Agnes Breedlove, Foreperson."

***

Eight weeks after trial, Andrew Smith was sentenced to Life plus 40 years without the possibility of parole for the double-homicide in his home.

A week later, he was sentenced to an additional 83 years in formerly suspended sentences after a judge found that he had violated the conditions of the suspended sentences.

Subsequent appeals of the murder convictions, focusing solely on the issue of self-defense, were each denied. There was no appeal on the re-imposition of the suspended sentences.

Andy remains incarcerated.

POSTSCRIPT

The title of this novel reads 'The Threesome" but this story was not about three men. This story was really about the life of Andrew Smith, good ole Andy, who is now growing old in a cold dark cell somewhere deep within the folds of the Virginia Department of Corrections. He will remain there forever, assuming he's real.

Andy truly isn't real, though. Of course, you already know that. I invented him. Andy, as well as any other character in this book, has no existence outside my imagination. They are not related to anyone bearing the same name or names, nor are they even distantly inspired by any individual known or unknown to me, and all incidents are pure invention.

But just think for a moment: Doesn't Andy at least seem real? To me, he does. I became so wrapped up in his character that part of me died—using his word—with him. He seemed like my shadow, my best friend, a reflection of my very own being. Yet, while his story has now been told and 366 days along with 555 hand-written pages have been utilized to tell that story, I can still feel Andy. I mean really feel him. I kinda care for him still. For sure, I will always respect and admire his determination. Nothing—and I mean nothing at all—could ever, ever, ever change that. I simply wanted—and needed—to tell his story, whether he's real or not.

Take care, Andy. I love you, man.

January 1, 2004
Dion Gooden-El

ABOUT THE AUTHOR

Dion Gooden-El is a Moorish-American who lives in Virginia. He has been down the aisle several times and has six children and step-children: Butterry, Bettina, Ahmar, Darius, LaQuetta, and Diamond. Gooden-El is currently writing his next two novels, Serena's Return, (the sequel to A Question of Intent) and Sexless Love, both of which will be released jointly as one book entitled Tales of Distinction.

S. W. Greene, aunt of Dion Gooden-El, encouraged her nephew for years before he finally wrote his first book, A Question of Intent. Greene is an employee of the U. S. Department of Agriculture. She has served as a civil servant in various positions for more than 30 years and has gained much experience in writing effectively.

Greene is a native of Portsmouth, Virginia; lived in Europe for three years, and currently resides in Maryland with her husband. She is pleased to have the opportunity to collaborate with her nephew.